Dedication

For those who are strong enough to walk away.

Playlist

Listen to The Honey Trap playlist on Spotify!

In order of appearance -
Run the World (Girls) – Beyonce
Cry Me A River – Michael Bublé
Hotel – Cassidy ft R.Kelly
Pony - Ginuwine
I Believe In A Thing Called Love – The Darkness
Livin' On A Prayer – Bon Jovi
Hot In Herre – Nelly
We Don't Have To Take Our Clothes Off – Jermaine
Stewart
Bump n' Grind – R.Kelly
You've Got a Friend In Me – Randy Newman
I Kissed a Girl – Katy Perry
Let's Get It On – Marvin Gaye
Despacito – Luis Fonso ft Daddy Yankee & Justin Bieber
Sexual Healing – Marvin Gaye

The Honey Trap

By Karli Perrin

Caroline,

Take the risk
or lose the
chance!

Karli Perrin
xo

honeytrap

noun

a stratagem in which an attractive person entices another person into revealing information or doing something unwise.

Prologue
Sophia

In the beginning, I used to feel guilty when I seduced a married man.

I used to feel dirty when I kissed them.

I used to feel ashamed when their wives divorced them.

But now I feel nothing.

I am not to blame.

I am merely the catalyst.

I am the loaded gun.

I am *the honey trap*.

Chapter One
Sophia

I focus on his wedding ring right before I close my eyes. His eager lips meet mine and I can almost taste his excitement. My mind goes into distraction mode as his tongue darts in and out of my mouth.

Tonight is what we call a half trap. This is where our clients are satisfied by photographs of their boyfriends or husbands kissing another woman. We wear a wire at all times so they also receive a recording of their partners planning to go home with us. Most women believe that planning to cheat is just as bad as actually cheating but some women need more. Some women refuse to believe that their man would actually go through with it. In other words, some women are stupid.

A full trap is where we take the men back to our place. Only, it's not *our* place. It's actually an apartment which the Honey Trap Agency (HTA) rents. Waiting inside are their scorned girlfriends or wives and sometimes the occasional lawyer. We also have an agency bodyguard on standby just in case things get heated but usually the men are too busy begging for forgiveness.

Our safety is a priority. If it's a full trap then we always insist on ordering a cab. Our driver, who is actually another bodyguard, will be parked up around the corner. They take our call then wait for five minutes before picking us up, which is always from a public place. On the rare occasion that a man insists on driving or calling their own cab, we end the trap and only charge our client for a half trap. We make a lot of money but nowhere near enough to put ourselves in any real danger.

I finally pull away when his hands begin to work their way down my back. I open my eyes and watch him for a moment, looking for any signs of indecision or guilt but they don't come. This guy's willing to go all the way. He smirks. "Wanna come back to my place, darlin'?"

I'm pretty sure he doesn't want to take me home to talk about the weather but I ask anyway for the recording. "What have you got in mind?"

He leans closer. "Have you ever had a multiple orgasm?"

I stop myself from rolling my eyes. "No," I reply, feigning innocence. Guys love the whole virginal act.

"Then I'll be your first."

Only in his dreams. If his wife doesn't leave him after tonight then they deserve each other. I grin seductively. "Let me go and freshen up first. I'll be back in a minute." I wink at him before walking away, swaying my hips as I go.

As soon as I step inside the restroom, I reach into my purse and take out my mini bottle of mouthwash. I always use too much but I like how it burns the taste of them away. After successfully numbing my entire mouth, I remove my wire and place it inside my purse just as the door opens. One of the agency photographers walks in and checks that we're alone before stopping in front of me. "Are you okay?"

I nod. "Did you get it?"

"Of course I got it." She takes out her camera and scrolls through several photographs. The first few are close-ups of his face so he can be clearly identified. The rest are shots of us kissing.

I call my boss as we both exit out of the back. "It's done."

Chapter Two
Mason

I hit the reject button on my cell for the fifth time today. I've had a shitty day and I'm not in the mood to talk to Emily right now. I lean back in my chair and spin around so that I'm facing the floor to ceiling windows which line the back wall of my office. Even after six years, the view never fails to take my breath away. Right in the heart of the city and almost fifty floors up, I have a perfect view of the Golden Gate bridge. Every time I look at it, I'm reminded of how lucky I am. I've worked my ass off to get where I am today and I'm damn proud of it.

I groan when I hear the sound of a phone ringing once again. At least this time it's my assistant calling on my office line. I push the little flashing button and put her on speakerphone. "Yes, Natalia?"

"Mr Hunter, I have a call for you on line one."

"Who is it?"

"Miss Louisa Wright."

"I don't know who that is. Take a message."

"She said she's calling from your lawyers office. Jewels and Stoneman?"

They must be calling for more information after our meeting last week. "Okay, put her through." Michael Bublé begins to serenade me for what feels like the hundredth time today. I make a mental note to change the hold music. There's only so many times you can listen to *Cry Me A River* without wanting to jump into a goddamn river so you don't have to listen to it anymore. The music stops, thank god. "Mason Hunter."

A woman clears her throat. "I can't believe I have to pretend to be somebody else to get you to talk to me."

I sigh. "What's up, Emily?"

"Why have you been ignoring me?"

"I've been busy. I still am."

"But you're the boss."

I glance at the huge pile of paperwork on my desk. "Yes, I'm well aware of that."

"So then why can't you take a break to call your wife?"

My head falls back against my chair. "I can't do this right now."

"Fine, we can talk about it when you come home. Speaking of which; any idea when that may be?"

"I'm not coming home." I pause, tempted to leave it at that, but it would only lead to more questions. "You know how things are, Emily. Look, it's getting late and I still have to prepare for a meeting."

"Another one?"

"Like you said, I'm the boss."

"Do you want me to swing by? I can bring food."

"No. I've already ordered take-out," I lie. "It should be here any minute."

"Well it sounds like you've got everything covered."

"Yeah. Thanks for the offer."

"Okay well I guess I'll just see you tomorrow."

"Tomorrow?" I have no intention of seeing her tomorrow.

"Don't tell me you've forgotten." When I don't reply, she sighs. "We're meeting Joanne and Pete for dinner at Scoma's."

"We are?"

"Yes, *we are*. We arranged it months ago, before Pete left for Dubai. He got back yesterday. I can't believe you forgot."

"Can we reschedule?"

"*Again*?" she asks, losing her patience. "All I ever do these days is reschedule. It's just dinner, Mason. I'm not asking for much."

In fairness, I can't remember the last time we went out for dinner. I guess there are only so many times I can get away with using the same excuses. "What time?"

"Six thirty."

"I have a meeting in the afternoon so I'll probably be a

little late."

"That's fine. The three of us can have a few drinks while we wait for you to arrive. We have a lot of catching up to do." Even though her voice is sickly sweet, her warning is received loud and clear. If I don't get there on time, she can't guarantee what she might let slip.

I sigh. "See you at six thirty."

Chapter Three
Sophia

"Honey, I'm home," I shout as I close the front door behind me.

A few seconds later, Lori appears. "How many times do I need to tell you? Stop calling me honey, you're going to blow my cover." Lori has been working for the agency for a little over five years. Within hours of first meeting, we became best friends as well as roommates. Her heart may be full of gold but her mind is full of filth. I blame it on her obsession with romance novels. She has zero interest in men unless they're fictional. She once told me that book boyfriends were God's way of apologizing for men in real life. She winks at me. "So, how was it?"

"Like taking candy from a baby."

"That's my girl." She looks at her watch. "Just under two hours, we have a new record."

When I first started working for the agency, a trap would usually take me around four hours. Now that I know the tricks of the trade, that number has halved. I hold up the pizza that I grabbed on my way home. "I've bought celebratory pizza. Let's get fat, drink wine, and watch *The Bachelor*."

"See, this right here is why I believe in fate. We belong together."

"Are you talking about you and me or the pizza?"

"Of course I'm talking about the pizza." She takes the box off of me and leads me into the living room.

I sit down before taking off my five inch heels. "Oh, that feels so good."

"If you think that feels good, wait until you take off your bra."

"I'm not wearing one."

"Ah ha! So that's your secret weapon? I'll have to try it next time." She takes a big bite of pizza. "So yu no wurnex tap his?"

"I have no idea what you just said." She rolls her eyes and begins to chew faster. "You do know that you could just wait until after you finish eating before asking me a question, don't you?"

"And waste precious reading time later on? No thanks. I *said* do you know when your next trap is?"

"Nope, I'm swinging by the office tomorrow."

"Well fingers crossed you get somebody young and hot this time."

"Your fingers have been crossed for a very long time." My last ten traps have been with older men. And by older men, I don't just mean a few years older than me. The youngest was double my age at forty eight. It doesn't bother me as they are usually the easiest to trap. Most of them can't believe that somebody my age would actually be interested in them. "As long as I get paid, I don't care how old they are."

"Yeah but surely you'd rather flirt with a young handsome guy than an old wrinkly one?"

"A cheater is a cheater. Plus, the handsome ones are usually the most arrogant."

"When you've been doing this job for as long as I have, you learn to make compromises. I don't mind a bit of arrogance if it's wrapped up in a pretty little package."

I shrug. "You know I don't care about that kind of stuff."

"I know, I know, you're doing it for the greater good. Justice, feminism, world peace. Yada, yada, yada."

I started working for the agency two years ago, after I graduated from college. It turns out that while I was busy busting my balls in a different city, my ex-boyfriend was balls deep in another woman. On the last day of the semester, I decided to surprise him by going home a few days earlier than planned. I think it's safe to say that we were both surprised when I walked in on him fucking somebody else. I spent a whole week
wallowing in self pity until I woke up one morning with a clear head and knew what needed to be done.

I needed to chop off his dick.

But since I've never been cut out for prison, I settled on pinning up hundreds of posters around our neighborhood. It had a photograph of him accompanied by the following –

MISSING: Scott Parker's respect for women.
If found, please shove it up his lying, cheating, good for nothing ass.
$1,000,000 reward.

The search is still on.

I also posted flyers in our neighbors mailboxes. This time I was feeling quite creative so I Photoshopped his face onto a cheetahs body.

WARNING: Cheater on the loose.
Approach with extreme caution.
Lock up your daughters.

What can I say? He deserved it.

A few weeks later, I started working for the agency. Never underestimate the power of a broken heart and a stupid amount of college debt.

To begin with, I was on a huge revenge rampage but once the hurt and anger wore off, I quickly realized that a woman's happiness should never depend on little boys like Scott Parker. From that moment on, my outlook changed and my focus shifted. The job became less about the men and more about the women who they didn't deserve. Now I do my job for three reasons and three reasons only.

1. I'm good at it.
2. It pays well.
3. Girl power.

Chapter Four

Mason

I lied.

I finished preparing for my meeting over half an hour ago. The truth is, I don't want to go home. Actually, that's another lie. I want to go home; I just don't want to see my wife. I'm not in the mood for another argument. I shoot off a few emails before reaching for my suit jacket and keys.

It's warm out so I decide to walk. It's nice to get some fresh air after being cooped up in my office all day. After about ten minutes, I stop in front of the hotel and pull out my cell. I scroll to the letter 'I' in my contacts before hovering over her name. I hesitate, like I always do before calling her. I should probably just try to get some sleep but I'm not in the right frame of mind and she always manages to take my mind off of things. I push the call button as I make my way inside. I nod in greeting to the doorman as I wait for her to pick up. She answers after a couple of rings. "Hello?"

"Hey," I reply. "Are you free to talk?"

"Yeah. Do you want me to come over?"

"Only if you're not busy."

"Where are you?" she asks.

"The usual."

"Okay. Give me half an hour."

Chapter Five
Sophia

The next day, I wake up early and go for a run. It started off as a way to keep in shape but now I use it as an escape. It's nice to clear my head and not have to think about work. Dealing with cheating men on a daily basis can really mess with your mind. I concentrate on nothing but the wind in my hair and the air in my lungs.

After having a shower and taking care of some errands, I head to the office for my next assignment. I check my reflection in a nearby mirror while I wait for the elevator to take me to the tenth floor. My blonde hair, which is in desperate need of a cut, has a slight curl to it from letting it dry naturally. I run my hands through it then apply some lipstick.

The elevator doors open and a middle-aged woman steps out. Her eyes are red and puffy as if she's been crying and my gut is telling me that she's one of our clients. She looks up and down before shaking her head. "You're so young. We have a daughter around your age." I have no idea how I'm supposed to respond so I stay quiet. A lone tear trickles down her cheek. "Thank you," she says before walking away. Wait; did she just thank me for trapping her husband? It takes me a few seconds to realize how completely fucked up that is.

I step into the elevator, feeling a little taken aback and punch the button for the tenth floor. We never meet our clients. That part is left up to our boss, Kristen. Even when it's a full trap and they are waiting for us at a specific location, we always leave immediately afterwards. As soon as a man proves that they are willing to go home with us, our job is done. Meeting our clients would only complicate matters.

When the elevator doors open, I'm greeted by the large company logo. HTA is written in a black, elegant font. It could easily pass for some kind of design company or advertising agency. I carry on walking until I see a woman sitting in the small waiting area. Kristen usually tells us to drop by at a time when she's completely free to avoid us bumping into clients. Could this be two in one day? The woman glances up and catches me looking at her. I suspect she's used to it. Her eyes are the color of dark chocolate and her long black hair looks like silk. I would guess that she's only a few years older than me and it's obvious that she comes from money. She's dripping in jewellery and is head to toe in designer clothes. "Hello. Can I help you?" I ask.

She leans her head to one side. "I don't know, can you?"

"Have you got an appointment to see Kristen?"

"Yes. I'm early."

"No problem. I'll go and let her know that you're here." I smile politely before making my way to my boss's office.

"Come in," Kristen shouts after I knock several times. I step inside and take a seat in front of her huge desk. "Sophia, how are you today?" Before I even get the chance to answer, she carries on talking in true Kristen style. "Great work last night. My client was shocked that he took the bait. I think she's been in denial for a long time. Did you pass a woman on your way up here?"

"Um, I saw a woman getting out of the elevator and there's another woman waiting outside who says she's got an appointment with you."

She nods. "The one in the elevator, that was his wife. When I showed her the photos, she couldn't believe how young you were. She's filing for divorce today." She says it like it's the most normal thing in the world and to her, I guess it is. Although my job has taught me to have quite a thick skin, it's never nice to hear that I'm one of the reasons why somebody is getting divorced. But what's even worse is listening to a married man talk about giving me a multiple orgasm while his wife is at home washing his goddamn underwear.

Kristen roots through her papers before handing me

a file. "Here's your next trap." After a few moments, she gestures to the folder. "Well? Aren't you going to take a look?" I narrow my eyes. She knows that I always wait until I get home. I like to sit down with Lori and come up with a plan of action. We treat each of our traps differently. Some require a slow and steady approach whereas others benefit from being more aggressive. I favor the ones like last night - minimal work, maximum results. When I don't answer, she continues, "I want you to know that I've spent a lot of time thinking about this. It might seem a little daunting at first but I think you're the right woman for the job." Why is she saying these things? "Sophia, your next trap is high profile and my client is offering us a lot of money." She leans in closer to me. "And when I say a lot, I mean *a lot*. More than ten times the usual rate."

My stomach does a somersault. I've heard Lori talk about these kind of traps. High profile means that I could end up being in the public eye, which in turn means that somebody could recognize me. If my cover was blown, it would be game over. Was I ready to leave the agency for good? Maybe it's finally time to move on and put my degree to good use. I decide to keep an open mind and weigh up all of my options before making a decision.

I open the file and get my first look at him. I swear that in a matter of milliseconds, the sun shines brighter, the birds chirp louder and the room gets hotter. I see dark hair, blue eyes and stubble. Olive skin, a chiselled jaw and stubble. High cheekbones, full lips and *stubble*. If you can't tell, I kind of have a thing for stubble. Some people call it an obsession but I call it a healthy appreciation for facial hair. It's not as if I spend hours
trawling Pinterest looking for hot guys with beards and stubble.

I've become so used to opening files and seeing graying, middle aged men that I begin to wonder whether this is some kind of practical joke. Either that or Lori must have crossed her fingers for me after all. I read his short bio.

Mason Hunter.
27 years old.
6'2. 182 lbs.
Brown hair. Blue eyes.
Business owner.
Married since 2016. No children.

"Do you need some time to think about it?" Kristen asks.

My brain is saying yes but my ovaries are screaming no. It says a lot about my life when I've forgotten what it even feels like to be physically attracted to someone. I remind myself that I'm a professional and even though he's hot, he's probably a cheating douchebag and it's my duty to help his wife discover the truth. After convincing myself that he's the devil and my decision has nothing to do with the fact that he's stupidly handsome, I close the file. "I'll do it."

Kristen grins. "Excellent. I knew I could count on you. Now, I must warn you that this trap is going to be a little different."

"Different how?"

"Well first of all, his wife wants to meet you."

A feeling of unease washes over me. "But that's not how it works..."

"My client is paying us a lot of money. It works however she wants it to work."

"But why does she want to meet me? What difference would it make?"

We're interrupted by a knock on the door. "You can ask her yourself."

I immediately begin to regret my decision when the woman from the waiting area enters the room. Kristen stands up to greet her. "Mrs Hunter, it's good to see you again."

"Call me Emily."

"Of course. Emily, allow me to introduce you to Sophia, she's agreed to work with us."

I can feel the hostility radiating off of her as she looks me up and down. "Hmmm, I think she looks too young for Mason. I was hoping it wasn't her when she walked by a few minutes ago." I frown. I've always taken good care of my skin but I've never been told that I look young for my age. If anything, my curves have always made me look older than I actually am. "She looks too innocent. Find somebody older."

I can't keep quiet any longer. "I'm twenty four. Your husband is only three years older than me."

She smirks. "Wow, it sounds like somebody is very eager to seduce my husband."

"Well that's kind of my job," I reply, starting to feel defensive.

"So what's your real name?"

"Sophia."

"Why don't you use a fake name?"

"Because I don't need to. I never tell people my last name."

"But strippers use fake names."

"Well I'm not a stripper."

"It's the same line of work."

"*No*, it isn't."

"You both seduce men."

Is she trying to piss me off on purpose? "I keep my clothes on."

"That's a shame. You could probably make a lot more money if you didn't." I'm ready to get up and leave when she turns her attention to Kristen. "I thought I asked for a brunette?"

"You did but Sophia is one of my best girls. I trust her to do the job. She can dye her hair whatever color you want."

Gee, thanks.

Emily waves her hand dismissively. "Leave it. It'll be interesting to see if he likes blondes after all." She turns to face me. "How much do you weigh?" I laugh in response. "What's funny?" she asks.

15

"Oh, you're actually being serious? I thought you were joking."

"None of this is a joke to me. I'm asking you because I know what my husband likes."

Other women, apparently. I sigh. "Around one forty five."

"Hmmm, you have a good fifteen pounds on me. Stand up." Is she being serious? I turn to Kristen and raise my eyebrow in question. She nods so I stand up and perform an overly dramatic twirl, jazz hands and all. "How tall are you?"

"Five eight," I reply, which has to be at least four inches taller than her.

"Bra size?"

I roll my eyes. "Thirty four double d. I'm an only child and my favorite color is midnight blue. I don't smoke and I like to sing Disney songs really loud in the shower. Anything else? How about my blood type?"

She smiles but it fails to reach her eyes. "You've got a sharp tongue. Whereas I find it irritating, no doubt Mason will find it endearing. I guess this could work."

"Thanks for your approval," I reply sarcastically.

She stares at me for a long time but I refuse to be the one to look away first. "You have one shot so make sure you impress me." I stop myself from saluting her. "You need to be at Scoma's restaurant tonight at six o'clock. Wait at the bar for my friend Joanne to come and get you. It's supposed to be a double date but I'm going to cancel at the last minute. You're going to pretend that you went to school together and take my
empty seat at the table. Joanne and her husband will excuse themselves shortly after, leaving you alone with my husband."

I nod. "Is it a full trap?"

"Am I supposed to know what that means? In English, please."

"If he's willing, do you want me to take him home with me? You'll get the location so you can get there first."

She tosses her hair over her shoulder. "Put it this way,

I'm not paying your company ten grand to have a friendly chat with my husband."

Chapter Six

Mason

"Guess who got laid last night?"

I turn around to see Buzz walking towards me, high-fiving people on his way. "Your mom?" I ask.

"Close. *Your* mom. Don't worry, we cuddled afterwards."

"Go fuck yourself."

"I would but your mom's stopping by later for round two."

"This conversation is over." I head towards my office but he catches me up.

"Aww, come on. Don't you want me to be your new daddy?"

"I don't want anything to do with you at this moment in time."

He laughs. "I fucked Victoria last night."

"Which one is Victoria?"

"The hot blonde from Pulse. You know, the one who's training to become a Victoria's Secret model."

"You have to train to do that?"

"Yeah, apparently it's really hardcore. She practically lives at the gym."

"So her name is Victoria and she wants to become a Victoria's secret model?"

"I don't know what her real name is. That's just what I call her."

I laugh. "You're such a dick."

"I have a huge what?" He winks at my assistant as we walk past her desk. "Good morning, Natalia. You're looking lovely today."

She gives him a dirty look and I'm pretty sure I hear her whisper a chain of curse words under her breath. I close my office door behind us and hold up two fingers. "Number one – stop having sex with my assistants. You've already made three of them leave and Natalia is very good at her job."

He wiggles his eyebrows up and down. "She's good at a different kind of *job* too."

"Jesus, stop with the blowjob gestures. I'm trying to be serious here. It takes time and money to train them up."

"You should be having this conversation with them, not me. It's not my fault that I'm irresistible to women."

"I think sometimes you forget that I'm your boss."

"And I think sometimes you forget that I'm your best friend. Stop hiring pretty assistants, problem solved."

"Thanks for that, Einstein. Number two - what's that on your neck?"

He grins. "Turns out that Victoria's no angel. You should see the rest of my body." He begins to unzip his pants. "Look what she did to my..."

I hold my hands up. "Woah, woah, woah! I'll pass. Just cover it up, it's unprofessional."

"My neck or my..."

"Both!"

"Okay, *Dad*."

"Hey, if I'm your dad, does that mean I get to fuck your mom? Don't worry, I'll make sure I cuddle her afterwards."

He grimaces. "Okay, I get it. Mom's are off limits. So where were you last night? I tried calling you."

"I was at the hotel."

"Alone?"

"No, with Indiana."

"Well you could have still answered your phone. What happened to bro's before ho's?"

"I'll tell her you said that. I switched my phone off."

"Why? Has Emily been calling you again?"

I sigh. "Yep."

"You up for drinks after the meeting?"

"I wish I could but I'm going for dinner."

He raises an eyebrow. "With who?"

"Emily. She's already arranged it with Pete and Joanne."

"Thanks for my invite," he says sarcastically. "I guess I'll just have to go home with another hot blonde instead. Oh, I have such a hard life. What about tomorrow night instead? You'll need it after your cozy little dinner date."

"I think you might be right."

"I'm always right." He begins to walk away but stops when he reaches the door. "Actually, I was wrong about one thing. You know when I said that you shouldn't hire pretty assistants? Don't listen to me, it was a stupid idea."

Chapter Seven
Sophia

"How did it go?" Lori asks as soon as I step through the door.

"It was...different."

"Good different or bad different?"

"Meeting the wife different."

Her eyes nearly pop out of her head. "Nooooo! Are you joking?"

"I wish I was."

"But why? We never meet the clients."

I sigh. "It's high profile."

"Oh my god!" She grabs hold of my hand. "Have you agreed to it?" I nod, still unsure whether I've made the right decision. "Come and sit down, tell me everything." She drags me into the kitchen and we sit down opposite each other. "So who's the guy?"

"Mason Hunter."

She laughs. "Good one. I wonder who I'll be trapping next, Channing Tatum?" When I don't reply, she waves her hand around. "Well come on, don't keep me waiting. Who is it?"

"I've already told you. It's Mason Hunter."

Her smile fades. "Are you actually being serious?" I nod. "No way! Mason Hunter? *The* Mason Hunter?"

"I hope he's not expecting me to address him as that."

"Are you sure it's him?"

I pull his file out of my purse and pass it to her. Her mouth falls open. "Holy shit, it *is* him."

"Seriously, his ego would love you."

She rolls her eyes. "I'm guessing you don't know who he is."

"And I'm guessing you do."

"Of course I do. He's a big deal in the business world. He was listed in Fortune magazine's forty under forty for being one of the most influential men in business. You probably walked past his hotel on your way home."

"Well I've never heard of him and I'm pretty sure I would have remembered his face. Does he have paparazzi following him?"

"I don't think so. He's high profile in the business world but he tries to stay out of the public eye as much as he can. He seems like a very private person and I think the paparazzi respect him for that. He's featured in quite a lot of newspaper articles and magazines but he's never been front page news and he's very rarely in gossip magazines. It's probably because he's married and on a tight leash."

"Perhaps not tight enough if she thinks that he's cheating."

"Touché."

"How do you know so much about him?" I ask.

"Because some of us haven't been living under a rock for the past few years. Plus, my friend knows him."

"Which friend?"

She laughs. "Google. So what was his wife like?"

"Well she started by saying that I looked too young and innocent then went on to ask about my bra size and how much I weigh."

"Woah, complete violation of girl code right there. How much is she paying?"

"Ten grand." We get a 50% cut.

"Woah. Not bad for one nights work."

"I know, that's the only reason I'm doing it."

She smirks. "Are you sure that's the only reason?"

"Of course."

"So the fact that he's gorgeous didn't influence you at all?"

Maybe. "Nope."

"Not even a little bit?"

I shrug. "You know me, I'm a professional."

She laughs. "Then why are you blushing, Miss Professional?"

"Oh, shush." I stand up. "I need to choose an outfit.

I'm meeting him in a few hours."

"A few *hours*? I thought you were going to say a few days! Do you want to go over a plan of action?"

"I already did with his wife." I realize how strange that sounds. There's definitely a reason why we're usually kept apart.

"Oh, so it's like that now, is it?" She coughs the word traitor.

I wink. "Yep, she's my new BFF. We share everything, even her husband." I leave the room and make my way upstairs.

"Sophia?" she shouts from the kitchen.

"Yeah?"

"You're going to add him to your Pinterest board, aren't you?"

I take a sip of my virgin mojito before glancing around the room. I've been sitting at the bar for around twenty minutes waiting for Emily's friend to make her move. There's no sign of Mason and I'm beginning to wonder whether Emily has backed out.

The bartender breaks my train of thought by asking if I want another drink. He's tried to strike up a conversation with me at least three times but each time I give him a one word answer. I don't want to come across as rude but I can't allow myself to get distracted. I like to keep my head in the game when I'm working. I decline but that doesn't stop him from complimenting my outfit. I decided on my white figure-hugging dress which falls just above the knee. Lori thinks that because I'm wearing white, Mason will subconsciously see me as a beacon of light and hope. She even mentioned an angel and devil analogy. I stopped questioning her theories a long time ago. I jump when somebody taps me on the shoulder. I turn around to see a woman with flaming red hair glaring at me. "Are you

Sophie?"

"Sophia," I correct her.

She waves her hand dismissively. "Whatever. I'm Joanne, Emily's friend."

"Hi Joanna." *Two can play that game.*

"Joanna? It's Joanne. Are you trying to be funny? Mason will be arriving soon so we need to run through what's going to happen."

"I've already discussed it with Emily."

"Oh. Awesome. The less time I spend with you tonight, the better." She looks me up and down. "I'm only doing this for her. Don't think for one second that I actually like you. Just wait here until I come and get you then act like we're old friends."

"That might be a little difficult if you keep acting like a dick."

Her eyes go wide. "Emily was right, you *are* a smart-ass. And correct me if I'm wrong but isn't it part of your job to love dick? I bet you see a lot of them in your industry, if you can even call it that." She grins, looking pleased with herself. I can see why she's friends with Emily.

I smile sweetly. "You're right. I do see a lot of dicks." I lean in closer to her. "The *biggest* are usually the ones who are married. Speaking of which, isn't your husband here tonight?" I feign innocence as I look around the restaurant.

"Don't even think about it, skank. If I catch you looking in my husband's direction, your pathetic excuse for a career will end tonight. Remember that you're here for Mason and nobody else."

I watch her walk away and thank the lord that this will all be over in a couple of hours.

Chapter Eight

Mason

I walk into the restaurant at exactly six thirty. I had to leave my meeting early but at least I can trust Buzz to hold down the fort. He might be a pain in the ass but he's a total beast at work. I quickly scan the room but there's no sign of Emily or the others. I head in the direction of the bar but there's only one blonde woman with her back to me. The bartender is completely in awe of her, which makes me curious to see what she looks like. I start to walk in her direction when I hear my name being called. "Mason, it's good to see you." I turn around to see Pete making his way over to me, arms wide open. He gives me an awkward man hug complete with several pats on the back.

"Good to see you too, Pete."

"It's been way too long; we hardly see you and Emily these days."

"I've been busy with work, you know how it is."

He grins. "No rest for the wicked, eh?" I follow him as he leads us over to our table. Joanne nods when she sees me. "Mason."

"Joanne, how are you?" I ask to be polite, not because I actually care. I've never liked her. She has a talent for sucking the happiness right out of you and she feeds off of other people's misery. She's basically a Dementor in disguise.

"I'm good. How's Emily? Is she feeling any better?"

I frown. "How do you mean?"

"She's sick. She called me about an hour ago to say she couldn't make it but that you were still coming." She leans her head to one side. "Wait, has she not told you?"

"No, she hasn't."

Pete looks from me to Joanne. "This is the first time I'm hearing about it. Why didn't you mention something earlier?"

"Excuse me, I'll be right back." I walk out of the restaurant and can already feel the anger building up inside of me. I take a couple of deep breaths to try and calm myself down but it doesn't work. I can't believe she guilted me into coming then cancelled without telling me. I pace up and down but start to attract unwanted attention from passersby so I sit down on a nearby bench. I pull my cell out of my jacket pocket and call Emily. She picks up immediately, as if she was waiting for my call. "I left an important meeting to be here," I say through gritted teeth.

She coughs pathetically. "Aren't you going to ask me how I'm feeling?"

"No, you sound fine."

"Just because I *sound* fine doesn't mean that I *am* fine. There's a difference."

"Cut the bullshit. Why didn't you call me?"

All traces of being ill disappear as her voice turns harsh. It was only a matter of time. "What's the point? You never answer my calls."

"That doesn't usually stop you. Did you not feel like pretending to be from my lawyer's office today? Or how about my doctor's? You have a full array of occupations to choose from."

"I'm going to ignore everything you're saying because I know you're stressed out from work. I just wish you wouldn't take it out on me."

"It isn't work that stresses me out, Emily." *It's you.*

"Well now that you're there, just relax and have a little fun."

"With *your* friends?"

"They're your friends too."

"No they're not. You know I've never liked Joanne."

"What's wrong with you? Why are you acting like this?"

"Because I could have stayed in my meeting. We have important clients visiting. I'm only here because of you. You're quick to remind me how little we see each other these days but then when I do show up, you cancel."

"Yeah well it's not very nice when somebody cancels, is it?"

I take a deep breath and try to keep my voice level. "Are you insinuating that you cancelled on purpose?"

"Maybe you needed a taste of your own medicine."

I throw my free hand up. "For fuck's sake, Emily! We're not twelve years old so stop playing games! You know I take my work seriously. If I didn't, you wouldn't be sitting in a ten bedroom house right now. Do you really think pulling shit like this will achieve anything? It's not exactly going to help our relationship, is it?"

"At least I'm trying *something*. I'm not sure the same can be said about you."

"Oh believe me, I'm trying. I'm trying really fucking hard right now." *Trying not to lose my shit in broad daylight.*

After a few seconds, she sighs, "I don't know what else to say."

"An apology would be nice."

"Well here's the thing Mason...I'm not sorry. So what if you had to leave your meeting early? Stop acting like a little bitch and get over it."

Her words are like gasoline, feeding the flames burning inside of me. I can't bear to hear her voice for even a second longer. I hang up and slam my cell down on the bench next to me. Then I slam it down a few more times for good measure. I know I need to cool it, especially when I'm in public, but she's really gone and done it this time. And what's worse is that this is just the tip of the iceberg. I place my head in my hands and desperately try to think of something else to distract me. A song pops into my head. *Cry Me A River*. Fucking typical.

"Try holding it up," I hear somebody say from nearby. I look up to see a woman standing a few feet away from me. She's beautiful in an almost ethereal kind of way. She has to be the woman from the bar because I'm pretty sure I'm staring at her just like the bartender was. She has long blonde hair all the way down her back and is wearing a white dress which showcases her curves perfectly. Her heart shaped face and bambi eyes make her look sweet and innocent but her body is a walking contradiction. My greedy eyes can't decide where to look first. She laughs, which breaks my train of thought. Shit, what did she even say?

"Try holding your phone up. I'm guessing you can't get service either? It's annoying, isn't it?" She holds her cell high in the air which makes her dress ride up, revealing smooth, toned thighs.

Eyes up, Mason.

Chapter Nine
Sophia

Like what you see, Mr Hunter?

He swallows hard, his eyes finally meeting mine. "It's working fine," he replies, sounding a little confused.

"Oh, so do you always end your calls like that?"

His brows furrow. "Like what? Have you been watching me?"

"Watching you smash your phone against a bench? Nope."

His face relaxes a little. "Well that's a relief. I've never been good at coming up with excuses."

That's probably why your wife has hired me. I shake my phone around in the air, doing all of the stereotypical things people do to try and get service. "I need to make a call. Is it okay if I borrow your phone?" He frowns and I can tell that he's about to say no. "I promise I won't steal it or anything." I hold up my purse. "Here, you can hold my purse while I use it if you want, kind of like insurance."

He laughs. "That's hardly a fair swap. My cell in exchange for a sparkly purse?"

"A sparkly *designer* purse. It's probably worth more than your cell." In reality, it was only ten dollars from Target but he doesn't need to know that. This wasn't part of the plan but neither was Mason storming out of the restaurant. It was pure luck that I glanced over my shoulder at the exact same time that he was walking outside. A girl's gotta do what a girl's gotta do and right now I need to try and seduce an angry man who is only just meeting me for the first time. He stands up and closes the gap between us. Jesus Christ, he smells good. I have to stop myself from leaning in and taking a huge sniff of him. He hands me his cell. "I trust you."

Bingo. This might be easier than I first thought. "Thank you." I look down at his cracked screen. "Wow, it's in excellent condition. Not a scratch in sight. You must take good care of it." A hint of a smile appears on his face. I

29

dial Lori's work cell and hope that she has it with her. We both have one for times like this when we don't want to expose our personal numbers. Just when I think it's about to go to voicemail, she picks up. "I'm here, I'm here! Is everything okay?"

"Hey. Yeah, everything's fine. I just wanted to let you know that I can't get service on my cell. I didn't want you to worry if I didn't text you back. Also, did you remember to feed the dog?"

We don't have a dog. About a year ago, we came up with a secret question, kind of like a codeword, so that the other person would know we were on a trap and in earshot of the guy. I have no idea what to say next but I needed a quick way of stopping Mason from leaving and I'm pretty sure he won't leave while I'm using his phone. "Yay! I've been waiting to have this conversation for ages." She giggles. "Yes, I fed the dog. Whose phone are you using? Is it his?"

Of course I have to play dumb. "I'm not sure, just some guy's. He let me borrow it to call you."

"I'll take that as a yes. You've only been there for half an hour and you're already using his phone. Bravo, my friend."

I ignore her and turn towards Mason. "She's asking me who you are in case you end up being an axe murderer."

"Yes, that's exactly what I'm fake asking," Lori says in my ear.

Mason smiles. "Don't worry, I don't have an axe."

"Did you hear that?" I ask Lori. "He doesn't have an axe. I'm safe."

"Let's play a little game," she replies. "Pretend that I don't know what he looks like. How would you describe him to me?"

"Um, he's around six three, maybe six four."

"Oh he's going to love you for saying that. All men wish they had an extra couple of inches." She begins to snort and I have to bite my lip to stop myself from laughing. "Sorry, carry on," she says when she finally stops giggling.

"Brown hair, blue eyes. Wait, they could be green." I take a step closer to him. "Nope, they're just really light blue."

"Rate him out of ten, boost his ego."

I laugh. "I'm not going to rate him out of ten, he's standing right in front of me." I say it purposely to peak his interest and it works. He raises his eyebrow and leans his head to one side. "Please go ahead," he says. "Don't let me stop you."

"Well this is a little awkward."

He shrugs. "It's only awkward if your answer is below a six."

"No pressure then?"

"None at all."

"I need a minute to think. Something this important requires careful consideration."

He nods. "I understand. Take as much time as you need."

I take a step back and begin to peruse every single inch of him. I start at his feet and slowly rake my eyes upwards. His suit is tailored to perfection, accentuating his broad chest and strong shoulders. What is it about men in suits? Even though every inch of him is covered, I can't help but wonder what's underneath. By the time our eyes meet, I'm pretty much a puddle on the floor.

"Satisfied?" he asks, his voice noticeably huskier than before.

Very. "Hmmm, I guess so."

"So what's the verdict?"

"A solid six point five."

He laughs. "I'll take it."

"Maybe even a seven when you smile."

"Wow, only half a point for my smile? In that case, I'm not sure it's worth the effort. All those muscles that are involved."

"Well shit," I hear a distant voice say. It takes me a second to realize that I still have his phone held up to my ear. "I was planning on starting Colleen Hoover's new book tonight," Lori says. "But I think I'll just listen to you two instead. Who needs fiction when you've got the real thing? I could do with a little more description though. How would you describe the sexual tension right now? Are you *aching* for him? Is he *smouldering*?" The only words I hear are 'sexual tension' and 'aching'.

Mason drags a hand across his jaw. "It's the stubble isn't it?" he asks. "Would you give me a better rating if I was clean shaven?"

I laugh. "Actually, you'd be a six without the stubble."

He raises his eyebrows. "Ah, so you're a stubble kind of girl." He taps the side of his forehead. "I'll try to remember that."

"Maybe I should record this and try to upload it to Audible." Lori's voice breaks me out of my trance. "My bookish friends would kill for it. Do you actually need me to do anything or shall I just sit back and enjoy the show?"

"I have to go," I reply. "I'm not sure what time I'll be home. My date decided to stand me up so I'm probably going to stay here and drown my sorrows. See you later."

"Have fun trapping that handsome son of a bitch."

I hang up and pass the phone back to Mason. "Thank you and sorry about my friend."

"No worries. It's saved me at least five minutes of shaving time tomorrow."

I laugh. "Can I buy you a drink? You know, to say thanks."

"You don't have to do that."

"I insist. Besides, I could use the company."

"So you're just using me? Am I your plan B?" He grins and I'm pretty sure I have this in the bag until his phone lights up in his hand. We both look down at the same time and I catch Emily's name flash across the screen. It's a text message but I can't see what it says. He swipes his finger across the screen and his eyes turn serious. There's nothing I can do except stand there and watch as he shuts down and builds his wall back up. "I have to go. I'm sorry."

"Are you sure? You really look like you could use a drink."

"You're right, I could, but I should leave."

"Okay, well I guess I'll just stay here for a while and make sure the bench doesn't piss off anybody else."

He smiles but it looks forced. "Have a nice evening." He begins to walk away. After taking a couple of steps, he holds up his cell. "Thanks for not stealing it."

Before I get the chance to reply, he's gone. And just like that, I once again have a new record for the shortest trap, except this time I failed. I can't help but think about the money I've just lost out on. It would have easily paid for a few months rent. Because I failed to trap Mason, I don't receive a dime. Kristen does it on purpose to make us work harder. The last thing I want to do is spend several hours seducing a man only to go home with nothing to show for it. That's why I can count the number of times I've failed on one hand but for some strange reason, this time feels different. I usually hate failing but a part of me is secretly pleased that Mason didn't take the bait. Maybe it's because he seemed like a nice person or maybe it's because Emily didn't. Or maybe, just maybe, it's because I like the thought of a man being able to say no. It gives me a little bit of hope that one day I'll allow myself to have a normal relationship and put my trust in a man once again.

Pain is real, but so is hope.

Lori claps excitedly when I arrive home. "You're in love with him, aren't you? You're in love with him and you're going to have his babies!"

I roll my eyes. "Stop it right now. You read way too many books."

"Can I be your Maid of Honor?"

"For somebody else's wedding, far away from me, then

yes."

"You're perfect for each other."

"You're crazy, do you know that? Like actually certifiably crazy."

She shakes her head. "I'm not. I failed an online psychopath test the other week. Anyway, stop trying to change the subject. You can't deny it. I heard it all. Hell, I *felt* it and I was on the other end of a telephone."

I try to escape into the kitchen but she follows close behind. "Go on then, humor me. What did you *feel*?"

"Your connection."

"I was faking it. It's all part of the job, remember?"

"Nobody's that good at faking it."

"Trust me, after years of dating my ex, I'm good at faking a lot of things."

She wiggles her eyebrows up and down. "I bet you wouldn't have to fake it with Mason."

I can't help but blush. "Oh my god, Lori! Stop it right now!"

She holds her hands up. "Just saying."

"Well I'm sorry to burst your bubble but he left."

Her eyes go wide. "What?"

"He left. I asked if I could buy him a drink when I got off the phone to you and he said no then left."

She squeals. "This is perfect!"

"What the hell?"

"You can marry him after all!"

"Are you on some kind of drugs?"

"No. I was secretly hoping that you wouldn't trap him because if you did then he would hate you forever but now you can have your love story."

"Earth to Lori. This is real life, not some cheesy Nicholas Sparks movie. He's married and that's the end of it. I'll never see him again."

Famous last words.

Chapter Ten

Mason

I call Buzz into my office the next morning. "Woah, what happened to you?" he asks as he closes the door behind him. "You look like shit."

"Thanks. You really know how to make a person feel good, don't you?"

He grins. "Oh believe me, I do. In fact, I made Stacey feel *very* good last night."

"Psycho ex-girlfriend Stacey?"

"Correct."

"I thought you said you'd rather cut off your balls with a blunt knife than ever see her again? And that you'd rather be celibate for the rest of your life than..."

"Bro!" he shouts, interrupting me. "Don't use the C word." Buzz once applied to be on the TV show *Fear Factor*, stating that his number one fear was celibacy. He was genuinely surprised when he didn't get a call back.

I laugh. "I thought you two were over for good this time."

"We are but it was Thursday yesterday."

"What's that got to do with anything?"

"Throwback Thursday. I'm allowed to sleep with my exes, no strings attached."

"I'm seriously contemplating firing you for saying that."

"Why? It's a real thing. Just like today is Follow Friday." He draws a hash tag in the air. "Or what I like to call hash tag FF."

I pretend to hit my head against the desk. "Please tell me you didn't just do that."

He ignores me. "As I was saying, Follow Friday is where I allow a hot girl to follow me home."

"Oh, so you're going to *allow* them to go home with you rather than spending hours *persuading* them?"

"Yep, you'll see exactly how it works tonight. Are we still on for drinks?"

"Yeah but only if you stop being lame."

"I will if you will. Anyway, how did it go last night? Is that why you look so rough?"

"Again, thank you. But yeah, it was bad."

"Do you want to talk about it?"

"Not really."

"Good, I'm not in the mood to listen to you whine today."

"Remind me, why are we friends again?" I hand him the piece of paper. "Here, go and make yourself useful."

"What's this?" he asks.

"A phone number."

"I can see that, but whose? Is it your assistants? Has she finally fallen for my good looks and boyish charm? They always come back for more."

I ignore him. "I want you to trace it and find out as much as you can."

His face turns serious. "The last time you asked me to do this, somebody ended up dead."

"What the hell are you talking about?"

He begins to laugh. "Sorry, I couldn't resist. I've been watching too much Netflix recently."

"Just trace the number."

"Okay but a little more information would be nice."

"I met somebody last night."

"What do you mean you *met somebody*? A woman?"

I shrug. "It's no big deal."

"So then why are you asking me to trace her number?"

"I'm not. I'm asking you to trace her friend's number."

"You're making no sense. Why have you got her friend's number?"

"Because the woman I met used my phone to call her friend."

He goes from looking confused to looking like a kid in a candy store. "Dude, why was she using your phone? You fucked her, didn't you?" He's practically bouncing up and down.

"She borrowed my phone at the restaurant. Nothing else happened."

"Liar! At least now I know the real reason why you look like shit."

I point to the door. "Just trace the damn number, Buzz."

Chapter Eleven
Sophia

I groan when I walk into Kristen's office the next morning and see Emily staring back at me. Twice in as many days? Lucky me.

"Thanks for coming, Sophia. Emily has asked to sit in on our debrief, is that okay with you?"

Do I really have a choice? "Yeah that's fine," I lie. I can already feel the tension in the air.

"So, how do you think it went last night?" she asks as soon as I'm sitting down.

I shrug. "You've listened to the recording. How do *you* think it went?" After analyzing every little detail in my head after I got home yesterday, I can't be bothered to rehash it all.

"I think it went well," she replies.

"Wait, what? But I failed."

"I think you did great given the circumstances."

"Are you sure you listened to the right recording? I offered to buy him a drink and he said no. We were on our own, if he wanted to cheat then he could have. He obviously wasn't interested."

"I disagree," Emily says, shaking her head. "Last night was my fault. I got it all wrong. I thought my plan was a good way for you to meet but it backfired. He just ended up being pissed at me."

"Exactly, pissed at you for cancelling which means he obviously wanted you there."

"No, he was only angry because he left an important meeting to be there. He wasn't bothered about me at all. I don't think it helped that I text him telling him to grow up after he hung up."

"But if he was so angry then why didn't he stay? If anything, you gave him a motive to cheat last night but he walked away. He passed the test."

Emily stands up. "All I know is that he didn't come

home last night. He switched his phone off after you used it and I haven't heard from him since. He might have passed your test but he certainly didn't pass mine." She begins to pace up and down. "Does that sound like something a trustworthy man would do? Does it sound like something a good husband would do?" She stops in front of me. "I'm going to be honest with you, Sophia. I need your help. I have a unique proposition for you."

"What kind of proposition?"

"I want you to try again."

My mouth falls open. "I'm sorry, what?"

"Nothing has changed. I'm in the exact same situation as I was twenty four hours ago. I want you to try again. I want you to trap Mason."

"Is this some kind of joke?"

"The only joke right now is my marriage."

"I don't know what to say."

"Then say yes."

Kristen clears her throat. "You didn't get a fair shot yesterday. Nobody would have been able to trap him."

My cell buzzes loudly from inside my purse. I ignore it and turn to my boss. "But we never try to trap the same man twice, we both know that."

"Why not?" Emily interrupts. "Is that because nobody has actually asked you to try until now?"

"She has a good point," Kristen replies.

"Or maybe it's because our clients are usually happy when their husbands say no. Why can't you just be satisfied that Mason walked away?"

"Just because he walked away last night doesn't mean he will continue to walk away. I listened to the recording and you two definitely had a connection. You must have felt it." *Here we go again.* "For starters, he would never allow a stranger to use his cell. Jesus, he won't even let me use it. And don't get me started on the cute little jokes. We haven't joked around like that in a long time. If he's like that with you after five minutes, what would he be like after five hours? Or five days?"

"I don't think it's a good idea. Now that we've already met, it would look suspicious to just bump into each other again."

"Well we can wait a week if that's what you're worried about. But like you said, he's already met you so it'll be easier this time around. He should feel more comfortable talking to you."

I reach into my purse when my cell buzzes for a second time. "I'm not sure. I think you should ask somebody else instead." I look down at my phone and see one missed call and a text, both from Lori. I open her message.

"OMG!!! Call me!!!"

Emily perches on the edge of Kristen's desk. "Let me ask you a question. How many men have you trapped?"

I look up from my phone. "Um, I'm not sure. I don't keep track."

"Roughly?"

"Hundreds."

"And how many times have you failed?"

Where is she going with this? "Five, including Mason."

"Exactly. Those numbers speak for themselves. You're the best at what you do. I don't want somebody else to try. I want you. Please help me, Sophia."

For the first time since meeting her, I actually see sincerity in her eyes. I can't help but feel a tiny bit sorry for her. I sigh. "Look, my job is to try and tempt a man. I can't force somebody to cheat if they don't want to. If I'm being completely honest, I don't think we would get a different outcome if I tried again. I'm struggling to see what would change in the space of a day or even a week."

Emily nods. "I agree and that's why I said I have a *unique* proposition for you. Mason is different to most of the men you've trapped in the past. He has more to lose than most people. He's a well known businessman with a reputation to upkeep. Even if he wanted to cheat last night, he wouldn't have. He can't risk jumping into bed with the first attractive woman he sees. What if you were a journalist? Or working for a rival company?"

"Or a honey trap?" I interrupt.

"Exactly. He wouldn't risk a one night stand but that doesn't prove that he's not a cheater. So here's my offer - I don't want you to try and trap him in one night, that's unrealistic. I want you to take things slow. I want you to get to know him and establish some kind of relationship with him. I'm giving you five weeks to trap him. Five weeks to do whatever it takes. Five weeks for fifty grand."

Did I just hear her right? Fifty grand. Fifty. Thousand. Dollars. That's a whole lot of money and a whole different ball game. I can feel the adrenaline pumping through my veins as I try to process it all. Even though it sounds pretty crazy, I'd be lying if I said I wasn't intrigued by her offer. "Why five weeks?"

She shrugs. "Five weeks will give you enough time to form some kind of relationship with him without making me wait too long for the outcome. Ten grand a week sounds about right. You already have a connection, now you just need to build on it. Five weeks should be a fair test."

"A fair test for who?"

"For my husband. Calling it a trap suggests that the man is somehow getting the raw end of the deal but like you said, you can't force somebody to cheat. If he's not interested then he can carry on with his life as normal and none of this will affect him. No harm, no foul."

I've got to admit that what she's saying makes sense but I still have some doubts. "How would it work?"

"I'll find out where he's going to be and give you the heads up. I know for a fact that he has a charity event next week so we could start there. Beyond that, it's up to you how it works. I don't care what you do as long as you get results."

"What if I fail?"

"Then I'll walk away."

"What about the money?"

"I don't expect you to work for free. You'll get your money regardless of the outcome."

"What if she traps him on the next attempt?" Kristen asks.

"Don't worry, you'll still get your fifty grand."

She looks more than pleased by Emily's answer. My cell buzzes for a third time but I ignore it and instead look to Kristen. "Would I still be sent out on other traps?"

"Of course not. You can concentrate solely on Mason."

I nod and stand up. "I don't have any more questions right now but I need some time to think about it."

"That's fine," Emily replies. "But if my husband is cheating on me, I would like to know sooner rather than later."

"Why don't you take a day or two to think about it?" Kristen asks.

"Okay. I'll call you with my decision." Both pairs of eyes follow me as I walk over to the door.

"I wouldn't be wasting my time if I didn't think this could work," Emily says as I push down on the door handle. I don't look back as I close the door behind me. I carry on walking, taking several deep breaths as I go. What was supposed to be a routine debrief turned into something else entirely. I pull my phone out of my purse and head over to the elevator. I'm about to call Lori when I notice another text from her.

"Mason Hunter just called me!!! He was asking about u & has invited us for drinks tonight!! 3 words - Maid. Of. Honor."

Is this real life? I don't even know what to think anymore. Five minutes ago I was defending Mason but now he's calling my best friend and inviting us for drinks. The elevator doors open and I have a decision to make. Do I step inside and let my doubts and fear of the unknown hold me back or do I turn around and take the biggest risk of my career so far?

Chapter Twelve

Mason

"Do you want the good news or the bad news?" Buzz asks when we finish eating our lunch.

"Bad first," I reply.

"I traced the number but I couldn't get a name or address because it's a burner phone."

"So what's the good news?"

He grins. "Well I could have triangulated the signal but I decided to save time and just dial the number instead. The good news is that she sounds really fucking hot. Thanks for helping a brother out. I've saved her number for my own personal use."

The sandwich I've just eaten begins to churn inside my stomach. "You called it?"

"Yep. She's got this husky voice thing going on. She could make a shit ton of money working for one of those phone sex chat lines."

I place my head in my hands. "Why? Why would you do that? I could have just called her if I knew that's what you were going to do."

"Yeah you could have but you didn't."

"For fuck's sake, Buzz. I asked you to trace the number, not call it."

"You also asked me to find out as much information as possible which is what I was trying to do. What's the problem?"

I sigh. "The problem is that you never follow instructions. Just tell me what you know. Did she mention her friend?"

"Yeah, it's her roommate."

"I thought so. Last night she said something about feeding their dog. Did you get an address or anything?"

"Let me think about that for a second...oh yeah, she told me her address after giving me her social security number and bank details." He laughs. "I didn't ask for her address. That would have been weird, even for me." He puts on a creepy voice. "Do you like scary movies?" He starts to breathe heavily. "What are you wearing?"

I ignore him. "What else did you find out?"

"Nothing. She wouldn't tell me anything, not even her name. It was like talking to the secret service."

"So let me get this straight. You called the number even though I didn't ask you to and the only thing you've found out is that they're roommates?"

"Correct."

"Well thanks for being so helpful."

"You're welcome."

"Did you mention me?"

"The world doesn't revolve around you, boss."

"Answer the question."

He shrugs. "No, I didn't *mention* you."

I groan. "Oh no, what did you do?" I can already tell that it's bad by the look on his face.

"If I tell you, you're not allowed to fire me. I was only trying to help."

"Just tell me."

He winces. "There's a small chance that I pretended to be you."

It's even worse than what I imagined. I close my eyes and take a deep breath. "Get out."

"Aww come on, it's not that bad. I thought there was more of a chance of her telling me something if she believed it was you."

"Well clearly it didn't work, did it?"

He shrugs. "I didn't anticipate her being so guarded. Chicks before dicks and all that crap."

"Just get out. Go somewhere far away and stay there for a while."

"Awesome, does that mean I can work from home this afternoon?"

"No. Now get out before I come over there and kick your ass."

"You couldn't kick my..." I stand up which makes him rush out of the room midsentence.

Knowing Buzz, he's bound to have said something stupid or offensive...or both. Should I call back and apologize or just act like it never happened? Act like last night never happened? Even if I wanted to, there's a part of last night that I don't think I'll be able to forget any time soon.

A few seconds later, Buzz sticks his head around the door. "There's one more thing you should probably know. I've invited them to come for drinks with us tonight."

Chapter Thirteen

Sophia

"Six weeks for six figures," I announce as I walk back into the office. "I want one hundred grand."

Kristen looks surprised to see me but Emily simply raises one eyebrow. I don't expect her to agree to that amount of money but it's worth a try. I remain poker faced. "You have balls, Sophia. Big ones." She pauses for a few seconds. "I like it." She crosses the room and stops in front of me. It feels like a whole minute passes before she finally holds out her right hand. "We have ourselves a deal. Six weeks for six figures." Kristen lets out a sigh of relief while we shake hands. "What made you decide to do it?" Emily asks.

"Your husband. He's invited me for drinks tonight."

Her eyes widen. "When did this happen?"

"Just now. He called my roommate. He had her number after I used his phone last night."

"Well, well, well. It didn't take him very long, did it? This is why I need your help, Sophia. I need you to find out what else he's willing to do."

"Okay, but if we're doing this, we're doing it on my terms," I tell her.

"That's fine."

"Our relationship needs to feel as natural as possible. Wearing a wire and having a camera following us around isn't natural. Plus, I can't risk the wire falling out or being exposed. "

"But then how will we get the evidence?"

"Text messages, emails, phone conversations. I can take photographs on my phone too. I'll get your evidence."

"Okay then, no wires or cameras." She pulls some paper and a pen out of her purse and starts to write.

"We communicate via Kristen to keep things professional. I'll check in with her after each meeting then she can pass on any information to you."

"Anything else?" Emily asks, still writing.

"Not that I can think of right now."

"Okay, good. I have a few rules of my own. The first is that you have to see him at least twice a week. Anything less than that is unacceptable. I'm not paying you six figures for nothing. Obviously I would like you to see him as much as possible so you can prove whether or not he's willing to cheat but I also don't want him to get suspicious. My next rule is that you have to see the six weeks through to the end unless you trap him before then. You can't change your mind and back out half way through. I will be your new boss for the next six weeks. And last but not least, you can't tell anybody what we're doing. That's why I need you to sign this." She hands me the piece of paper that she's just been writing on.

"What's this?"

"A non-disclosure agreement."

"What's it for?"

"Protection. To make sure nobody finds out about this. I added in your stipulations at the end so you'll need to sign and date those too."

I take a minute to skim-read both pages. "So basically this is just a fancy way of saying that I'm not allowed to tell anybody what we're doing or you'll take legal action."

"Yes. I can't risk Mason finding out."

"Well it wouldn't exactly be ideal for me either. If the paparazzi found out, I'd be out of a job. I'm not going to say a word." I sign and date the paper in several different places before handing it back to her.

"Excellent. Now I just need Kristen and your friend to sign it too."

"Lori?"

"Yes, she already knows too much."

"What's in it for her?"

"I'll be sure to reward her for keeping her mouth shut."

"I'll ask her to sign it the next time she's in the office," Kristen tells her.

"Are we done here?" I ask. I've spent more than enough time with Emily for one day. Now it's time to go home and try to process everything before I spend the evening with her husband.

"Yes, that's everything," Emily replies.

I nod and tell Kristen that I'll call her tonight. Just as I'm about to open the door, Emily calls my name. I turn back around. "Good luck for tonight."

"I don't believe in luck," I reply before leaving the office once more.

No. I believe in hard work and killer heels.

Chapter Fourteen

Mason

"Why do you keep looking over at the door every two minutes?" Buzz asks with a shit-eating grin on his face.

"Shut up and drink your beer," I reply.

"She might not even show up. I hope you're not going to sulk for the rest of the night if she's a no show."

"I have no idea what you're talking about."

He laughs. "You know exactly what I'm talking about." *Of course I do but I'm not going to admit that to him.* "Are you ever going to tell me what she looks like? You know, so I can look out for her."

"What who looks like?"

"Your woman from last night. Stop playing dumb."

"My woman? What are we, cavemen?"

"Pretty much. Trust me, women love alpha males. They eat that shit up like it's going out of style."

"Isn't that just an excuse for men to act like crazy motherfuckers and get away with it?"

"Yeah pretty much. Why do you think *Fifty Shades of Grey* is so popular? The main character is a moody bastard who treats that poor chick like shit but hey it's fine because he's an alpha male."

"How do you know so much about *Fifty Shades of Grey*?"

"I went to see the movie."

"Why?"

He winks. "Because I knew there would be hundreds of horny women leaving the cinema at the same time as me."

I laugh. "You're such a creepy bastard."

"I think the word you're looking for is *genius*."

"Nah, I'll stick with creep. So was it worth it?"

"Well let's just say that I went to watch it every day that week."

"And there's me thinking that women appreciate a gentleman."

"Not anymore. Open a door for a woman and you're

too nice. Call her back and you're too attainable. Pay for dinner and you're sexist. These days you've gotta treat 'em mean, keep 'em keen. You've been out of the game for too long."

"I guess so."

"Don't worry, just follow my lead."

"Even if I *was* back in the game, I would never follow your lead."

He nearly chokes on his beer. "Even if you were back in the game? Have you heard yourself? You're either in denial or full of shit. I'm leaning towards the latter. You wouldn't have chosen a table directly opposite the door if you weren't back in the game. Your legs wouldn't be nervously bouncing up and down if you weren't back in the game and don't get me started on that fancy-ass cologne you're wearing. Not only are you back in the game, you're about to bat for the fucking Yankees, my friend." He holds up his bottle of beer. "On behalf of the entire female population, welcome back."

I ignore him and down the rest of my Jack and Coke. "Oh look, it's time for another drink. I guess that means I'll have to go to the bar...*alone*." I quickly stand up before he can say anything else and begin to weave my way through the sea of people on the dance floor. Pulse is one of the busiest clubs in town and tonight is no exception. I came close to buying it last year but Emily talked me out of it. She said it attracts the wrong type of crowd but what she really meant was that it attracts other women.

When I finally make it over to the bar, I'm actually relieved that there's a wait. I'm in no rush to get back to Buzz and his theories, even if there is some truth behind them. I spend the next five minutes debating whether or not to go and wash off some of my 'fancy-ass' cologne.

"Hey Mason," Tarryn shouts from behind the bar when I make it to the front of the line. She's been working at Pulse for a couple of years but I've known her for a lot longer. She throws a bottle of liquor high in the air before catching it upside down and pouring some into a glass.

"Show off," I joke. "When are you coming to work for me instead?"

"I'm not a good fit for your business, I keep telling you this."

"You're an awesome bartender so that makes you the *perfect* fit."

She walks over to the cash register. "How many of your staff have tattoos?"

"I have no idea."

She hands somebody their change. "Exactly. So that means they either don't have any or they are in places where they can be covered up. I might have a problem doing that." She kisses the pin up girl which covers the whole of her right forearm. "Besides, I wouldn't want to."

"And I wouldn't ask you to. I don't care what my staff look like as long as they're good at what they do."

She snorts. "*You* might not care but I'm pretty sure your customers would. Suits and tats don't mix." She hands me my usual Jack and Coke without having to ask. "Anything else?"

"Just a beer, please."

She rolls her eyes. "Let me guess, you're here with Buzz?"

I laugh. "Afraid so." Tarryn and Buzz used to be good friends until the night he took her little sister's virginity. He swore that he had no idea she was a virgin until afterwards, not that it would have stopped him. I regularly remind her that it could be worse…he could have ended up being her brother-in-law. That always seems to make her feel better.

She gets a bottle of beer from the fridge and removes the cap. "Can I spit in it?"

"You know what Buzz is like, he would probably like it."

"I bet he would, the asshole." She places the bottle down in front of me and then shakes her head when I try to hand her a fifty dollar bill. "On the house," she tells me. I wink at her and drop it into the tip jar instead. "Have you seen much of Indiana recently?" she asks. "I'm meeting up with her once I've finished my shift. We're going to check out that new sushi place around the corner." She laughs when I scrunch my nose up in disgust. I don't understand why anybody would spend money on that crap when God gave us pizza.

"Yeah, I saw her a couple of nights ago. She came over to the hotel."

"The hotel?"

"Don't ask. Make sure she stays out of trouble tonight, okay?"

She laughs. "Since when has your sister ever listened to me?"

"How about the time you persuaded her to skip school and get a tattoo instead? You took her to that crappy little studio that ended up getting shut down a week later for failing health and safety checks. I still remember the look on your faces when I walked in."

"You turned up just in time." She holds out her thumb and forefinger. "We were *this* close."

"Hey lady!" Somebody shouts from the other end of the bar. "Can we get some service down here?"

"You'd better go," I tell her. "Call me if you need a ride home later. I don't care what time it is. I'll send a car for you both."

"Okay, thanks Mason. Have a good night."

"You too." I pick up our drinks, one in each hand, and make my way back to Buzz. Surprise, surprise, he's not alone when I reach our table. He's talking to two women; a blonde and a brunette. I don't think it's physically possible for him to go longer than a minute without hitting on somebody. I pause and consider
leaving him alone but it's too late, he's already spotted me. He wiggles his eyebrows up and down before motioning for me to join him. The two women turn around to see who he's looking at.

Holy shit.

It's her.

Chapter Fifteen
Sophia

It's him.

He's standing a few feet away, eyes wide like he's surprised to see me. Maybe he thought I wouldn't show up. I didn't think that it was possible but he looks even more handsome than he did last night. The realization of what I've agreed to do kicks in and for the first time in a long time, I feel nervous on a trap. I can't decide whether my sweaty palms are because I know how much is at stake or because of the way Mason is staring at me.

"Are you just going to stand there?" Buzz shouts over to him.

I hope not. I'm already getting bored of Buzz's cheesy pick-up lines and lame attempt at flirting. At least Lori seems to like it. She noticed him as soon as we arrived which isn't surprising seeing as though he has the 'Three T's'. A guy must be tall, toned and have tattoos or else Lori isn't interested. I was just about to excuse myself and go in search of Mason when he found us first.

He finally breaks out of his trance and walks over to us. He places a couple of drinks down on the table and I notice that he isn't wearing his wedding ring. He was definitely wearing one last night when he thought he was meeting his wife. Forget six weeks, this might be over a lot quicker than that.

"Ladies, this is my friend, Mason," Buzz tells us. "Mason, meet my new friends, Lori and Sophia."

"I'm Lori and this is Sophia," Lori clarifies since I never told him my name last night.

"Hello," Mason replies, concentrating solely on me. He looks like he's about to say something else but Buzz beats him to it.

"The ladies were keeping me company seeing as though you ditched me."

Lori laughs. "You're a big boy, I'm sure you can be left

alone for ten minutes."

"You're right," Buzz replies. "I am a big boy. *Very* big."

"Yeah, what are you, about six foot four?" she asks.

He winks. "I wasn't talking about my height, sweetheart."

"I know, I was joking. Just like you were joking about being big, *sweetheart*."

He looks surprised and even a little bit excited by her response. "How do you know I was joking if you've never seen it? Maybe you should take a look so you can set the record straight."

She shrugs. "I would but I've left my microscope at home."

I can't help but laugh. Mason leans in closer to me. "Hello again, *Sophia*."

The hairs on my arms stand up. Who knew my name could sound so sexy? "Hello, Mason."

"Well now that we've been formally introduced, how are you?"

"Relieved that I don't have to third wheel with those two anymore."

He laughs. "I swear I need to keep him on a leash."

"I'm sure Lori will have a few spare."

"Ah yeah, what breed of dog do you have?"

"I'm sorry, what?"

"Your dog. What breed is it?"

"My dog?" What is he talking about? I don't have a...*ohhhh*. "That's right, I have a dog." Shit, shit, shit, my mind goes completely blank. Why can't I think of anything other than how much of an idiot I must look right now? "Um, it's a...it's a...black dog. It's black. I mean, she's black. She's a black la...lab...labrador! Yes! She's a black labrador." *Thank god for that.* I say it with a little too much enthusiasm. Talk about being put on
the spot. Rookie mistake, Sophia. "This is a nice place," I say as I look around, trying to change the subject.

"I'm sorry about last night," he tells me, ignoring my

comment about the club.

"Sorry for what exactly?" I ask.

"For acting like a dick."

"Oh yeah, you were such a dick when you let me borrow your phone," I reply sarcastically. "I can't believe you did that."

"And I can't believe I left you on your own without checking that you had a ride home, especially when I knew your phone wasn't working properly. I couldn't sleep last night. I couldn't stop thinking about you."

"Oh?" I hold his gaze and it suddenly feels like I'm just a normal girl with a normal job talking to a normal guy. An *insanely hot,* normal guy.

"You know, because I was worried."

"Right." I wave him off. "It's fine. I didn't have any money left for a cab so I just crashed in the parking lot. No biggie."

His eyes go wide. "What?"

"It was actually pretty fun, kind of like camping but without all of the fun stuff. I did find an old blanket in the dumpster though, it was surprisingly comfortable. Moldy but comfortable." He looks like he's about to have a heart attack. "Mason, I'm joking. I got home fine."

"Jesus, don't do that to me."

"I'm sorry, I couldn't resist. You should have seen your face."

He laughs. "Well I'm just glad you were okay. Seriously though, I'm sorry if I came across as rude yesterday. I wasn't having the best day as you could probably tell."

"Yeah, I kind of guessed when I saw you assaulting the bench."

"I'll admit that wasn't one of my finest moments."

"I hope you didn't take it out on your furniture when you got home."

"I didn't go home," he replies.

I know, your wife has already told me. "Couldn't trust yourself?" I joke.

He shakes his head. "I couldn't take the risk. I really like my coffee table."

"That's very sensible of you. And what about tonight?"

"What about it?" he asks.

I drop my gaze then look back up at him through lowered lashes. "Do you think you'll be able to trust yourself?"

Chapter Sixteen

Mason

I'm pretty sure we're not talking about coffee tables anymore. I try to think of something flirty or funny to say but my mind goes completely blank.

Just say something...

Anything...

The longer you stay quiet, the more awkward it will be.

Words, remember them?

She laughs. "Do you need some time to think about it?"

"Apparently so."

"Well don't keep me waiting too long, will you?"

I blurt out the first thing that comes into my head. "Did your date show up?" *Smooth.*

"Excuse me?"

"Last night. Did your date show up after I left?"

She laughs. "No but thanks for bringing it up."

"It's his loss."

"Hmmm, I didn't have you down as a cliché kind of guy."

"I'm not. I'm an *honest* guy," I reply.

She shakes her head. "He probably walked in, saw me, and then left."

"I'm pretty sure that wouldn't have happened."

"It might have, you never know."

"Trust me, it didn't happen."

"How are you so sure? Wait a minute..." She gasps, feigning shock. "Oh my god, it was you, wasn't it? You were my blind date?"

I play along, holding both of my hands up in surrender. "You've got me."

"So you're horny guy sixty nine?"

I laugh. "Yes, yes I am."

"Well it's nice to finally put a name to a face. How did you come up with your charming username?"

I don't know if it's the alcohol kicking in or the adrenaline pumping through my veins but I haven't felt this kind of a connection with anybody in a long time. It feels like the old me is coming back. "I wanted to pick something meaningful and sixty nine just so happens to be my favorite number."

"What a coincidence, it's my favorite number too."

"Did somebody say sixty nine?" Buzz appears out of nowhere, Lori by his side. He leans closer and shouts over the music, almost deafening me. "Looks like you've forgotten all about the other girl you're supposed to be meeting. I don't blame you, brother." If he was trying to keep the conversation strictly between me and him then he failed. It's obvious that Sophia and Lori heard him too. I wouldn't be surprised if Tarryn heard him all the way from the bar. I give him my best "be quiet or else" face but it's completely lost on him. "Why are you looking at me like that?" he asks.

I sigh. Sometimes he can be really hard work. "Sophia *is* the girl I'm supposed to be meeting."

He looks from me to Sophia then back again with a blank look on his face. "What are you talking about?"

"We met last night at Scoma's."

His confusion quickly turns to excitement. "No way! What are the chances of that? You come back from the bar and I just so happen to be talking to the right girls. Why didn't you say something sooner?"

"You didn't give me a chance."

"Wait a minute," Lori says, looking at me. "So you're who I spoke to earlier on the phone?"

I glance at Buzz who has a huge grin on his face. I'm about to tell her the truth when he decides to answer for me. "I bet you were surprised to hear from him, weren't you?"

She ignores him and instead narrows her eyes. "You sound different in person."

"I wonder why," Buzz says, laughing. He stops when I elbow him in the ribs.

"Where do you both work?" Lori asks.

"And here come the questions," Sophia says, shaking her head. "I'm sorry."

"It's fine." I shrug. "I own a business."

Buzz laughs. "Business? As in just one? You modest son of a bitch."

"What kind of business?" Sophia asks.

"Um, I own a couple of hotels."

"A couple? More like hundreds," Buzz says.

"Will you shut up?" I ask, wishing that he was at the opposite end of the room. Even though I'm extremely proud

65

of what I've achieved, I don't like telling people who I've only just met because it usually makes them
act differently around me.

"Yes boss." He looks at Lori. "I work for Mason. I'm his bitch."

"What's Mason like as a boss?" Sophia asks, grinning.

"Well I haven't had a pay rise in two years so go figure."

"You have to earn it," I tell him.

"Why? It's so unfair. If I was a woman, I could just sleep my way to the top."

Lori scowls. "You're such a pig."

"It's okay, you'll learn to love it."

"That's never going to happen," she replies, before turning to me. "Will you tell us the story behind his nickname? He won't tell us."

I laugh. "Good luck with that one."

"Come on, it can't be that bad," she says.

"Ah, I don't know about that. He's had it since he was seventeen."

"Dude, you're already saying too much."

"Is it because you used to have a buzz cut or something?" she asks him.

"Nope."

"Do you have a weird fetish for bees?"

"Is that even a thing?" I whisper to Sophia.

She laughs. "I don't know but if it was, Lori would know about it."

"Why do you want to know so much about me?" Buzz asks her. "You like me, don't you? If you want my phone number, all you need to do is ask, sweetheart."

"In your dreams. And stop calling me sweetheart."

"In my dreams? When I dream about you, you won't be asking for my telephone number. You'll be asking me, no, *begging* me for something else."

"Why does it always have to be about sex with you?" she asks.

"Who said it was anything to do with sex?" He grins.

"You have a dirty mind."

In the corner of my eye, I see somebody approaching us. I groan when I realize who it is. I tap Buzz on the shoulder. "Incoming, nine o'clock."

"Fuck," he says before quickly whispering something to Lori.

She rolls her eyes then places her hand in his. "You owe me big time."

"This should be interesting," I mumble under my breath.

"What's happening?" Sophia asks.

"Buzz's ex-girlfriend is heading this way."

Chapter Seventeen
Sophia

I shoot a worried look in Lori's direction. "Behave."

She winks. "I always do."

"Hey Buzz," his ex says without even looking at him. She's too busy burning holes into Lori's skull.

"Hey Stacey, how are you?" he asks.

She finally looks at him and winks. "A little sore after last night." Mason chuckles when he spots my raised eyebrow. "Who are your friends? Aren't you going to introduce us?"

Buzz points to Mason. "This is Mason. I might have mentioned him once or twice."

"Very funny. I already know Mason." She points to Lori. "And who might this be?"

"This is my girlfriend."

She laughs. "Your girlfriend? Since when?"

"Since ten seconds ago," Mason whispers to me.

"Does she know that you fucked me last night?"

"Well if she didn't then she does now."

Lori smiles. "Yes, I already knew."

"And you're okay with it?"

She shrugs. "It was Throwback Thursday."

Buzz's jaw hits the ground as soon as the words leave her mouth and I'm pretty sure I can see little hearts floating around in his eyes. "Come here, *sweetheart*." He leans in and kisses her like he's been waiting to do it all of his life. When he finally pulls away, Lori looks a little taken aback but recovers quickly.

Stacey shakes her head. "So let me get this straight. You don't mind that your boyfriend cheated on you?"

"We only became official tonight so technically he didn't cheat on me."

"Buzz doesn't know the meaning of the word official. He's not a commitment kind of guy."

"I am now," Buzz replies, looking only at Lori. "I don't

want anyone else."

"You won't be saying that when you're back in my bed next week."

Lori takes a step towards her. "You're right, he won't be saying that. He won't be saying anything to you because you won't be seeing him again. He's mine now. If you go anywhere near him, or me for that matter, then we're going to have a very big problem."

"Are you threatening me?"

"Oh, did I not make that clear enough?"

Stacey turns to Buzz. "Since when do you like prim and proper?"

"You know nothing about me," Lori says. "And I intend to keep it that way. Bye bye." She waves her away.

"Call me when you get bored of little miss vanilla." She looks at each one of us in turn before walking away.

Lori shakes free of Buzz's hand. "Kiss me again and I'll break your jaw."

"Oh my god, you're perfect," Buzz replies, ignoring her. "You're sexy when you're angry."

"Oh, please. It was all an act. How long did you date her?"

"Not long. I wouldn't even call it dating."

"Okay then, how long did you sleep with her for?"

"About nine months."

"She doesn't seem like your type."

He shrugs. "I had to occupy myself while I was waiting for you."

"Well you'll be keeping yourself occupied for a very long time."

"No I won't. We're official now, remember? You said so yourself."

"If we were official then I would know the story behind your nickname."

He laughs. "Where have you been all my life?"

"Avoiding you. My parents warned me about guys like you."

"Woah, woah, woah! Slow down for a second. Parents love me." He grins. "Tell her, Mason. Tell her how much your mom loves me."

"My mother despises him," Mason replies. "More drinks?"

"I'll come with you," I tell him. "I think we should give the new couple some time alone."

"Very funny," Lori replies as we walk away.

"So what are his odds looking like right now?" Mason asks.

"Hmmm, I'd say slim to none."

"Hey, that's pretty good for him. He'd be happy with that."

"He's definitely her type but I'm not sure his ex did him any favors. She kind of has a no baggage rule. What's the story with them anyway?"

He groans. "Where do I start? Do you want to hear about the fake pregnancy or the time she broke into his apartment and cut all the sleeves off of his shirts?"

"Oh my god, she faked being pregnant?"

"Yep, she even printed a fake scan picture off the internet. That's how he found out she was lying because it had some other woman's name and date of birth on it. Sloppy."

"Jesus. I thought that kind of thing only happened in movies. Why isn't he running in the opposite direction as fast as he can?"

"How can I put this? Buzz finds it hard to say no, especially when it's being handed to him on a plate."

"Hence the commitment issues?"

He nods. "It's weird, he seems to fall in love really easily but once the honeymoon period is over, he moves on to the next woman."

I definitely need to remember all of this to tell Lori. "So he's in love with the idea of love?"

"Maybe. Or maybe he just hasn't found the right woman for him, the one who can keep the spark alive for longer than a few weeks."

"Well he's never going to find her if he keeps going back to his ex."

"That's what I keep telling him."

By the time we reach the bar, I've lost count of the number of women who stopped what they were doing to stare at Mason. It's no surprise as he's easily the best looking man in the club. "Mason?"

"Yeah?"

"That bartender is staring at you."

He looks around then waves. "Oh, that's my little sister's best friend. I've known her forever."

I smile and it's a genuine one. It's nice to find out something that I didn't already know about him. "You have a sister?"

"Yes. Indiana. She's a year younger than me."

"Wow, small age gap. Are you close?"

"Very." I already knew what his answer was going to be. His face lit up when he started talking about her. "What about you, have you got any siblings?"

"Nope, I'm an only child. I used to beg my parents for a little brother or sister but it never happened. That's why I've always said that I want to have loads of kids one day."

He grins. "How many are we talking?"

"A lot. Five, six, ten."

"Wow, enough to make your own soccer team then?"

"That's the plan."

"Sounds like a good one if you ask me."

"What about you? Do you want children?"

His smile fades. "One day, when the time is right. I need stability first."

I nod but wonder what he means by that. Mason has a wife, a good job and a place to call home. If anyone has stability then surely it's him. But then I remember why I'm even here in the first place. His wife thinks he's a cheater. I've been so caught up in conversation that I've forgotten about trapping him. Maybe it's the talk of children or his candid answer but I suddenly feel very uncomfortable. I decide to amp it up and take a bolder approach. The sooner I get this over with, the better. I lean closer to him so that our bodies are touching. "Well I'm sure we can have lots of fun practicing in the meantime." His eyes turn dark.

Time to get this show on the road.

Chapter Eighteen
Mason

I'm not about to admit that I could count the amount of practice I've had in the last year on one hand. So instead, I play along. "You know what they say - practice makes perfect."

She smiles which makes the corners of her eyes crinkle. "I thought they say practice makes permanent."

"Even better," I reply.

She laughs. "You know, I'm a little rusty. I should probably start practicing as soon as possible, maybe even tonight."

"Correct me if I'm wrong but I'm pretty sure you'll need a partner for that." I can't focus on anything other than her mouth. Her blood red lips are making my own blood pump a lot faster, rushing to one body part in particular.

"You're right, I will. Do you know anybody who might be interested?"

I'm about to answer honestly when somebody taps me on the shoulder. I turn around expecting to see Buzz but instead come face to face with Stacey. "Hello, Mason."

"Hey. I'm not sure where Buzz is."

"I don't care. I actually wanted to speak to you." She glances at Sophia. "Am I interrupting?"

Yes. "What's up?" I ask.

"I want to apologize for being rude earlier, I didn't even acknowledge you."

Since when has she ever apologized for being rude? She must be up to something. "Don't worry about it."

She turns her attention to Sophia. "Hi, we haven't met properly. I'm Stacey."

"Sophia."

"It's nice to meet you. Are you a friend of Emily's?"

By the time I realize what's happening, it's already too late. "Who's Emily?" Sophia asks, falling right into her trap.

"Mason's wife." I've never seen a person look so smug.

"Wait, did you not know that he was married?" She looks down at my hand. "Then again, how are you supposed to know when he doesn't wear his wedding ring?"

My stomach churns. The thought of Sophia knowing that I'm married bothers me a lot more than it should. "Why are you doing this?" I ask her.

"I could ask you the same thing. Shouldn't you be at home with your wife?"

"I think it's time for you to go home, Stacey." Tarryn shouts from behind the bar.

"No thanks, I think I'll stay."

"I wasn't asking you, I was telling you."

"Oh please, you can't make me leave. You're just a bartender, not the boss."

"I might not own the place but this is *my* bar and I don't want you here anymore." She signals for one of the security guards to come over.

Stacey takes a step closer to Sophia. "Maybe now you'll think twice about fucking him. Or at least feel guilty about it afterwards." As the security guard pulls her away from us, I notice red wine running down the entire length of Sophia's dress. "Woops, it slipped out of my hand," Stacey says. "Tell your friend to stay away from Buzz."

Sophia groans and begins to dab at her dress with some napkins. "Are you okay?" I ask.

She nods but it isn't very convincing. "Where are the rest rooms?"

"Here, come and use the staff room," Tarryn says while punching a code into the door behind the bar.

"Thank you," Sophia replies before turning to me. "Will you come with me?"

"Yes, of course," I reply, a little too quickly. I follow her inside and watch as she walks over to the sink.

"Take as much time as you need," Tarryn says before leaving us alone.

"This is never going to come out. Jeez, she could have at least thrown *white* wine at me."

I can't help but think that if this had happened to Emily, she would be causing a huge scene, not making a joke. I perch on the end of a table. "I'm sorry."

"It's not your fault."

"She only did it because you were with me."

"Nah, I'm pretty sure she did it because she's a shitty person."

"Well that too."

"Why did I have to choose a lilac dress?"

"What she said out there…can I explain?"

She smiles politely. "You don't have to explain anything."

"I know but I don't want you to think that I'm a jerk who takes off his wedding ring just so I can go out and pick up other women."

"I don't think that at all."

"We're only just getting to know each other. It's not something that I usually tell people as soon as I meet them." I sigh. "It's complicated."

She laughs. "Is that your relationship status on Facebook?"

"I don't have one but if I did it would say single. We've been separated for three months."

Chapter Nineteen
Sophia

I stop dabbing at my dress and look up. I know that he's telling the truth as soon as our eyes meet. My stomach does a somersault. "Oh," is all I can say, trying to hide my shock. Why the hell didn't Emily tell me that they were broken up? And three months is a long time.

"That's why I'm not wearing my wedding ring. I wasn't trying to hide it from you like Stacey was suggesting."

My mind begins to race. I want to ask him a hundred questions but I don't want to raise any suspicion so I try to play it cool. "I'm sorry to hear that."

He shrugs. "Neither of us were happy. To be honest, it should have ended a long time ago."

"Then why didn't it?"

"I didn't want to give up without a fight. I wanted to walk away knowing that I gave it my all. I've always believed that marriage is a lifetime thing but I guess that's only when it's with the right person. Turns out she's not my person."

Wow. "So you don't think you'll work things out?"

"No. It's over. We tried therapy but it didn't help. If anything, it reinforced why we shouldn't be together."

"Are you still living together?" *Go easy on the questions.*

"No. I've been staying at one of my hotels."

"Well that's convenient. You won't even have to pay for the minibar. Shit, I'm sorry. I shouldn't be making jokes about it."

He laughs. "No, it's fine. I've had months to come to terms with it. It's the best thing for both of us. To be honest, it feels good to be talking about it. You're the only person that knows except for Buzz, my mom and my sister."

"Why haven't you told anybody else?"

"Emily keeps saying that she's not ready. I think she's in denial. I decline a lot of invitations and avoid as many social events as possible but sometimes, like last night, I have to wear my wedding ring and act like everything is normal. I hate lying to people. I've tried to be patient and respectful of Emily's feelings but I can't carry on pretending. It's been too long. I want to move on with my life."

"I don't know what to say." I genuinely mean it. This isn't what I signed up for. My phone buzzes in my purse. "I should probably answer it." He nods.

"Where are you?" Lori asks as soon as I pick up, her voice laced with worry.

"I'm in the staff room behind the bar."

"What the hell are you doing in there?"

"Stacey decided that she wasn't finished causing trouble."

"Buzz's ex? What did she do?"

"Poured red wine all over me."

"She did *what*?" she shouts, almost deafening me. "Is she still there?"

"No, she's been kicked out."

"Good. I'd rather not spend the night in a cell. Are you okay?"

I glance up at Mason. He's looking at the floor, his hands in his pockets. "I'm fine, but I'm going to head on home." He looks up at the mention of me leaving.

"Okay, I'll come with you," she replies.

"I don't mind if you want to stay."

"We're a team, remember? I'm walking over there now, see you in a minute."

"You're leaving?" Mason asks.

"Yeah, I need to get some baking soda on my dress or it'll stain." *And try and figure out why your wife has hired me to trap you even though you've been broken up for three months.*

"I can take care of your dress, if you'd like." I raise my eyebrow. "Wait, that sounded wrong. What I meant is that I can get it professionally cleaned for you. It's the least I can do."

"It's fine. I should try to get the stain out tonight. Besides, if I give you my dress, I'll have nothing to wear now, will I?"

Now it's his turn to raise an eyebrow. I desperately try not to blush. Now that I know the truth about his marriage, it feels different between us. Mason isn't in a committed relationship anymore so effectively I've been flirting with a single man. A hot, intelligent, single man. "I'd better go," I finally say, breaking the silence. "Lori will be waiting for me."

He nods. "Can I give you a ride home?"

"No. We can grab a cab. You should stay and enjoy the rest of your night."

"Are you sure? You're not going to crash in the parking lot, are you?"

I laugh. "No, I'm not going to crash in the parking lot and yes, I'm sure. I guess I'll see you around." *At least twice a week according to my contract.*

"I hope so."

"Goodnight, Mason."

"Until next time, Sophia."

Chapter Twenty

Mason

"Dude, what happened?" Buzz asks as soon as I leave the staff room.

"Your ex-girlfriend happened. Why did you have to provoke her like that?"

"Like what?"

"Pretending to be with Lori. Did you really have to kiss her? You know what Stacey is like."

"Exactly, I know what she's like and I wanted her to back off. Anyway, stop trying to blame me for everything and tell me what happened."

"She told Sophia about Emily."

He grimaces. "Sorry, brother."

"I would have told her at some point but now it looks like I was being shady and intentionally keeping it from her. To be honest, I'm more pissed that she threw a drink at her."

"Are you fucking joking?"

"No. Tarryn kicked her out."

"Is she okay?"

"She said she was but she's gone home." I shrug. "I guess actions speak louder than words."

He shakes his head. "Shit."

"I know."

"I can't believe my psycho ex just cockblocked us."

I wait for him to laugh but he doesn't. He's actually being dead serious. "You're a dick."

"Why? What have I done this time?" he shouts as I walk away.

"Mason...are you crying?" Buzz asks on our way home.

"No, I'm not crying."

"You don't have to lie," he says sarcastically. "It's

perfectly normal to cry. Let it all out." I give him the middle finger. "Do you want to talk about it?"

"There's nothing to talk about," I reply.

"Then why are you staring out of the window like you're in a fucking romcom? Jesus, I'm waiting for the depressing background music to kick in."

I turn around to look at him. "My options are pretty limited. I either look out of the window or I look at you."

"Please stop, you are way too funny...said no one ever. Seriously though, why are you being so quiet? Is it because of what happened with Sophia?"

"I've already told you, there's nothing to talk about."

"People only say that when there's *a lot* to talk about."

I sigh. "Just drop it or I'll tell Charlie to leave you here and you can make your own way home."

"Oh yeah, you've just reminded me..." He taps on the privacy screen which separates the front and back of the car. It opens slowly. "Yo Charlie, can we make a quick pit stop at Walmart?" Charlie finds my eyes in the rear view mirror. I simply nod before the screen starts to rise up once again.

"What do you need from Walmart?" I ask.

"*I* don't need anything. *You* need some ice cream for when you get home. You can eat it while you watch *The Notebook* and wallow in self pity. I'll buy you some tissues too so you can wipe away your tears."

I pretend to laugh. "Good idea. Then maybe I'll call Lori and tell her the story behind your nickname before finally hand delivering your pink slip."

He narrows his eyes. "You wouldn't."

"Try me."

"I can't believe you would do that to me."

"Well you better believe it."

"I thought we were bro's. You wouldn't really tell Lori, would you?"

"So I threaten to fire you but the only thing you're bothered about is whether or not I'll tell Lori your nickname?"

"Pretty much. I really like her."

"You always like them to start off with."

"Lori's different."

I laugh. "The past five girls have been *different*." He doesn't seem impressed by my use of air quotes.

"Yeah well I mean it this time."

"You said that last time."

"Fuck off." He turns away from me.

We sit in silence for a little while. It's nice. "Buzz?"

"What?" he asks, without looking at me.

"It's perfectly normal to cry. Let it all out."

"Fuck you."

"Don't worry. I'll let you share my ice cream."

Chapter Twenty One
Sophia

I call Kristen as soon I step out of the cab. She answers immediately. "Sophia, how did it go?"

"Did you know?" I ask.

"Excuse me?"

"Did you know?" I repeat, trying to rein my emotions in.

"What are you talking about? Did I know what?"

"Did you know that Emily and Mason are separated? Tell me the truth."

"I...Sophia..."

She knows. "Yes or no?"

"Yes. But not at first."

I follow Lori into the house. "Why didn't you tell me? This changes things."

"It doesn't change anything."

"Are you joking? It changes everything!"

"This is exactly why I didn't tell you; because I knew you would react like this. It doesn't have to change anything, they're still legally married."

"So what if they're *legally* married? They've been broken up for three months! Three months! Mason's just told me they're not getting back together. It changes everything and you know it."

"Okay, okay, just calm down. We can figure this out together."

"There's nothing to figure out. I'm done."

"Sophia, you need to think about this."

"Trust me, I've already thought about it. It's one thing trapping a married man but trapping one who is separated? That doesn't even make sense. I don't understand why she hired me. Who will I be trapping next? A bachelor? How about a gay guy?"

"I understand what you're saying but you've signed an agreement. There's no backing out now."

"Well I signed it under false pretences. Jesus, I know we signed a non-disclosure agreement but this is something that she definitely should have disclosed."

"Do you really think that Emily will let you quit?"

"I don't care."

"She won't think twice about suing you."

"Well what the hell am I supposed to do?"

She sighs. "They're still married, Sophia. You don't know what goes on behind closed doors. Can you not just treat it like a normal trap and get it over with?"

"No, I can't. And you can tell Emily that he was the perfect gentleman tonight. He was honest and respectful and didn't try anything even though he could have. We were all alone and the only thing he was bothered about was whether I could get home safe and if he could pay for my dry-cleaning. And can you also ask her why the hell she's hired me when they've been broken up for the past few months?"

"I already know the reason why."

"What do you mean?"

"You're not going to like this."

"Oh great, more surprises. Just tell me."

"About an hour ago, Emily called to see if I had any news. It was pretty obvious that she had been drinking. When I told her that you hadn't checked in with me yet, she started asking if I really believed that you could trap Mason. I thought maybe she was having second thoughts or needed some reassurance but then she mentioned that she *needed* you to trap him. The way she said it sounded strange. I asked her what she meant but she kept trying to change the subject. I carried on pushing until she finally told me why she's so desperate to catch Mason cheating."

I groan. "Go on..."

"It turns out they signed a prenup. If either one of them are caught cheating, the other person gets everything. And when I say everything, I mean *everything*. One hundred percent of all properties, savings, shares, you name it. The cheater would be left with nothing. Apparently Mason is huge on honesty and trust."

My head starts to spin. "Oh my god, so she actually *wants* Mason to cheat on her. She wants me to trap him so she can take all of his money."

"I would never have let you sign the agreement if I had known. We need to be clever about this."

"There's no chance in hell that I'm going along with her evil little plan."

"That's fine, but Emily can't know that. You still need to act as though you're trying to trap him. I can help with that too. I can tell her that it's best if we take things slow. We're getting the money regardless of whether you trap him or not so you just need to get through the next six weeks."

"I don't really have much of a choice, do I?"

"I'm afraid not."

I sigh. "He's not like the rest of them. He seems like a decent guy."

"Then we won't have a problem, will we? He won't take the bait and Emily's little plan will fail. Don't let your emotions get in the way. It's just business, remember?"

"How can I forget? I've signed a damn contract."

"Everything's going to be okay. Trust me, these next six weeks will fly by."

Famous last words.

Chapter Twenty Two

Mason

The next morning, I wake up to three missed calls and a text from Buzz. I open up the message which was sent around half an hour ago.

Bro, I need your help! It's important. Can you come get me? The address is 355 Berry Street. I'll explain when you get here. Come alone.

The fact that he wants me to go and get him myself probably means that it's either money or female related. I'm guessing the latter. I quickly throw on a T-shirt and some jeans and head downstairs.

"Good Morning, Mr Hunter," the doorman says as I pass through the lobby.

"Good Morning, Eric," I reply.

"You may need an umbrella today, sir," he informs me as he holds the door open. "Would you like one?"

"No thanks, I think I'll brave it." I instantly regret my decision once I step outside. By the time I make it to the car, I'm drenched. I consider going back inside and getting changed but I don't want to keep Buzz waiting any longer. Charlie quickly steps out of the car when he spots me and goes to open the back door. I hold my hand up. "I'm going to drive myself today, Charlie. Go and spend some time with your wife."

"Thank you, sir," he replies.

I climb inside the Mercedes and punch the address into the GPS. I think about the last time Buzz called me with one of his emergencies. Turns out he had been locked out of a girl's house for almost an hour...naked. I made him sit on top of an emergency foil blanket on the drive home.

Around ten minutes later, I pull up outside the address he gave me. I look around but there's no sign of him so I get out of the car and ring the doorbell. It's still raining but I'm already dripping wet so it makes no difference. When nobody answers, I check that I have the right house before knocking instead. I wait a few seconds but there's still no answer so I pull out my cell, trying my best to shield it from the rain. I call Buzz, which I probably should have done before I even left the hotel.

"I'm here," I tell him when he answers.

"Where?"

"At the address you sent me, getting rained on."

He laughs. "I thought you would have called me first."

"Just come out. I'll go and wait in the car."

"No, wait! I need you to come inside. I've got a little problem."

"Well come and let me in before you have a big problem."

"Knock on the door."

"I already have. Hurry up before I drown out here."

"Knock again."

I do as he asks. "I better be here for a good reason or I swear this is the last time I'm ever bailing you out."

"A good reason? It's a fucking *great* reason."

I hear footsteps then the sound of a chain rattling. "Someone's coming."

"Good. You can thank me later. Just remember that I'm your best friend and you're too pretty for jail."

"Wait, what do you mean? Why will I need to thank..." I stop midsentence when the door opens.

Oh.

Chapter Twenty Three
Sophia

Either my mailman just got a thousand times hotter or Mason Hunter is standing on my doorstep. I pinch myself to check if I'm dreaming.

I'm not.

Mason is standing in front of me, soaking wet. I watch as little drops of rain fall from his floppy hair and make their way down his face. I follow their path as they trickle from his chin onto his white T-shirt; which is now completely see through, revealing rock hard abs. I swallow hard as warmth spreads throughout my entire body. I don't know how long I stare at him but it must be a while as goosebumps begin to form on my arms from the chill outside. I finally manage to tear my eyes away from his body and look up to discover that I'm not the only one admiring the view. His eyes are wide and hungry as they peruse my silk cami and matching shorts. My nipples harden but this time it has nothing to do with the weather. I suddenly remember that I'm not wearing a bra and quickly fold my arms across my chest.

His eyes find mine. "Good morning."

"Morning," I reply, which comes out as more of a whisper. What the hell is he doing here?

"I didn't think I'd be seeing you again this soon."

"Me neither. I'm starting to think that you're stalking me."

"If I was stalking you, wouldn't I be hiding in your bushes?"

"I don't know, you tell me."

He laughs. "How are you?"

"Not bad. You?"

He looks down at his T-shirt. "Um, a little wet."

"Do you want to come inside?" I ask without thinking. Shit, what am I doing?

"Please." He takes a step inside and glances around before his eyes find mine once more.

"Can I get you anything? A towel? Rubber duck?"

He laughs. "A towel would be good."

"Okay, I'll be right back." I walk away but as soon as I'm out of sight, I run to Lori's room and let myself in without knocking. She's in bed, grinning at something on her phone. "Help," I whisper.

She looks up. "Well hello there, nipples."

"Mason's here."

"Is that your explanation or have you changed the subject?"

"Help me," I hiss. She gets out of bed and casually strolls over to her dressing table. "Why are you so calm?" I ask.

She laughs. "I'm sorry, am I supposed to panic?"

"Yes! Panic with me!"

"Well in that case..." She grabs hold of my hands and jumps up and down. "Why is he here? What the hell are we going to do? Who, what, when, where, why?"

I scowl. "You're such a sarcastic bitch." She laughs again. "Shhhh," I tell her. "He'll hear you."

"Oh noooo, god forbid he hears your roommate laughing in her *own house*." She passes me some gum. "Here."

"What's this for? Oh my god, does my breath smell?" I breathe into my hands.

"No but you asked me to help and I don't know what else to do."

"It'll look weird if I go back out there chewing gum."

"Well it's going to look weird anyway after disappearing for half an hour."

"You're not helping. Can I borrow a shirt?"

"No."

"No?"

"No. Free the nipple."

I roll my eyes. "Please just get me one."

"It's a real thing, Google it."

"I don't want to *free the nipple.*"

"I bet Mason would want you to."

"Gah, I hate you." I turn around and head for the door. "Thanks for all of your invaluable help. I don't know what I'd do without you."

"Free the nipple, free the nipple," she begins to chant as I close the door behind me.

I take a deep breath and try to compose myself before heading back to Mason, arms folded across my chest. He smiles as I approach and continues to wipe the rain off his forehead. *The rain.* Shit, I forgot the towel. It's too late to turn around now. "I'm sorry, I couldn't find a towel. I looked everywhere, that's why it took me so long."

"Oh. Don't worry about it, I'm not even that wet." A big drop of rain falls onto his cheek. "Okay, maybe that was a lie."

"Can I get you something to drink?"

"More liquid, why not?"

"Is coffee okay?"

"I don't drink coffee."

I gasp. "A businessman who doesn't drink coffee? But how do you stay awake?"

"Well there's this thing called sleep."

"Ah, I've heard about that. It's what I should be doing at three A.M instead of googling the entire history of the universe. I can get you a bottle of water?"

"Water would be good, thanks. Although I could probably just squeeze the water out of my T-shirt."

I laugh. "Come and sit down."

"Are you sure? I'll drip all over your floors."

"It's fine, they could use a clean."

He takes off his shoes and places them next to a pair of my own. The sight of them lined up makes my stomach flutter. It's such an insignificant thing, a picture of normality, but I didn't realize how much I craved normal until now. "I hope Buzz didn't cause too much trouble last night," he says as he follows me into the kitchen. He must be talking about what happened with Stacey.

"No, it's all good. He was just having fun and got a little

carried away. We could have probably stopped it from happening but it's not that easy when alcohol is involved. Anything can happen. I'll admit that I was a little unsure of him at first but he's harmless. I like him."

His face falls. "You do?"

"Yeah, he's fun and doesn't take himself too seriously. I could totally see us hanging out again."

"Oh," is all he says, looking disappointed.

I laugh, confused by his reaction. "Did I say something wrong?"

"Um, no...it's just...I'm a little surprised. I didn't think you two..."

"You didn't think we would get along? Yeah, he's a little full of himself but nothing I can't handle."

"Where is he?"

"Buzz? How would I know?"

"Has he already left?"

I frown. "Left where? I don't know what you're talking about."

"Buzz said that he was here…and judging by the look on your face, I've been set up. I am *so* going to kick his ass."

I laugh. "Buzz told you that he was here?"

"Yeah, he asked me to come and get him. I didn't know this was your address until you opened the door."

"Why would he do that?"

"I have no idea how his brain works and I'd like to keep it that way."

"Wait a second, did you think that Buzz spent the night?"

"Yeah."

I raise both eyebrows. "With *me*?"

"Well I would have guessed Lori after last night but then you said that you liked him and wanted to hang out again."

"He's not my type," I reply, a little too quickly.

"Good." His response comes just as fast.

I walk over to the fridge and pull out a bottle of water,

90

taking my time to hide the pink blush which is slowly spreading across my cheeks. If this was any other trap, I would like where our conversation was heading and use it to my advantage but now that I know the truth, I can't help but root for Mason. I don't want to do or say anything which could help his wife get the evidence she needs. But trying not to flirt with a man as handsome as Mason is an almost impossible task. "Lori must have given him our address," I say, changing the subject. It would explain why she was acting so weird just now. She didn't seem surprised when I told her that Mason was here, almost as though she was expecting it. "They must be up to something."

"Buzz is always up to something."

"They sound like the perfect match."

"He wouldn't shut up about her last night. Speaking of which, did you manage to get the stain out of your dress?"

"No, it's ruined."

"What's ruined?" Lori asks as she walks in the room. "Hey Mason, nice shower?"

"Very refreshing, thank you."

"You're dripping everywhere. Do you want a towel?"

"We don't have any," I tell her.

"What? There are loads in the bathroom."

"No there's not. We need to do laundry."

"I put about ten clean ones in there yesterday."

"Well they've all gone." I try to silently communicate with her but she ignores me and walks out of the room. When she reappears a few seconds later, she's holding not one, not two, but *three* towels. She hands them to Mason.

"Are you keeping a secret stash?" I ask. "I didn't see them."

"They were right in front of you, where we always keep them. I think you need to get your eyes tested."
She opens the fridge and buries her head inside.

"Sorry," I tell Mason as he towel-dries his hair, making it look all kinds of sexy and dishevelled.

He laughs. "It's fine. I'd be completely blind if I didn't

wear my contacts."

"I didn't know you wore contact lenses."

"Every day. I'm actually having laser eye surgery next month."

"Wow, you're a lot braver than I am. I would never let a needle near my eyes." I shudder.

When Lori reappears from the other side of the fridge, she has a huge grin on her face. I know she's up to something and my suspicions are confirmed when she winks at me. "Sorry to interrupt your riveting conversation but did you tell Mason about your dream?"

"What dream?" he asks.

"Yeah," I say, "What dream?"

"The one you had last night. Don't you think it's weird that you dream about Mason then he shows up a few hours later? I guess the law of attraction really does work."

I turn to Mason. "I have no idea what she's talking about."

"Don't be embarrassed," Lori continues. "I'm sure Mason would love to hear all about it."

"You're right, Mason *would* love to hear all about it," he adds.

This time there's no hiding my blush. I'm going to kill Lori. I decide to play her at her own game. "Okay, fine. I dreamt that we walked in on Lori and Buzz having wild sex." Her eyes widen. "Maybe Mason should call Buzz right now so I can tell him how you kept screaming that it was the best sex of your life." She looks half angry, half impressed.

"Well at least now we know that dreams don't come true," she replies.

"What about the law of attraction?"

"I'll know that's real when he moves to the other side of the world. Oh, before I forget, I can't make brunch today."

I frown. Why is she acting so strange? "I didn't know anything about brunch."

"Yeah you did, silly. I booked a table at that new

92

restaurant down the road. People book weeks in advance. Why don't you two go instead?"

What the hell is she doing? "I'm actually about to go for a run," I say quickly.

"In this weather?" Lori asks.

"Yes Lori, in this weather. It's only a bit of rain."

"A bit of rain? Have you *seen* Mason?" He shakes out his wet hair right on cue. "Do you run?" she asks him.

"Of course I run."

"Wow," Lori says. "It was only yesterday that you were saying that you wanted a running partner. Why don't you two run together?"

"Oh, I bet I'm too slow for Mason."

"I'll let you set the pace." His comment earns a grin off Lori. "Do you like to go fast or slow?"

My heart begins to beat a little faster. "It depends what mood I'm in."

He raises one eyebrow. "I see. And when do you usually run?"

"Every morning," Lori answers for me. "Nine o' clock. Weston Park."

"Well I might see you there tomorrow then."

"Oh, um, I'm actually busy tomorrow."

"Doing what?" Lori asks.

"A thing," I reply.

"Maybe another time," he says.

"Maybe."

"Well I better go before I get pneumonia. Sorry for interrupting your morning."

"It's fine," I reply. "Say hi to Buzz for us."

"Oh I will, after I kick his ass."

"I'll walk you out," I tell him.

He waves bye to Lori then follows me over to the door. He winces as he puts his shoes back on. "I think barefoot would have been a better choice."

I open the door. "At least the rain has calmed down now."

93

"It was nice to see you again." I want to reciprocate and tell him that it was nice to see him too. I want to be honest with him. I want to tell him that his wife is trying to take all of his money and that she's paid me to help. I want him to know how much I regret it already but of course I can't tell him any of those things. "Will you let me pay for your dress?"

"Nope."

He laughs. "I didn't think so."

"Goodbye, Mason."

"Until next time, Sophia."

I close the door behind him then slide to the floor. I stare at the solitary pair of shoes for a long time before Lori finds me.

Chapter Twenty Four

Mason

I call Buzz. "Hello?" he answers.
"You're fired."

Chapter Twenty Five
Sophia

"What are you doing in here?" Lori asks.

"I'm always going to be alone, aren't I? Just like the shoes."

"What are you talking about? What shoes?" She places her hand against my forehead. "Are you getting sick?"

"I should never have agreed to trap him. I'm a terrible person."

"Oh sweetie, of course you're not. This is your job. Just think of how many women you've helped in the past two years. You saved them."

I shake my head. "None of that will matter. Nobody will care about the hundreds that I've saved, only the one that I've ruined. I could ruin his entire life."

"Only if he allows it. It's his choice. Come on, you know how this works. I know it's daunting because it's high profile but you'll be fine, I promise."

I sigh. "Why were you acting so weird before?"

"What do you mean?"

"Oh come on, I don't need to spell it out. I'm surprised you didn't light a few candles and start playing love songs."

"I was just trying to help."

"Help how exactly?"

"I saw how angry you were last night, especially after Kristen's phone call. The sooner you trap him, the better."

"What happened to being Maid of Honor?"

"That ship sailed the second you agreed to spend the next six weeks trapping him." She sighs. "You'll never be able to marry him now. It's such a shame. Your babies would have been beautiful."

"Let's just concentrate on real life, shall we? I'm not going to trap him. I can't."

"Sorry to break it to you but you kind of have to. You've signed a contract. We both have."

"I can't do it. It's wrong."

"I get that it's a little weird because they're on a break..."

"It's more than a break," I interrupt. "He said they're not getting back together."

"Well that's what he's told you."

"What's that supposed to mean?"

"Maybe he's lying. You know what men are like. We've seen enough douchebags in this job to last us a lifetime. What if he's telling you one thing and telling Emily another? Maybe you should talk to her about it."

"I don't trust her to tell me the truth. I trust Mason more than her. Even if he is making their relationship out to be worse than it actually is, they're still separated. Emily has admitted that she wants to divorce him and take his money."

"If he cheats."

"No. No, Kristen said that Emily *wants* him to cheat. She needs him to cheat so she can take his money. I don't want to be a part of that."

"But you already are."

"Maybe, but I can still stop it from happening. If they want to get a divorce then fair enough but *I* shouldn't be the reason why. I'm not going to help Emily."

"You seem a little defensive."

"I'm not."

She laughs. "See."

"I can't do it, Lori. It doesn't feel right. My gut is telling me not to do it."

"Okay, just as long as you're not letting his good looks cloud your judgement."

"This has got nothing to do with Mason. I'd feel the exact same way if it was anybody else."

She nods. "So what are you going to do?"

"Maybe I could just tell him the truth and make him promise not to tell Emily."

"Make him promise? Are you back in kindergarten? He's a businessman, I don't think promises are his currency."

"Well maybe I can write him an anonymous letter so Emily can't prove it was me."

"So Emily hires you as a honey trap then a few days later her husband finds out about it. Let's face it, there would only be three suspects; me, you or Kristen."

"I could ask her to let me out of the deal. She could hire somebody else to do her dirty work and *then* I can tell Mason."

"You know she won't let you out of the deal."

I sigh. "Then I guess I'll just have to ride it out. I'll see him as little as possible. She said a minimum of twice a week but she didn't specify how long for. Then when I do see him, I need to do the opposite of what I'm being paid to do. I need to do everything in my power *not* to trap him. I'll just pretend that he's a friend and we're hanging out."

"And you think you'll be able to do that?"

"I'll have to."

"You're serious about this, aren't you?"

"Yes."

She wraps her arms around me. "You're a good person, Soph. I'm lucky to call you my best friend."

I can't help but wonder if she will still feel the same way in six weeks time.

Chapter Twenty Six
Mason

"It's nice to see you like this."

"Like what? Shopping?" I wink.

"No, idiot. Happy."

I ruffle her hair. "It's because I'm spending time with my favorite sister."

"I'm your *only* sister."

"Yeah but you're still my favorite."

"Hmmm, your sweet talking doesn't work on me remember?" She picks up a pair of display shoes and starts to bend them in all different directions. "So what's the real reason?"

I laugh. "Does there have to be a reason? Am I not allowed to be happy these days?"

"Of course you're allowed to be happy. I just want to know who I need to thank for putting you in such a good mood."

"You don't need to thank anybody."

She holds up the shoes. "These ones look good."

"I'll take them."

"Don't you want to try them on first?"

"No, I trust you."

"Remind me again why we're shopping for running shoes when you hate running?"

"I don't hate it, it's just never been my favorite thing to do."

"Until now?"

"Until now."

"What's changed?"

"I want to start trying new things. Plus, I'm getting bored of the gym."

"That's what happens when you go twice a day."

I shrug. "It'll be nice to get outside and do a little cardio. Get the heart pumping."

"Maybe we can run together."

"No thanks. I like to work out alone." *Or with Sophia.*

"What's wrong? Am I not cool enough for you?"

"You're too cool, that's the problem."

"Hmmmm." She narrows her eyes. "Tarryn mentioned you were at the club last night." I nod. "She also said that you were with a woman." When I don't respond, she continues. "A *beautiful* woman."

I laugh. "Ah, I see what's happening here."

"What?"

"You're fishing."

"I'm your sister, what do you expect? I'm just looking out for you."

"You're my *little* sister which means I'm supposed to look out for you, not the other way around."

"It works both ways. So who is she?"

I know for a fact that she's not going to let this drop. "Her name is Sophia. I only met her a couple of days ago before you get carried away. We're just friends."

She tries her best to play it cool but a grin breaks through. "I see. And will you be seeing this *friend* again?"

There's no way that I'm going to admit that she's the only reason why I'm buying running shoes in the first place. "I don't know."

"Do you *want* to see her again?"

Yes. "Maybe."

"Where did you meet her?"

"At a restaurant, now stop with the Spanish inquisition."

"Fine, but you better keep me in the loop."

"There is no loop."

She raises one eyebrow. "So what happened with Stacey? Tarryn said she had to kick her out of the club."

I groan. "She threw a drink at Sophia."

"Why?"

"Because that's what Stacey does."

"As long as you're not attracted to *another* trouble causer."

"It had nothing to do with Sophia. Now less talking, more shopping."

"You can't buy my silence, Mason."

"No?"

"No."

"Not even if I buy you shoes?"

"Nope, I'm not interested." After a few seconds, she sighs. "What kind of shoes are we talking about?"

I laugh and sling my arm around her shoulder.

Chapter Twenty Seven
Sophia

"What do you think about this?" I hold the sweater up.

"It's nice…for your grandma," Lori replies.

"My grandma wears vintage Dior, I'll have you know."

"Then why the hell am I not out shopping with her instead? You need to hook me up."

I roll my eyes. "She's too busy to shop. She has a jam packed social life."

"It's such a shame that you don't take after her."

"Have you finished insulting me yet?"

"It depends if you pick out any more ugly sweaters."

"If you need me I'll be over there with my real friends."

"The shoes?"

"Yep."

She laughs. "I'll come with you. I want to check out the new Manolo's."

Fifteen minutes later, she's still checking them out. "Can you please pay me some attention?"

"No," I reply as I continue to scroll through instagram. "I told you ten minutes ago that I prefer the black ones."

"But the blue ones bring out my eyes."

"So get the blue ones."

"But the black ones are…*shit*."

I look up from my phone. "Then what's the dilemma? Get the blue ones."

"Don't turn around," she whispers calmly. "But Mason just walked in."

Of course I do the complete opposite. He's only a couple of steps into the store but has already been stopped by a blonde sales assistant. I quickly duck down behind a display table and begin to flatten my hair.

"What are you doing?" Lori asks.

I pull her down to my level. "What does it look like?"

"It looks like you've gone crazy."

"I'm hiding."

"But why?"

"Isn't that obvious? Because I don't want to see him."

"Jeez, I knew you didn't want to see him but I didn't think you were this serious about it."

"Well I am. Why is he even here?" I gasp. "Do you think he's following me? First he showed up to our house and now this."

"Maybe he's following *me*." She winks.

"You're not helping."

"I was joking and no, I don't think he's following you. We live in the same city with the same stores. Besides, if he wanted you followed then he would pay somebody else to do it."

"We need to leave."

"How? We're trapped."

"We can crawl out."

"I'm wearing a skirt, I'm not crawling anywhere."

"Okay, I'll see you back at the house."

"Soph, just wait a second. Would it really be a big deal if you had to talk to him?"

"I've already seen him once today. That's three times in as many days. This isn't part of the plan."

"Well he might leave soon. There's no need to go all Mission Impossible on my ass."

"Or he might catch us hiding and that would be one hundred times worse."

"Are you ladies okay?" A store assistant asks as she walks by.

"Great, thanks," I reply.

"Can I help you with something?"

"Oh, um, no. We're fine. We're just…admiring the floor."

"The floor?"

"Yeah, we're redesigning our kitchen and wanted to…"

"We're hiding from someone," Lori interrupts.

"I thought so. The hot guy who just walked in?"

"Yeah so you can either join us or move along."

"He's still at the front of the store being hit on by Candace. Good luck." She smiles as she walks away.

"Why did you tell her the truth?" I whisper angrily.

"She was drawing attention to us. I got rid of her, didn't I?"

"Why do I have a feeling that you've done this before?"

"Oh, this ain't my first rodeo."

"I wish I'd never agreed to any of this. Why can't I just go back in time and say no to Emily?"

"Because unfortunately we live in the real world so you need to put on your big girl panties and deal with it."

I roll my eyes. "Why is he here? This is a *women's* store."

"Maybe he's buying something for his mistress."

"Even if he *is* seeing somebody, would she still be classed as his mistress even though he's separated from Emily?"

"I guess so. He's still married."

"Hmmm. Will you check to see if he's left yet?"

She stands up slowly then ducks straight back down. "Oh my god."

"What? He's coming over here, isn't he? Kill me now."

"He's with a woman."

I feel a twang of something in my chest. Disappointment? Anger? Jealousy? "Who is it?"

"How the hell am I supposed to know?"

"Well maybe it's Emily."

"It's not. I've seen photos of her online."

"I want to see." I reach up and pull a hat off the display table. It's a huge floppy one which will probably end up drawing more attention to me but at least it covers most of my face. I adjust it then slowly rise up until I can see them. They're mid conversation and looking through a rail of dresses. I'm full on staring at them when the mystery woman turns around. I quickly look down and busy myself with the accessories on the display table. I could work here for all she knows. When I dare to glance back up, they're making their way out of the store. Thank god. I crouch back down just to be safe. "They're leaving," I tell Lori.

"Good. Did you know who the woman was?"

"No. I've never seen her before."

"Well at least you know that he likes blondes. You should have taken a video of them and been done with it."

"A video of them doing what? Shopping? We don't know who she was. It might have been one of his friends."

"Or it might have been his long-term mistress. Maybe she's the reason why they broke up and why Emily wants to take his money. Maybe he deserves it."

I shake my head. "I don't believe that."

"Why not? You've only know him for forty eight hours."

"It's hard to explain. It's just a gut feeling."

She pulls the hat off of me. "What happened to the old Sophia? You're usually the cynical one. I'm not used to playing bad cop."

She's right, and maybe she's right about Mason too but for the first time in a long time, I'm choosing to see the good in people and it scares me just as much as it excites me.

Chapter Twenty Eight
Mason

"Hey, what was with the speedy getaway?" I ask Indiana once we've left the store.

"There were some paparazzi inside."

"Paparazzi? Are you sure?"

"Well no but there were people hiding behind a table. They were probably trying to take photographs of you."

I laugh. "I'll bet that had nothing to do with me. You're giving me too much credit. I hardly ever get photographed these days. Plus, nobody came into the store after us which means they were already in there. If it was paparazzi, how would they have known we were going to shop there?"

"Maybe they got a tip off from one of the other stores."

"You're being paranoid."

"Mason, there were people hiding behind a table. One of them was wearing a huge floppy sun hat *indoors*. I'm surprised she didn't have a fake moustache too."

"Maybe she just likes to wear hats."

"When it's cloudy outside? You're too naïve for your own good. I wanted to leave anyway. Blondie was annoying me."

"She was just being friendly."

"Oh, come on. She pounced on you the second you walked in. I'm surprised I didn't slip on her big pile of drool. Don't you ever get tired of women treating you like a piece of meat?"

"Nah, I'm used to it." I wink.

"Arrogant ass. Can we go home now? I'm getting bored of looking at dresses."

"Well that's a sentence I never thought I'd hear you say."

She sighs. "We've been in nearly every single store possible. It's not as fun when I'm not shopping for myself."

"We've only got a couple of stores left then I'll call it a day, I promise."

"Fine, but you're buying me dinner afterwards."
"Deal. As long as it isn't sushi."

Chapter Twenty Nine

Sophia

"Rise and shine, sleeping beauty."

I groan and bury my head under the sheets. "Go away, it's too early."

"I can't hear you," Lori replies as she yanks the sheets off me.

"I *said* go away, it's too early."

"It's eight fifteen."

"Exactly. Too early."

"Are you sick? You usually get up at the crack of dawn."

"I stayed up late last night."

She raises an eyebrow. "Doing what?"

"Stuff."

"What kind of stuff?"

Googling Mason. "Just stuff. Why did you wake me up?"

"Mason's here."

I sit up at lightning speed. "What?! Why?"

She bursts out laughing. "Calm down, I'm joking."

I place a hand on my chest. "Jesus, don't do that to me."

"I'm sorry, it's cute how worked up you get over him."

"It's not cute, it's annoying."

"A package arrived for you." She retrieves it from the hallway and hands it to me. It's a rectangular box sealed with a big red bow. "I've been staring at it for the last fifteen minutes wondering what it is. I can't take the suspense any longer."

"I should make you wait until tomorrow for almost giving me a heart attack."

"Please open it."

"Hmmmm, I'm not sure, you *did* wake me up."

"I'll do your laundry for a week."

I don't take much convincing. "Deal." I untie the bow and carefully remove the lid. The first thing I see is a little card with my name on it. I stare at the handwritten message.

Sophia, let's drink the wine next time.

My stomach flips. I read it aloud for Lori. "Is that it?" she asks. I nod. "No name?"

"No." I don't need a name.

"Open it!" I do as she says. She gasps when she see's what's underneath the mound of tissue paper. "Is that what I think it is?"

"It depends. If you think it's the dress that I was wearing on Friday night then yes."

She grins. "Well played, Mason. Well fucking played."

"He asked if he could pay for it and I said no."

"Well it looks like he doesn't take no for an answer."

"I wonder how he knew where to get it from. I bought it from that little boutique off of Union square."

Her eyes widen. "Maybe that's what he was looking for yesterday when we saw him shopping."

"I doubt it. I'm sure he has staff who run around after him."

"Wait a minute. Check the size."

I lift it out of the box and check the label. I sigh. "Of course he got the right size."

"Holy shit. You're screwed."

"Why?"

"Because he's going to make it near impossible for you not to fall for him. Jeez, if he keeps this kind of thing up, *I'll* fall in love with him."

I roll my eyes and put the dress back in the box. "Calm down. He bought me a dress, it's not a big deal."

"He didn't just buy you a dress. He *found* the dress then picked out the right size."

"It must have been a lucky guess."

"Either that or he's been paying a lot of attention to your body." She wiggles her eyebrows up and down. "Memorized all of your curves."

"He only bought it because he feels guilty about what happened with Buzz's ex."

"He definitely feels *something* but I'm not sure that guilt is the overriding emotion."

I close the box and throw the card and ribbon on top. "I can't accept it. I'm going to return it to him."

"Of course you can accept it. It's an expensive dress and your other one is ruined."

"Then I'll buy myself a new one. I need to shut it down and let him know that I'm not interested."

"But you *are* interested."

I narrow my eyes. "No, I'm not."

"Well can I keep it if you won't? I earned it. I'm the one who pissed Stacey off, remember?"

"Seriously?"

"Seriously."

"I can throw a glass of wine over you if that would make you feel better."

"If I get a new dress out of it then go ahead."

I stand up and walk over to my wardrobe. "I'll drop it off at his hotel before my run."

"I thought you had *a thing* this morning."

"What are you talking about?"

"You told Mason you wouldn't be running today because you had *a thing*."

I pick out a sports bra and matching leggings. "Yeah well plans change. Just like how I was planning on sleeping in today but that hasn't happened, has it? Now go and make me a smoothie while I get changed."

"I forgot how grumpy you get in the morning." She huffs. "I should have just opened the damn box and kept the dress for myself."

As soon as the door closes behind her, I walk over to the bed and pick up the handwritten card. I trace the letters, wondering if Mason wrote it himself or if he got somebody else to write it. Hopefully it's the latter. The less effort he makes, the better. I don't want him to care about the dress.

I definitely don't want him to care about me. And I sure as hell won't allow myself to care about him. The last time I cared about somebody, my heart was shattered. In my line of work, it's inevitable that somebody is going to get hurt but I'll try my damned hardest to make sure it isn't me.

Chapter Thirty

Mason

"Buzz is calling you," Indie shouts from the kitchen.

"Don't ans…" Too late. I sigh and go to find her. "Tell him I'm busy."

"My brother doesn't want to talk to you. What have you done to piss him off this time?"

I roll my eyes and hold out my hand. "What do you want?" I ask him.

"Good morning to you too."

"What do you want?" I ask again.

"I was just calling to see if you're off your period yet?"

"Goodbye."

He laughs. "Wait! Drinks later?"

"No. I'm still deciding whether I should fire you."

"Aww, come on. I'm sorry I lied to you. At least you got to see your girl again."

"Lori said you were a terrible kisser," I reply before hanging up.

Indie laughs. "Have you two had a lovers tiff?"

"Nah. He's just being his usual self."

"Who's Lori?"

"His latest victim."

"Poor girl. Mind you, he probably needs the distraction this month."

I nod. "The anniversary is in a couple of weeks."

"How long has it been now, three years?"

"Four."

She bows her head. "It doesn't seem like he's been gone for that long. Tell him that I'm here if he ever needs to talk."

"I will. You're the best."

"I know. It must be so horrible for you knowing that I'm the favorite child."

I laugh. "Well clearly I got the good looks so I can't have it all."

She throws a cushion at my head. "I'm leaving."

"About time."

She ignores me as she picks up her purse. "I have a lunch date with Ted."

"Which one is Ted?"

"Which *one*? You make it sound like I'm dating more than one person."

"You know what I mean." I hold the door open for her. "I'll walk you out."

"Can't wait to get rid of me, can you?" I wink in response. "Ted is the movie director."

"Ah yeah, I remember now. Ted Spielberg."

"Not quite."

I punch the button for the elevator and the doors open immediately. "Want me to run a background check on him?" I ask as we step inside.

She groans. "No, I don't. Not everybody is a creep who has something to hide."

I grin. "If he has nothing to hide then what's the harm in checking him out?"

"Leave him alone. It's like being back at school when you used to threaten my boyfriends."

We step out once we reach the bottom floor. "That's what big brothers are for."

"Any plans for today?" she asks, changing the subject.

"I'm driving over to the house."

She raises her eyebrows. "Oh?"

"I thought I'd already taken Grandpa's watch but I can't find it."

Her face visibly relaxes at my reason for visiting. "It doesn't help that most of your stuff is still in boxes. Does Emily know that you're visiting?"

"No." I lead her outside and over to the car. Charlie exits when he sees us approaching. I hold a hand up. "I've got it, Charlie. Take Indiana home, please." He nods and gets back into the driver's seat.

"Well if you see her, be sure to pass on my regards. Or, you know, mono. Either is fine by me."

113

"Ah, there they are. I wondered where you were hiding them."

"Hiding what?"

"Your claws."

She pouts. "I'm just looking out for you. She's caused enough trouble recently."

"If I remember correctly, the last time you *looked out for me*, it ended up being world war three between the two of you."

"If you're referring to the lovely family dinner we had last year then no, you don't remember correctly. That was all her fault. I won't sit back and watch her treat you like a piece of crap."

"Of course not. I'd be the same if it were you. But I'd rather you not get involved in my mess."

"I'm always going to be involved whether you like it or not." She smiles sweetly. "That's what little sisters are for."

Chapter Thirty One
Sophia

I slow to a jog and eventually a walk as I approach the hotel. There's no mistaking who it belongs to. 'Hunter's Hotel' is displayed in huge blue letters some fifty floors up. I've passed by it hundreds of times before, mostly when I've been running around the park across the street but I've never given it a second thought. Never given Mason a second thought.

I try to steady my breathing as I glance down at the box in my hands, my palms noticeably sweatier than usual. I'll drop it off at the front desk then be on my way. In and out in less than half a minute. I remind myself that I'm doing the right thing by returning the dress. Doing the right thing for *him*. If Emily ever found out that he bought me a gift, she would use it as ammunition against him and no doubt pressure me to work even harder to get the evidence which she so desperately needs. The evidence which I so desperately *don't* want to give her.

I stop dead in my tracks. I've been so caught up in my own thoughts that I don't notice him until I'm about twenty feet away. He's standing next to a parked car outside the entrance to the hotel. Good, maybe he's about to leave. He takes a step to his right and that's when I see a woman with him. A woman with blonde hair. The same woman he was with yesterday. I watch them for a few seconds as they laugh and then everything turns to slow motion as Mason leans towards her. Relief floods through me as he wraps his arms around her in a friendly embrace. I watch as she climbs into the car and wait for him to follow suit but instead, he closes the door and taps the top of the car. We both watch as it pulls away. Frozen to the spot, I silently will him to go back inside the hotel. But as if he can sense somebody watching him, he turns around and looks straight at me. My heart stops. I spin around as quickly as possible and collide with somebody carrying a tray of coffee in each hand.

115

The young girl looks mortified as I jump back, gasping in pain and surprise. I drop the box with the dress inside and frantically try to pull at my soaked T-shirt but it's completely stuck to me. Stupid skin-tight workout clothes. I have no choice but to take it off before the steaming hot coffee has chance to do any permanent damage. I throw it onto the floor just as Mason appears in front of me. I thank the lord that I wasn't lazy today and wore a sports bra instead of one of my everyday bras. His eyes go wide as he takes in all of my bare skin. "Are you…are you okay?"

"I think so," I reply as I quickly assess my arms and stomach. The latter is a little red and blotchy but it's my left wrist which took the brunt of it. Small blisters have already started to form on the soft underside.

Mason notices it too. "We need to get you checked out."

I wave him off then bend down to pick up my soaking wet T-shirt. "It's nothing, I'll be fine."

"Sophia, your skin is bubbling. *Literally* bubbling."

"It's just a couple of blisters."

"At least come over to the hotel so we can run it under some cool water."

"I'll just jog home. I don't want to bother you."

"Bother me?" He gestures to the hotel. "It's right there. ETA twenty seconds."

"Okay," I reply but only because it's starting to sting like a son of a bitch.

Mason turns to the young girl who is still watching us in shock. "Did you get burnt too?"

"I…no, I didn't…I'm sorry." She bites her lip. "My boss is going to fire me."

"Are you an intern?" She nods. "It was just an accident. It wasn't your fault." He reaches into his jeans pocket and pulls out a fifty dollar bill, followed by
another. "Use this to buy some more drinks."

"Wow, um, thank you but I don't have time. I'll be late if I have to get in line again. It's only my first week."

"What company do you work for?" he asks sounding rushed, his eyes going back and forth between the girl and my wrist.

"Clayton Law."

"David Clayton? The law firm?" She nods. "Tell David you're late because of Mason Hunter. Explain what happened." He hands her a business card. "I know David. He should be fine, but if he gives you any grief, you're welcome to come and work for me instead."

"Oh, wow. Thank you so much. And sorry again," she says, wide eyed, before scurrying off.

"That was nice of you," I tell him. "Thank you for that. It was completely my fault."

He shrugs. "I just did what anyone would do."

"No, you didn't."

He bends down and retrieves the box which is now splattered with coffee. He obviously recognizes it as he says, "Wow, you must either be extremely attached to this dress or you were on your way to tell me I got the wrong size."

I cringe and wish that the ground would open up and swallow me. "You got the right size."

He grins. "So then you really do have attachment issues?"

"I can't accept it," I reply as I follow him over to the hotel.

"Do you mean to tell me that I visited twenty four stores yesterday for nothing?"

My eyes snap to his. "You…you went shopping for it yourself?"

"Yes. How else was I going to find it?"

"I thought…" I shrug. "I thought you would have *people* for that kind of thing."

"I do. My sister."

"Your sister helped you look?" I ask as we walk through the revolving doors.

"Yes. We were shopping all day. I lost count at store number twenty four. It was probably closer to thirty."

"And this was yesterday?"

"Yes but I've only just managed to get rid of her. She sometimes stays at the hotel. She says it's to keep me company but I think she only does it for the free food and drink." He raises an eyebrow. "It was my sister who you saw getting into the car just now." He nods in greeting to several members of staff before leading us through a set of double doors and into a large bar area.

"I wasn't watching you. I know it looks like I was but I was just…"

"Coming to return the dress. Got it." He lifts up a panel allowing us access to the space behind the bar. He walks over to the sink, turns on the tap then holds out a hand, waiting for me. He must sense my wariness as he gives me a little reassuring nod.

My heart starts to race as I place my hand in his. How is it possible for something so innocent to feel so emotionally charged? I've had to kiss a lot of men in the past but this feels different. More intimate. I gasp as he gently strokes the area above the burn with his thumb. I mentally curse myself for being so stupid and clumsy. Seeing Mason was never part of the plan and being inside his hotel was definitely not part of it. He places my wrist under the cool water and I feel instant relief. "That feels nice," I tell him, unable to think of anything else to say.

"It should help."

"So how long do we stay like this?"

He looks down at my hand in his. "However long you want." I don't allow myself too long to think about the meaning behind his words. We stay silent for what feels like minutes and then, "I didn't expect to see you today. I thought you were busy this morning."

"Oh, um, yeah, I was but the…the thing…it got cancelled."

"I see. So it was fate which brought us together."

No, it was actually your wife. "So you believe in fate?"

He crinkles his nose. "To an extent. I believe that most

things happen for a reason but I also believe in freewill. Fate can only do so much. I think we could choose to ignore it, if we really wanted to. Take today for example. Fate may have brought us together but we're standing here through choice."

"So is it fate that I got covered in twelve cups of coffee?" More like an omen, I think to myself. Bad karma for what I've been hired to do.

He grins. "You've had a drink thrown over you twice while I've been with you. If that's not fate trying to tell you something then I don't know what is."

"So it's telling me that I should take my clothes off?"

"Who are we to argue with fate?" he replies, his eyes twinkling with amusement.

I laugh. "It's a good thing we have freewill too then, right?"

"Ah, forget about that. That's just one of my theories. I think we should play it safe and just listen to fate." He grins as he checks my wrist then turns off the tap. "How's it feeling?"

"Better, thank you."

"Keep an eye on the blisters." He lets go of my hand and I instantly miss his touch. "Why can't you accept the dress?"

"It's too much."

"It was my fault that your other dress got ruined."

"It wasn't your fault."

"Well it certainly wasn't *your* fault. Just look at is as a replacement."

"But what would…" I shake my head, stopping myself.

"You don't need to censor yourself around me, Sophia. Please speak your mind. Ask me whatever you want."

"Okay. What would your wife think if she knew you were buying me gifts?"

"My soon to be *ex*-wife."

I try my hardest to appear calm and unaffected by what he's just said. "You're filing for divorce?"

"I've already filed."

"Does she know?"

"She hasn't been served with the papers yet but I doubt it'll come as a shock."

"When are you serving them?"

"As soon as I can. My lawyers are looking into a few things first."

I want to know more but I've already asked too many questions. "I don't know what to say. I'm sorry you're going through this."

"Thank you. Hey, let's make a deal. If the dress has been ruined then I'll happily accept your return." He grins. "If it's undamaged then you have to keep it."

Judging by the box, the odds are definitely in my favor. "Deal."

I watch as he slowly picks up the box and removes the lid. He takes his time checking over the dress then finally turns to me. His eyes burn into mine and a grin slowly makes its way across his face. "Looks like we have a keeper."

I swallow hard. "Maybe fate wants me to wear clothes after all."

"Maybe. Maybe not." He grins as he hands me the dress. "I meant what I said about the wine." He gestures to all of the different bottles of wine behind us. "I don't think I'm going to run out any time soon. You know where I am if you ever want a drink…or company."

I nod. "Thanks for your help."

"Any time."

"Well, goodbye, Mason."

"Until next time, Sophia."

I feel his eyes on me as I walk away.

I feel his hands on me as I shower.

Chapter Thirty Two
Mason

An hour later, I walk into the house with a genuine smile on my face, still riding the high from seeing Sophia. The fact that she happened to be wearing a sports bra and skin-tight pants was an added bonus. And seeing her so fresh faced, with her long hair tied back stirred something deep inside of me. Maybe it's because she looked even more beautiful than the last time I saw her, which I thought was impossible. Or maybe it's because it gave me a little insight into how she must look when she wakes up in the morning. And it's impossible to picture her in the morning without also picturing her in my bed. Adrenaline rushes through my veins as blood rushes to other parts of my body.

It feels strange walking through the house, like I don't belong here. It probably doesn't help that it's filled with furniture and artwork that Emily chose without me. It's always been a house but never a home. I can't say that I have many happy memories here and I won't be sad to see the back of it.

I take two stairs at a time and head for the master bedroom. I pass a few spare rooms on my way and notice the freshly painted walls and dustsheets. Emily didn't wait very long before deciding she wanted to redecorate. I open the door to the bedroom but stop in my tracks when I see her. She's standing in front of the mirror, wearing only a bra and panties. I quickly turn around and face the hallway. "I'm sorry," I tell her. "I thought you would be out."

"Hello to you too."

"I should have checked with you first."

"Turn around, Mason."

"I'll wait until you're dressed."

"Stop being ridiculous. It's nothing that you haven't seen a thousand times before. Turn around."

I slowly turn back around but keep my eyes on the window next to her. "I just came to pick something up. I'll be gone in a minute."

She slowly saunters towards me. "You don't have to rush off. Why don't you stay for a little while?"

"I don't think that's a good idea."

"Why not?" She traces a finger down my chest. "I miss you."

I bring my eyes to hers. "Emily…"

Her hand reaches the waistband of my jeans. "I miss your touch."

"Stop it."

She ignores my protest and moves her hand even lower. "I miss your…" Her eyes go wide when it meets its intended target. "It appears that you miss me too."

I push her hand away. "No, I don't."

"Your dick says otherwise, darling. Did you like walking in on me almost naked? Did it turn you on?"

"Stop. Just stop it."

"Why? Why are you trying to fight it? You're hard for me."

No, I'm really not. She tries to reach for me again but I take a step back. "No means no. Keep your hands to yourself. You don't get to touch me anymore, *darling*."

"So it's like that now, is it?"

"We both know what the situation is."

She reaches around her back then her bra falls to the floor a second later. "I *know* that you're still my husband. I *know* that I want you. And I *know* that you must want me too." She looks at my crotch but there's no trace of arousal left whatsoever.

"Put some clothes on. We went over this last time." I walk over to the drawers and begin searching for what I came here for.

"Have you met somebody else, is that what it is?"

I pause. Perhaps for a little too long judging by the surprised look on her face. "No."

"Are you sure about that?" I ignore her and continue to look through my remaining belongings. "Maybe we should give it another shot."

"We've given it plenty of shots."

"We can do more therapy."

"Please can you put some clothes on?"

"You wouldn't be saying that a few months ago."

"We're not the same people as we were a few months ago. The past is the past."

She finally slips on her robe. "We could take things slow."

I sigh. "It's over, Emily. We both know it."

"So you're not going to fight for us?"

"I've been fighting for well over a year and you know it. I've tried everything. I'm the one who suggested therapy in the first place, remember? Sometimes it's about knowing when to walk away."

"So what are you saying? That there's no hope for us?"

"It's time for us both to move on. We need to start being honest with ourselves and with other people. I don't want to hide it anymore."

"I'm not ready."

"I don't think you'll ever be ready. We've been separated for three months now." And emotionally separated for a lot longer than that. "I've filed for divorce."

Her face falls. Shock turns into panic. "Don't serve it. Please. I need a little more time. Give me an extra month. Six weeks tops."

"Why? What difference will it make?"

"As soon as you serve the papers, it'll become public record and everyone will know. I'm not ready for that yet. All this time I truly believed that we were going to get back together. Now I know that it's final, I need some more time to let it sink in and to somehow tell my family. Then we can tell everybody the truth. Please, Mason."

I nod. I've already waited several months so another few weeks isn't going to make any difference. "Okay. I want this to be as painless as possible for both of us."

"Thank you for understanding."

"I don't want things to turn bitter between us. I don't expect us to be friends but I don't want us to hate each other."

She smiles sweetly. A wolf in sheep's clothing. "Don't worry; things won't turn bitter on my end."

"That's good to know." I gesture to the drawers. "I'm trying to find my grandpa's pocket watch, have you seen it?"

"No. Are you sure you haven't already taken it with you?"

"I'm sure. I kept it in this drawer with my other watches." I check a few other places it could be.

"How strange. I'll have a look around for you."

"Please let me know if you find it. You know how much it means to me."

"Of course."

"Okay well I should go."

She swings the ties on her robe. "You know where I am if you change your mind or if you ever get lonely."

"Goodbye, Emily." I don't tell her that I've been lonely for a long, long time.

Chapter Thirty Three

Sophia

"He wanted me to pee on him," Lori says. "Jesus Christ, he wouldn't shut up about it. He kept ordering bottles of water to make sure that my bladder was full."

I can't help but laugh. "Why do you always get sent to trap the weird ones?"

"I have no idea." She covers her face. "But now I can't stop picturing him whenever I need to pee."

"I bet he would be *so* turned on by that."

She shudders. "I was thinking about ordering a take-out for…" Her eyes go wide when she spots the dress draped over a chair. "Did you change your mind about the dress?"

"No."

"I thought you went to return it this morning?"

"I did."

"And?"

"And I ended up in his hotel, half naked."

She jumps up and down. "Oh my god! It's happening!"

"Calm down, nothing is *happening*. It's not half as exciting as what you're imagining. Somebody spilled coffee on me so I went over to the hotel."

"What is it with you and drinks these days?"

"Right? It's a sign. A bad omen. It must be the universe punishing me for being a bad person."

"Or," Lori says, "Maybe it's the universe pushing you to get naked in front of Mason. Maybe it's written in the stars and you need to stop fighting it."

"I've been hired by his wife to catch him cheating. I'm pretty sure it's not written in the stars."

My cell starts to vibrate next to me. "Unknown number," I tell Lori.

"Oooh, maybe it's the universe calling."

"I'll make sure I ask for next week's lottery results. Hello?"

"It's Emily."

I cover the mouthpiece. "I told you I'm being punished. It's Emily."

"How did she get your number?"

I shrug. "Are you there?" Emily asks.

"I'm here." *Unfortunately.*

"I got your number off of Kristen."

"I think it's best if we communicate via her."

"Why? You work for me now, not Kristen. I think it's easier if we talk directly."

"And I think we should stick to the contract."

"Speaking of which, I want an update."

"There's not much to report. We went for drinks on Friday and nothing happened."

"Kristen has already told me about Friday. Have you spoken to him since then?"

I suddenly feel defensive and even a little protective of Mason. "No. Kind of." I don't want to tell her that he stopped by the house. "I saw him in passing earlier today. I was running through the park and he was outside the hotel with his sister."

"How do you know it was his sister?"

"Because he told me who it was."

"So you spoke to him?"

"Yes. Somebody spilled coffee on me. He saw it happen and came over to help."

"How very helpful of him," she says sarcastically. "Did you take a photograph of the woman?"

"No. I didn't have my phone with me."

"He could have been lying about it being his sister." I guess she's right. I didn't even consider that he could have been lying. My gut instinct is usually always right and I'm pretty sure he was telling me the truth. "What did she look like?"

"Tall, slim, blonde hair."

She sighs. "That doesn't really narrow it down. I guess it could have been Indiana. Take a photograph next time." I don't respond. "When are you seeing him next?"

"I don't know." It's the truth.

"He's hosting a charity event at the hotel on Friday. You should go."

"Wouldn't it look suspicious if I just showed up to one of his events without an invite?"

"No, it wouldn't. Hundreds of people attend and he has no involvement with the invites. He wouldn't even question it. He probably wouldn't even notice you were there but obviously we *want* him to notice you."

"Do we?"

"Yes, we do. That's the whole point of this, Sophia."

"I thought the whole point of this was to test if he was willing to cheat on you. Surely you would rather him *not* notice me."

There's a long pause, long enough to make me look at my cell to see if she has hung up. "You don't need to worry about my desires or motivations."

"Are you sure about that? Why didn't you tell me that you and Mason have broken up?"

Another long pause. "Mason is my husband. We're still married."

"But you're not together. Don't you think it was worth mentioning?"

"No, I don't. All couples go through rough patches. We took vows; for better, for worse. I need to know if he's willing to brave the storm or if he's just going to give up."

"So that's all it is? A rough patch?"

"Of course. We're just taking a little breather."

"So you think you'll get back together?"

"Yes, I do. Why? Has he said something different?"

Yes. "No. He mentioned that you were separated and I was caught off guard. I'd rather have full disclosure so I know what I'm dealing with."

"Full disclosure? Okay, let's do that. For your information, he's just been to visit me. We talked for a long time and he said that he wants to try more therapy." So one of them is definitely lying to me. Based on past experiences,

I would say that Mason was the liar but something feels different this time. "This is no different to any of your other traps," she says as though she can read my mind.

"As long as you're both on the same page. It wouldn't feel right trapping somebody who believed there was no hope."

"It wouldn't feel right? Oh, please. You break up families for a living. Don't pretend to have morals all of a sudden. Stop questioning everything and do your job."

Ouch. "Actually, I expose cheats for a living. If that leads to their family breaking up then that's on them, not me. From now on, we communicate via Kristen like it says in the damn contract." I hang up before she can respond.

"When this is all over and done with," Lori says, looking contemplative, "I think I'm going to pay her a little visit."

I laugh. "Pay her a visit? Who do you think you are, The Godfather?"

"In San Francisco, women are more dangerous than shotguns."

"Was that supposed to be an Italian accent?"

"Sicilian."

That evening she ropes me into watching *The Godfather* but I can't concentrate on anything other than Emily's words.

Chapter Thirty Four

Mason

"Why are you here?" I ask Buzz when I find him sitting at my desk on Monday morning.

"Somebody's got to make the millions while you're not here."

"I agree. But why are *you* here?"

He feigns laughter. "Still on your period?"

"Still an asshole?" I reply.

"You should be thanking me."

"Thanking you for what, exactly? I turned up at her house, dripping wet, for *no reason*."

"Does there have to be a reason to visit a beautiful woman?"

"When you've only known somebody for forty eight hours then yes, there has to be a reason or else it's just creepy. Jesus, at one point I thought…" I shake my head, trying to rid the mental image I've just conjured. "Forget it."

"No, go on."

I sigh. "At one point I thought you were there because you and Sophia had…you know."

"Fucked?" His grin threatens to take over his entire face. "I'm sure she would jump at the chance to ride the Buzz train but don't worry brother, I've got your back. I'll bow out gracefully and let you have her."

"Wow, how selfless of you," I reply sarcastically.

"She's all yours."

"Number one, stop talking about her as if she's a possession who *belongs* to somebody. Number two, you won't have to bow out because there's nothing to bow out *of*. And number three…get out of my chair." I decide not to tell him what's actually on my mind. I don't tell him that I fear I won't ever get a second chance at love, especially with a woman like her. Why would anybody want damaged goods? She probably thinks that I'm a huge failure.

Buzz finally stands up. "Okay, you keep telling yourself

that. I left you something in your top drawer, by the way." I take a look as he walks over to the door. "I came prepared," he adds with a wink.

I open the drawer and see a jumbo box of tampons. "Lori couldn't even remember you at first," I tell him. He stops walking and turns around. "You know, before she remembered how terrible you were at kissing."

He laughs and raises one eyebrow. "She wasn't complaining this morning." He dodges the box of tampons I throw at his head.

Chapter Thirty Five
Sophia

"So I've been thinking..."

Lori stops reading and looks up from her book. "Uh oh, do I need to sit down for this?"

I laugh. "You're already sitting down."

"You know what I mean."

"I have a new plan."

She closes her book, a sure sign that she means business. "Go on."

"So as you already know, I want to spend as little time with Mason as possible." She nods. "Well what better way to dodge Mason than go on a date with somebody else?"

"I'm not following."

"Mason is hosting a charity event this Friday. I looked into it and it's a date auction. We're going."

"Okay?"

"And I'm going to take part."

"What do you mean, take part? Are you going to bid on someone so you can go on a date? I guess that could work."

"No, I'm not going to bid on anybody. People are going to bid on me."

"Are you crazy?"

"No. I can tick off another meeting to satisfy Emily and there will be hundreds of people there so I probably won't even have to talk to Mason. Plus, the dates take place immediately after the auction. So if I take part, I don't have to hang around all night."

"Why can't we just go and then leave after an hour?"

"Because Emily would find out. I bet she sends Joanne to spy on me. If I was trying to trap him then why would I leave early?"

"I guess so but what if some creep bids on you?"

"They won't."

"How do you know?"

"Even if they do, it won't matter because *you* are going

to be the highest bidder."

"Me?"

"Yep. All you need to do is ask somebody in there to do your bidding. Tell them that you'll give them the money afterwards plus a little extra something for helping us out."

She raises an eyebrow. "A little extra something?"

"Jesus, no! I mean extra cash."

She laughs. "Good. I love you but not *that* much."

"So what do you think? Do you think you can pull it off?"

"Of course but why can't I just bid on you myself? Take the middle man out."

"Because we live together. We see each other every day so I don't think it would be believable for you to pay to take me out to dinner. Plus, I'm going to tell Emily that it's all part of my plan to try and make Mason jealous so she has to believe that I'm going on a real date."

"Okay. So what happens afterwards when you're expected to go on your date?"

"They'll see me leave with whoever you choose to do your bidding." I shrug. "Then we get to go home and order takeout."

"Sounds like a plan. How much are we bidding?"

"As much as it takes for you to be the highest bidder. A few hundred I'm guessing. Five tops."

She laughs. "A few hundred? Mason is a millionaire which means there will be other millionaires there too."

"And?"

"And you might end up paying a bit more than a couple hundred bucks."

"It'll be fine. Just bid up to five hundred."

"And if it goes over that?"

"If it goes over that then it looks like I'll be going on a real date."

Chapter Thirty Six
Mason

I try to steady my breathing as I run around the park for the fourth time. Or is this the fifth? I've lost count. My legs feel like jelly and my lungs are on fire. This is exactly why I don't usually run. It seems like too much effort to stay healthy. The music on my phone is interrupted by somebody calling me. I don't even look at who it is as I go to press decline but my sweaty finger swipes the wrong way. Great. "Hello?" I manage to get out.

"Dude, what are you doing?" Buzz asks.

"Running."

"From what?"

"Why do I have to be running *from* something?"

"Because why else would you be running?"

I stop and bend forward, hands on my knees. "Exercise."

He laughs. "You don't run."

"I do now."

"You sound like you're about to have a heart attack."

"That's because I probably am." I sit down. "What do you want?"

"Tomorrow night."

"What about it?" I adjust my shoes, loosening the laces. I'm pretty sure Indiana chose the most uncomfortable ones on the market. I can already feel the blisters starting to form on my toes.

"We're going to the movies."

"I think I'll pass. I've got some work stuff to catch up with."

"Okay, I guess it'll just be the three of us then."

"The three of you?" I ask, taking the bait.

"Me, Lori and Sophia."

My ears prick up at the sound of her name. "When and where?"

He laughs. "I thought you have work stuff to catch up

with?"

"I thought I fired you last week but for some reason you keep showing up. You know I'm not paying you anymore, don't you?"

"The three of us are going to have so much fun tomorrow. Tuesdays *are* for threesomes after all."

"Careful," I growl. "When and where?"

"AMC. Eight thirty."

"I'll be there."

"Of course you will, Yankee. Just don't overdo it with the fancy ass cologne this time."

I hang up then collapse into a pile on the grass. Even though my breathing is almost back to normal, my heart is still beating a mile a minute. I blame it on being so out of shape. I haven't been to the gym in a few weeks and even when I do go, I hardly ever do cardio. I close my eyes and try to stop myself from grinning like an idiot at the thought of seeing Sophia again. When my heart rate still hasn't returned to normal after a couple of minutes, I blame it on something else entirely.

Chapter Thirty Seven
Sophia

I call Kristen once Lori and I have fine tuned our plan. "Speak of the devil. I've just had Emily in my office. Did you really have to insist that you communicate via me? She's a pain in the ass."

"I told her yesterday that I had no updates for her."

"I know. She wasn't here about you."

"Well why else would she visit you?"

"She was looking through the portfolio."

My blood runs cold. "Why?"

She sighs. "She's thinking of hiring more girls."

"For what reason?"

"Because there's more chance of her trapping him, apparently. No more contracts, just a couple of one-off traps. Just in case one of them catch him on a good day."

"Are you joking? You can't let her involve more girls."

"I told her it's too risky but if she pays me then I can't say no, can I? There's nothing in your contract which says you'll be the only one to try and trap him."

"I thought the whole point I've got myself into this huge mess is because he won't be stupid enough to have a one night stand."

"I know but this is Emily we're talking about. She seems a little…"

"Crazy?" I offer. "Psychotic?"

"Unhinged. Just now she was bragging about pawning some of Mason's stuff."

"What do you mean pawning some of his stuff? What stuff?"

"She said she took a little trip to the pawn shop yesterday. Poor guy, they're not even divorced yet. She's a viper."

I groan. "A viper? More like a monster. I can't believe we're involved in all of this."

"I know but it'll all be over soon."

"I need you to ask her to do something for me."

"Do I have to?"

"Mason's holding a charity date auction on Friday. I need her to add me to the list of people being auctioned."

"Okay, I'll ask. What's your plan?"

"Lori's going to pay somebody to bid on me so we can leave straight after."

"What do you want me to tell Emily?"

"Tell her it's to try and make Mason jealous. Tell her anything you want, just make sure she gets me on the list."

"Got it."

"Now tell me exactly what she said about the pawn shop."

"Where have you been?" Lori asks.

"Walking."

She looks at her cell. "For four hours?"

"Pretty much."

"Are you okay?"

I sigh. "No. I want out."

She walks over and wraps her arms around me. "Aww sweetie, I know you do."

"She pawned his stuff."

"What?"

"Emily. She pawned Mason's stuff. And a load of her own jewellery that he probably bought for her. There was a painting and a watch and some silverware. I couldn't afford to get it all back."

"What do you mean get it *all* back?"

I lift the small box out of my purse. "I could only afford the watch."

Her eyes widen. "How much did you pay for that?"

"Not a lot. Three fifty. Everything else was at least triple that."

"Sophia…"

"Don't bother with the lecture. I tried to walk away but I couldn't. What am I supposed to do? Send him an anonymous letter and enclose a map with a big cross over the pawn shop? This watch is old. It was different from the other stuff. The guy at the store said it's probably more of a sentimental piece. She's trying to ruin his life and what's worse is that she's using me to do it."

She lifts the watch out. "How did you find out about it?"

"Kristen told me. I went to four different pawn shops before finding the right one."

"And how did you know which things were Mason's?"

"I showed the owner a photo of Emily then gave him fifty bucks to tell me what she had pawned."

"Mason is going to be a hundred times better off without her."

"A thousand times better off."

"He needs somebody like you."

I raise my eyebrow. "I agreed to work with her which makes me almost as bad as she is."

"You agreed to do it without knowing all of the details. Now you're doing everything you can to stop her from screwing him over. She's the villain in all of this."

"Then what am I, the sidekick?"

"Did you not listen to a word I just said? You're the hero. You're just undercover."

I laugh. "Thanks for trying to make me feel better."

"We'll get through this, I promise. How many times does it say you need to see him in the contract?"

"Twice a week."

"Okay so that's only another ten times or so. You could arrange to go for a run with him, that way there shouldn't be too much talking."

"Yeah, I guess so."

"And we can do things as a group. You, me, Mason and Buzz. At least you won't have to be alone with him."

"You'd do that for me?"

"Of course I would. In fact, Buzz asked if we wanted to see a movie tomorrow night. I didn't think you would want to so I told him I'd think about it. It might be a good opportunity. The movies plus the charity event would meet your quota for the week."

I nod. "It sounds like a good plan."

"But?"

"But I'd rather not involve you in this mess."

She laughs. "I'm already involved. You're my best friend. If you're in a mess then I'm right there with you, shovel in hand."

"A shovel? To dig my grave?"

"No, smarty pants. To shovel all the shit away."

Chapter Thirty Eight
Mason

I look down at my watch for what feels like the hundredth time tonight. When did time decide to move so slowly? I run a hand through my hair then pick at an invisible thread on the hem of my T-shirt. "I don't think they're coming."

"They're coming," Buzz simply replies.

"How are you so sure?"

"Because I haven't seen Lori since Saturday."

"And?"

"And she's having major withdrawal symptoms." He flexes both of his biceps. "She's dying for some more Buzz. But then again, who isn't?"

"I hope they don't show up now just to wipe that cocky grin off of your face."

"You don't mean that."

No, I don't. I check my watch again. Maybe I need a new battery because it still says eight twenty nine. I zip up my jacket only to unzip it again a few seconds later.

He laughs. "Chill out, Yankee. You're acting like we're about to rob a bank."

He's right. I've never been good at hiding my emotions. I don't know why I feel so nervous about seeing Sophia again. Maybe it's because I haven't been able to stop fantasizing about how soft her skin is. Or maybe it's because my dream about her had been so vivid that I woke up this morning and expected to see her lying next to me. Whatever the reason, I was desperate to see her again. Desperate to feel that invisible force which seems to push us together. I clear my throat. "Stop calling me Yankee."

"Whatever you say...Yankee." He nods to the opposite side of the street. "I told you they'd come."

I instantly relax when I see Sophia walking towards me. She's wearing jeans and a baggy shirt but she still looks impossibly beautiful. I notice that her expression is softer than usual, perhaps a little apprehensive. Maybe I'm not the only one who is feeling nervous. "Mason thought you were going to stand us up," Buzz announces before I can even say hello.

I roll my eyes. "I *thought* that you were bound to find something better to do but Buzz reassured me that you would come. What was it that you said? That somebody was gag…"

"Let's go inside," Buzz interrupts, throwing a warning glance in my direction. "The movie will be starting."

Lori pouts as she follows him inside. "Aww, the trailers are the best part."

"Hi," I finally say when we're alone. "How are you?"

She hesitates. "I'm…fine." Her eyes are full of sincerity as she asks, "How about you?"

"I'm doing okay." A truth to contrast her lie. We stand in silence for a moment but it's clear that she doesn't want to talk about whatever is on her mind. "How's your wrist doing?"

She pushes her sleeve up. "I forgot all about it to be honest. It doesn't sting anymore."

"That's good," I say, eyeing the burn. "It looks like you might be left with a little scar."

"Oh well, I guess it'll add a bit of character."

"That's true. And hey, at least people won't mess with you if you have a scar."

"Well they don't anyway because of my badass butterfly tattoo, but now I'm taking intimidation to a whole new level."

I laugh. "I've got to admit, I'm pretty scared of you right now."

"You should be," she says completely straight faced before laughing. "We should probably go inside."

I hold my hands up. "I'm not going to argue with somebody who has a butterfly tattoo." I fall into step beside her. "What movie are we even watching?"

"I have no idea. I was going to ask you the same thing."

We make our way over to the ticket booth just as Buzz

turns around, holding four tickets up in the air. "There's been a slight change of plan," he tells us. "The new Tom Hanks movie has sold out."

"So we're watching Beautiful Disaster instead," Lori says, clapping her hands excitedly. "It's based on one of my all time favorite books. I know the movies are never usually as good but I'm still excited to see how it turned out. I can't wait to see Colton Haynes as Travis."

I smile politely as she continues naming different characters. Sophia is biting her lip, looking deep in thought. "Are you sure you're okay?" I whisper.

She shakes her head as though trying to break free from her thoughts. "Oh…yeah…yeah, I'm fine."

"Long day?" I ask.

"You could say that."

I don't push any further. "Do you like ice cream?"

She grins. "Are you joking? I *love* ice cream."

Buzz hands me two tickets then whispers, "Back row seats, motherfucker. We'll see you in there."

"Ice cream it is then," I say, ignoring Buzz as we walk over to the concession stand. "What's your favorite flavor?"

"Oh, I don't discriminate. I like them all."

"How considerate of you."

"What's yours?"

"I'm very loyal to mint chip. I've tried other flavors but I always regret it afterwards. I feel like I'm cheating."

Something flashes across her eyes but it's gone in the next second. "Good choice," she replies.

"What can I get for you?" The cashier asks Sophia, his eyes roaming all over her body.

"They all look so good. Go ahead and surprise me. I'll take three random scoops."

"Ah, so you're a risk taker?" I ask.

"I've never really thought about it before but yeah, I guess I am."

"It's a good thing."

"I'm not so sure these days."

"Take the risk or lose the chance."

"But what if you take a risk and it backfires?"

"Then at least you'll learn from it."

She looks contemplative as the cashier hands her a cone with three large scoops. She thanks him then turns to me. "The polite thing would be to hold off until you get yours, right?"

"And risk it melting? Go for it." Her eyes light up as she assesses each scoop carefully. "Difficult decision?"

"Sometimes the order in which you eat the scoops can be more important than the actual flavors."

"Wow, you're a real ice cream connoisseur."

"Meh, I guess they'll all end up in my mouth anyway." *Is it possible to be jealous of food?* She takes a lick and then moans. "Oh. My. God."

I laugh, mostly to distract myself from replaying the sound of her moaning over and over again in my head. "Is it good?"

"Good? It's the best thing I've ever had in my mouth." I raise an eyebrow and she laughs as a faint blush creeps across her cheeks. She holds the ice cream out to me. "Here, you need to try it."

I know that I shouldn't and I'm about to decline but Jesus Christ, the way she's looking at me right now, I would do just about anything she asked. All logic goes out of the window as I take the ice cream off of her.

Chapter Thirty Nine
Sophia

I watch as he takes a long, slow lick of my ice cream. I've got to admit, it's a major turn on. I'm tempted to let him eat the whole thing just so I can watch his masterful tongue at work. He pulls back and frowns.

"What's up? Do you not like it?" I ask, shocked.

"No, I do. It's just that…" He turns to the cashier. "What flavor is this?"

"I thought the game was to guess," he replies in a monotone voice.

"Just tell me."

"Pistachio."

Mason's shoulders stiffen. "Do you keep an EpiPen on site?"

"I don't even know what that is."

"Please go and ask a manager. Quickly." The cashier sighs as he walks off.

"What's happening?" I ask. "Are you okay?"

"I'm allergic to pine nuts."

"Oh, shit." I drop the ice cream on top of the counter, not caring that it's going to melt everywhere. "Shit, shit, shit. Are you okay?"

"For now, but I've left my EpiPen at home. It can turn pretty serious if I don't take a shot." He pulls his cell out of his pocket and hands it to me. "Will you call an ambulance?" He must notice my reaction as he adds, "You know, just as a precaution."

I nod and do as he asks. My hands are shaking and by the end of the call all I keep thinking is that I might have accidently killed Mason Hunter. I can already see the headlines tomorrow. *Bitter and twisted honey trapper murders her millionaire target.* "They're on their way," I tell him. "Now what do I need to do?"

He looks up from where he's now sitting on the floor. "Do you know CPR?"

My eyes nearly pop out of my head. "Why would I need to know CPR?"

"You won't but I was just wondering if you would know what to do."

"I know the basics."

"That's good. Maybe I can give you a refresher lesson some time. You know, when I'm not busy having an allergic reaction."

"You're going to teach me CPR?"

"Yes. You know, mouth to mouth resuscitation and that sort of thing."

I laugh. "So you're having an allergic reaction but still hitting on me?"

"I'm just being responsible."

"Well it wasn't very responsible of you to taste my ice cream when you're allergic to nuts."

"Pine nuts," he clarifies. "I'm fine with some ice creams."

"It looks like I'm not the only risk taker."

His laugh turns into a cough. "I hate this part."

"What part?"

"The part where my throat narrows."

"Maybe you should stop talking and focus on your breathing until the ambulance arrives." He nods as I sit down beside him.

The next few minutes feel like hours, especially when the manager comes to tell us that they don't have an EpiPen. Both Mason's mood and health seem to deteriorate with the news so relief rushes through me when I hear the sound of a siren getting closer. "The ambulance is here," I tell Mason. He nods, looking a lot paler than he did five minutes ago. "Do you want me to go and get Buzz?" A small shake of his head this time.

I stand up when I see two paramedics approaching. I explain what happened while they quickly check Mason over. "What's your name, buddy?"

"Mason," he whispers.

"We're going to take you in, Mason. You're having an anaphylactic shock. Your blood pressure is too low and you have a rapid heartbeat. I'm just going to put this oxygen mask on you to help with your breathing. Just breathe as you normally would."

"Is he going to be okay?" I ask.

"We're going to do all that we can to help him," one of them replies as the other jogs back over to the ambulance. "Are you his wife?"

"Oh, um, no. I'm his…I'm his…" *What the hell am I?* His wife's employee? His honey trapper? Mason's eyes find mine as I settle on, "His friend."

"Okay, well we're going to be taking him to St. Mary's Medical Center."

We both turn to Mason when he makes an unintelligible noise. He takes off his oxygen mask. "Stay with me?"

I look at the paramedic who nods. "If that's what you want."

"Of course I'll stay," I tell Mason. He nods and puts his oxygen mask back on just as the other paramedic reappears with a wheelchair. They help him get into it before we make our way outside.

We pass a small group of men and I get majorly defensive when I notice that one of them is pointing his cell straight at Mason, presumably taking a photo or video. "Have some respect," I tell them as we walk by, purposely keeping my face away from the camera. I hear a few of them laughing and joking about him getting burned by a woman and I can't help but think that if the tables were turned, Mason would be doing everything he could to help them. He may be the most beautiful man I've ever seen but no beauty shines brighter than that of a good heart. I climb into the ambulance and wish more than anything that we had met under different circumstances.

Chapter Forty

Mason

I panic when I open my eyes and see nothing but darkness. I'm lying down but I know for sure that I'm not in my own bed. I jolt up and look around the room. It takes me a few terrifying seconds to remember that I'm at the hospital then a few seconds longer to remember why. Somebody clears their throat and I've never been so goddamn happy to see Buzz. "So I'm not dead after all?" I ask.

"I fucking hope not because if you are then I must be too. Either that or I can talk to dead people which I definitely didn't sign up for."

"Sophia?" I ask as memories of last night come flooding back.

"She left with Lori about half an hour ago. The poor chick must have been bored stiff. Whatever the doctor gave you made you really tired. I've always said that you're terrible company."

"What time is it?" I ask, my throat still sore and swollen.

"Just after three A.M. The doctor wanted to monitor you for five hours. Sophia stayed with you the whole time. She didn't even go outside to call us until an hour ago when the doctor had discharged you. Lori was freaking out. She was ready to report her as missing."

I groan. "I ruined everybody's evening. Damn pine nuts."

"Don't say that, it's not your fault that you're nuts about her."

"How long did it take you to come up with that?"

"*Nut* that long." I press the call button on the remote next to my bed. "What are you doing?"

"I'm going to ask the doctor to give me another dose of whatever that stuff was so I don't have to listen to you anymore."

"Okay, okay, I'll stop." He grins. "No need to bust a

nut."

Chapter Forty One
Sophia

That night I dream about Mason.
And his tongue.
And it doesn't involve any ice cream.

Chapter Forty Two
Mason

It's not until I wake up several hours later, this time in my own bed, that I realize I don't have my cell. Maybe Buzz has it, unless it's still at the hospital. I go in search of my work phone instead then type myself a quick message.

Hey Mason, it's Mason. Thanks for not dying yesterday. Death by ice cream would have been pathetic. Please find your way back to me soon because I'm irresponsible and haven't backed you up in a really long time.

I grab a bottle of water and wince when I swallow the tablets the doctor gave me. I feel one thousand times better than I did last night but I still have a lingering headache and sore throat. I guess that's what happens when your throat constricts. I head back to my bed and turn Netflix on. I start browsing the latest shows when my phone vibrates beside me. I open up the text message.

Death by pine nuts, actually.
Buzz? I text back.
No. It's Sophia. I forgot to give you your cell back after I called the ambulance yesterday. How are you feeling?
M: Ah, I remember now. I'm feeling a lot better now that I can breathe.
S: Yeah, breathing is pretty important.
M: I'm sorry we didn't get to watch the movie.
S: I'm sorry I almost killed you with the ice cream.
I laugh at that. *M: Thank you for staying with me last night.*
A minute passes before she responds. *S: I'm not going to turn down the chance to ogle hunky doctors.*
I'm caught off guard by how jealous that makes me. *M: Every cloud has a silver lining. Same time next week? I could try the Nutella ice cream.*
S: Aww, that's sweet of you but I'd rather you stay alive.

M: Let me make it up to you.
S: There's no need. I'll drop your cell at reception later.
M: I can come get it.
S: No. Rest.
M: Yes Ma'am.

Chapter Forty Three
Sophia

"Morning," I say to Lori as she walks into the kitchen.

"I'm not talking to you."

"Um, I think you just did."

"I'm still mad at you."

"But I made you coffee. Coffee makes everything better."

"It's going to take a lot more than coffee. I thought you were dead."

"I'm sorry, I should have called. It all just happened so fast, then I couldn't get service at the hospital."

"They do have pay phones, you know?"

"I know, but I didn't want to leave him. The doctor gave him something which made him sleepy so I didn't want him to wake up and be alone. I called you as soon as they gave him the all clear."

"I legit thought he had murdered you."

"Ever the drama queen."

"I'm being serious. I thought he must have found out what you were doing and chopped you up into tiny pieces."

"Well I'm still here, still in one piece."

"For now."

"This isn't one of your crime documentaries."

She raises her eyebrows. "It has the premise to be. You need to be careful. People with money have *contacts*."

I roll my eyes. "I doubt that Mason has a hitman on speed dial. Anyway, did you at least have fun with Buzz last night?"

"No, I was too worried."

"Well it was nice of him to stay with you until I called."

"He only did it to try and get into my panties."

"And did it work?"

"Almost." She groans. "His tattoo's drive me crazy. But no, we actually made a pact."

"What pact?"

"Well it's more of a challenge for him really. No sex."

"And he's agreed to it?" I ask, both eyebrows raised.

"Yep."

"For how long?"

"Six weeks."

"Why six weeks?"

"Because that's when your contract ends so I figured I won't carry on seeing Buzz when you stop seeing Mason."

My heart sinks at the thought of never seeing Mason again. "You could still see him if you really wanted him to. You could tell him the truth about what you do."

"How many times have we talked about this? Nobody will ever be okay with what we do."

"I just want you to be happy."

"I *am* happy."

"Are you sure?"

"Yes. It's my choice to do this job, just like it's yours. *If* and when I want a boyfriend, I'll quit. Until then, as long as my books have a happily ever after then I'll be fine."

"So are you and Buzz just going to be friends?"

"We're definitely more than friends but I don't want it all being about sex. I guess we could do other stuff. To be honest, I'll be surprised if he sticks around for six weeks."

"Well if he doesn't then he's an idiot."

"Speaking of idiots, I wonder how Mason's doing today. I still can't believe he tried the ice cream."

"He said he's feeling better. He just needs to rest."

Her eyes go wide. "You've spoken to him?"

I pull his cell out of my jeans pocket. "Yeah, I forgot to give him his cell back."

"So wait a minute, if you have his cell, how have you spoken to him?"

"He's using his work cell."

"Have you looked at his photos?"

"No, of course I haven't."

"Why the hell not? Pass it here."

"Lori, no. I'm not going to look at his private photos."

She wiggles her eyebrows. "He might have taken naked selfies."

"Exactly."

"Exactly!" she echoes. "Aren't you a little bit curious?"

Yes. "No."

"You're so boring. At least look at his messages. There could be incriminating evidence. You've been giving yourself a hard time about trapping him but what if he has texts from another woman on there? They could be from months or even years ago."

"I guess you're right."

"Of course I am. Do you want me to look?" I nod and pass her the cell. "I wonder if he has any celebrity friends."

"Just look at the messages."

"I need to have a quick look through his contacts first. What if he has somebody saved as hot lips or fuck buddy? Oh my god, no way!"

My stomach flips. "What?"

"Bradley Cooper. *The* Bradley Cooper." I roll my eyes. "Shut the front door! He has Leonardo Dicaprio's number too! I've been in love with him since Romeo and Juliet. The fish tank scene gives me all the feels!"

"Just get on with it."

I wait, watching her gasp and squeal when she spots other celebrities. "No hot lips," she announces a minute later. "But he does know Taylor Swift. I wonder if any of her songs are about him."

I laugh. "Check the calls and messages."

She begins tapping and scrolling. "Oooh, lots of calls from somebody called Indiana."

"His sister."

"Oh. Um, a few random numbers. Some to Emily and Buzz but nothing that sticks out."

"When was the last time he spoke to Emily?" I don't know why I'm asking.

"Last Friday but he has missed calls from her after that."

"What about messages?"

More scrolling. "Mostly Buzz and Indiana."

"When do they date back to?"

"Um, about six months. So he's either a good boy or good at covering his tracks."

"Innocent until proven guilty."

"I wonder why Buzz calls Mason Yankee."

"Are you reading their messages?"

"Yeah, I want to see if they mention me. Huh, that's weird."

"What?"

"Buzz asked Mason if he enjoyed watching *The Notebook*. I thought men only watch that if they're forced to. Maybe he's been seeing a woman after all."

I hold my hand out. "I think that's enough, Sherlock."

"Please let me look at his photos."

"Lori…" She sighs and hands me the cell. "Ask Buzz to send you some nude pictures if you're that bothered. I'm sure he would oblige."

She rolls her eyes. "When are you giving it back?"

"I'm going to drop it off at the hotel later." I finish my coffee then rinse out the cup while she serenades me to *Hotel* by R.Kelly. "Finished?" I ask.

She holds the note for a few seconds then takes a bow. "You should keep his cell for a little while longer. You know, to see if anybody calls or texts him."

I laugh. "I'm not going to change my mind about the photos."

She sticks her tongue out. "It was worth a try."

Chapter Forty Four

Mason

Netflix: Are you still watching Sons of Anarchy?

"I've just watched six episodes back to back, of course I'm still watching." I'm just about to start the next episode when there's a knock at my front door. My mind instantly jumps to Sophia. Even though she said she would leave my cell with reception, my imagination runs wild and I'm flooded with mental images of her coming over wearing a nurse's uniform. I throw on a T-shirt and rearrange the contents of my boxer shorts before I open the door. I try to hide my disappointment when I see Emily standing in front of me.

"Well, aren't you going to invite me inside?" I open the door wider and step to the side. She looks around the room. "It's been a long time since I've been in the famous penthouse suite." She points to the grand piano. "Do you remember when we christened that thing?"

I ignore her and instead ask, "What can I help you with?"

"What can you *help me with*? This isn't a business transaction, Mason."

"Okay then, why are you here?"

"I heard you had a little trip to the hospital last night."

"Where did you hear that?"

"I'm listed as your emergency contact, remember?"

"The doctor called you?"

"Yes."

And yet she didn't show up at the hospital, not that I would have wanted her there. "Well I'm sorry if it disrupted your evening."

"It's fine. I asked if you had somebody there with you and they said yes so I didn't think you needed me there too. I presumed it would have been Indiana or Buzz or maybe even your assistant Natalie."

"Natalia."

She waves her hand dismissively. "But then I saw

this…" She holds up her cell. It's a photograph of me being pushed in a wheelchair with Sophia beside me. Luckily she has her back to the camera.

"Where did you get that?" I ask.

"It's all over the internet. Every single news site is speculating on who the mystery woman is." She scrolls down and a video begins to play. It's not the best quality but I watch myself getting wheeled towards the ambulance. Something stirs deep inside of me when Sophia's voice suddenly fills the room. "Have some respect," she tells the person recording. I smile even though Emily is watching me like a hawk. I need to thank Sophia for having my back, not many people do these days. The video comes to an abrupt end. "Who is she?" Emily asks.

"She's a friend."

"A friend who you take on a date to the movies?"

"It wasn't a date." At least, I don't think that it was. "We weren't alone. There were a few of us including Buzz."

"Then why didn't he ride to the hospital with you instead?"

"Because he was already inside the movie and didn't know what was happening."

"Do you have feelings for her?"

Yes. "We're not together anymore, Emily."

"Answer the question."

"I don't see why it matters to you."

"It matters because we're still married."

"Well that doesn't seem to stop you." I shake my head. "I noticed the other day that you've been redecorating."

She swallows hard then raises her chin as if she's trying to keep her mask from slipping. "And?"

"And we both know what happened the last time you wanted a change."

"That was a mistake."

"Which time? The first, second or fifth?"

"I don't know why you're bringing it all up again. It's in the past."

"The past *and* the present."

"I'm not fucking him this time."

This time. "Well you were when it mattered." When I still cared.

"Are you jealous of him? It's not too late for us to try and work things out."

"No I'm not and yes it is. I don't belong to you anymore. I don't appreciate you coming round here interrogating me when you're the one who is already *redecorating* when I haven't even finished moving all of my stuff out. Hey, at least this time you can fuck him without worrying about me walking in on you."

"That's not fair."

"Life isn't fair." I walk over to the door and open it as wide as possible. "Thanks for your visit."

She takes another look around and then slowly walks towards me. "TMZ are claiming that you and the mystery woman have secret children together. You might want to shut that down. It could be bad for business."

I close the door behind her without saying another word.

Chapter Forty Five
Sophia

I'm doing laundry a few hours later when my ass starts to vibrate. I pull Mason's cell out of my pocket, forgetting that I still had it with me.

M: Sophia, are you there?
S: I'm here. Still holding your cell hostage! Just doing some errands then I'll return it. Unless you need it right now?
M: No. Don't bring it back here.
S: ?????

I don't have much time to guess what he's talking about as he calls me a few seconds later. "Hello?" I answer.

"Hey." His voice sends a shiver down my spine.

"Is everything ok? Why don't you want your cell back?"

"Apparently you've been keeping secrets from me."

My heart stops. "Wh...what?"

"TMZ are claiming that we have secret babies together."

"What are you talking about?"

"We were photographed together last night and now there are tons of paparazzi waiting outside the hotel. You have your back to the camera in all of the photos I've seen so you shouldn't be recognized."

Thank god. I take a deep breath. "I think I know who took the photos. There was a group of men at the movies and it looked like one of them was recording you on his phone."

"Yeah, my lawyers are already on it. There's a video online too. I heard you telling them to have some respect. Thank you for that, I really appreciate it."

"It's bad enough that he recorded it, but selling it to some stupid gossip website is downright disrespectful."

"Yeah, all the usual suspects have it. TMZ, Perez Hilton, People Magazine. Hey, we even made it onto E

News."

"It must be annoying having to deal with this kind of stuff."

"It doesn't happen a lot. I don't think it helped that somebody started the rumor about me being your baby daddy because now everybody wants to get involved."

"My baby daddy, huh? So how many children do we actually have?"

"Three."

"Three? Wow, we've been busy."

"Right? I think it might be time to start trying for baby number four."

"Oh, you think so?"

"You're the one who said you wanted your own soccer team."

"Hmmm, that's true."

He laughs. "I'm glad we can joke about it. I know they can't see your face but I was worried about how it might affect you if they somehow found out. It made me realize that I don't know much about you. I'd like to change that." *I wouldn't.* I don't want him to know the real me. I don't want him to hate me. "I've been trying to guess your job for the last hour." A huge wave of guilt washes over me and I have the urge to come clean and tell him everything. I have a feeling it would save at least one of us from being hurt further down the line. "I keep picturing you as a nurse."

I wish. "I'm a writer," I tell him, which isn't strictly a lie. I studied English and Creative Writing at college with the dream of becoming a published author. Catching my boyfriend cheating on me was the ultimate plot twist which led me to begin a new chapter in my life. One which didn't involve writing. From past experience, telling people that I'm a writer usually limits the amount of questions asked and it helps that I'm not
expected to have an actual place of work.

"Wow, that's awesome. What do you write?"

"Romance."

159

"Ah, that's so cool. I'd love to read some of your work."

I feel like such a horrible person. "I'm kind of in the middle of something at the moment."

"That's fine. I'll wait and get a signed copy whenever it's finished. Hey, if you need any inspiration, you know where I am."

I laugh. "Thanks for the offer."

"I could be your muse."

"Have you warned your wife about the photos?" I ask, changing the subject.

"She's the one who told me about them. She came over to ask me about them but didn't care to ask how I was feeling."

Typical Emily. "Was she upset?"

"No and even if she was, she hasn't got a leg to stand on."

"What do you mean?"

"I think she's seeing somebody."

It's a good thing he can't see my shocked facial expression. "Who?"

"Her decorator. The same guy she cheated on me with last year."

"Emily cheated on you?" She *cheated*? And now she has the audacity to try and trap Mason when they're not even together.

"Yes, more than once. We're getting divorced and I'm *so* over it but I don't like her being hypocritical, telling me what I can and can't do when she's clearly always done what she wants."

"I'm sorry you went through that. I know exactly how it feels."

"You do?"

"Yeah, that's why I broke up with my ex."

He sighs. "Your ex cheated on you?"

"Yep. I saw it with my own eyes."

"What an asshole."

"We both have asshole ex's. Go us!"

"Hey, look on the bright side. At least we both got out."

"That's true. You deserve to be happy, Mason." And once I'm out of your life, you can be.

"So do you."

I'm not so sure about that. I clear my throat. "How do you want me to return your cell?"

"Just keep hold of it for now until the media circus calms down."

"Wow, do you trust me with it for that long? What if I look at all of your naked selfies?"

He laughs. "You mean you haven't already?"

"No. Sometimes I like to test my self control."

"And how long does that usually last?"

"Not very long."

"I'll have to keep that in mind."

I blush even though I'm alone. "Goodbye, Mason."

"Until next time, Sophia."

Chapter Forty Six

Mason

"Oh, so you *are* alive," Indie says as soon as I pick up.

"Of course I'm alive."

"I wake up to photos of my brother being wheeled into an ambulance and then he doesn't answer any of my calls. What was I supposed to think?"

"I'm sorry."

"Why didn't you call me?"

"I didn't want you to worry. I'm perfectly fine."

"You didn't look fine on the photos. I called your cell about fifty times. I was starting to get worried. I don't think I've ever had to call you on the penthouse line before."

"I haven't got my cell with me. I might not get it back for a couple of days."

"Why not? What the hell happened yesterday?"

"I had an allergic reaction."

"To what?"

"Ice cream."

"Why the hell were you eating ice cream?"

"I thought it would be okay."

"Since when? You know how risky ice cream is. Did you use your EpiPen?"

"I didn't have it with me."

She sighs. "I swear I'm going to come over there and kick your ass. You're supposed to carry it with you all the time, idiot. That's the whole point of having one."

"I know, I know."

"Wait until I tell mom."

I laugh. "We're not kids anymore, Indie."

"So you don't care if I tell her then?"

"Slow down. I don't want her to worry."

"If I don't tell her then somebody else will. Have you seen all the stories today?"

"Yes. Vultures, all of them."

"You could have at least told me that I was an aunt."

162

"Ah yeah, my three secret children. It somehow slipped my mind. You know how busy I've been recently."

"*Very busy*, apparently. So who's the mama?"

"I'm still waiting for TMZ to tell me."

She laughs. "Who's in the photos?"

"Indie…"

"What? I'm your sister!"

"I don't want you getting carried away like you usually do."

"I won't. Is it Sophia?"

"Yes."

"I knew it. Were you on a date?"

"No, Buzz and Lori were there too."

"Oh, so it was a double date?"

"No, I don't think so."

"You *don't think so?*"

"Indie, stop."

"Okay, okay. Did she go with you to the hospital?"

"Yes, she stayed with me the whole time."

"That's nice of her. She must really like you."

I hope so. "Am I free to go now? The doctor told me to rest."

"Yes, as long as you promise me that you won't have any secret babies."

"I promise."

"Good. Do you need me to swing by or anything?"

"Nah, I'm fine. I'll be back to work tomorrow."

"Okay, make sure you take it easy. Dinner on Friday?"

"I can't, it's the charity auction."

"Oh yeah, I totally forgot."

"You should come."

"Is Emily going to be there?"

"Yes."

"Actually, I've just remembered that I've got plans on Friday night. What a shame."

I laugh. "With who?"

"Anybody, anywhere, doing anything."

"Hmmm, do you think that excuse could work for me too?"

Chapter Forty Seven

Sophia

"How did it go?" I ask Lori when she arrives home from her latest trap.

"It was fine. Different."

"Oooh, tell me more."

She sits down opposite me and lets down her hair. "I trapped a woman."

"Wow. Why didn't you tell me this morning?"

"You've got enough on your mind at the moment. I don't want to bother you with my traps as well."

"Don't be silly, it would be a welcome distraction. So how was it?"

"It was actually kind of nice. Is that weird? We had a good chat. She seemed like she was genuinely interested in what I had to say and she didn't spend the whole night looking at my boobs. Oh and her lips were really soft."

I laugh. "Should Buzz be getting jealous?"

"No, but I made the stupid mistake of telling him that I kissed a girl and now he won't shut up about it. He keeps calling and texting me."

"Who does he think you kissed?"

"I didn't give him any details, just that I kissed a woman."

"You tease! Poor Buzz."

"I think he's half jealous, half horny."

"More like one hundred percent horny. So how did her girlfriend take it?"

"Her *boyfriend* seemed very upset."

I raise my eyebrows. "Oh."

"Yeah. Apparently he's had his suspicions for a while now. It started out as drunken kisses with her girlfriends but then he found flirty texts to one of them."

"Wow."

She nods and slides a newspaper across the table. "Here, I picked this up on my way home. You made page five."

I flick through to see the same two photos which have been circulating all day. "*The hunt is on for Hunter's mystery woman.* Is that the best they can come up with?"

"Take a look at the next page." I do as she says and my entire body comes alive at the sight of a shirtless Mason. As if his washboard abs and sculpted V wasn't enough, he's biting his goddamn lip and staring at me with bedroom eyes. "See what you're missing out on?" she asks with a grin.

Yes. Yes, I do.

That evening, I'm in bed scrolling through instagram when Mason's cell vibrates. I jump and almost end up liking somebody's photo from ten months ago - total creeper territory. I smile when I see that it's from Mason's work cell.

M: Hey :)
S: Hey yourself.
M: Am I interrupting?
S: No, I'm just in bed.
A few seconds pass. M: What are you wearing? ;)
I laugh. S: Minnie Mouse pajamas!
M: Wow. Let me take a minute.
S: What are YOU wearing?
M: Nothing...
S: You win.
M: Wait, are we sexting?! He asks.
S: LOL, not quite.
M: Tell me something about yourself.
S: What do you want to know?
M: Everything. Greatest fear?
S: Spiders. Original, I know.
M: Guilty pleasure?
S: The Bachelor.
M: Pet peeve?
S: When people misuse the word 'literally'.

M: I agree, it's literally the worst thing on earth.
S: Very funny.
M: Last time you cried?
I don't tell him that I shed a few tears the night that I bought
his watch back from the pawnbrokers. *S: I can't remember,*
probably a few weeks ago at a sad movie or something.
M: One place you would love to visit?
S: London.
M: Biggest flaw?
S: I'm very impatient. Hurry up with the next question ;)
M: How old were you when you lost your virginity?
S: 18. What about you?
M: 16.
S: How was it?
M: I can't remember. It was over so quickly.
S: And is that your personal best?
M: Nah, I can last at least five seconds longer these days.
S: Lol! Good to know.
M: Weirdest place you've had sex?
S: In an elevator.
M: That's wrong on so many levels. See what I did there?
I laugh. *S: I didn't think very highly of it.*
M: Good one.
S: You're desperately trying to think of more elevator puns aren't you?
M: No. Maybe.
S: It's okay, I'll wait.
His reply comes about a minute later. *M: You could say that it*
failed to push your buttons.
S: You're right. My mood was a little up and down afterwards.
M: I'm floored by the quality of our puns.
S: I haven't even started on the shaft yet.
M: I told you we were sexting!!!
I quickly google pictures of elevator shafts then send one to
him. *S: Now we're sexting.*

He calls me less than two seconds later. "Did you just
send me an elevator dick pic?"

I laugh. "Yes, I think I did."

"Am I supposed to send you one back?"

"I'm not too sure what the etiquette is."

There's a long pause and I suddenly become extremely aware of the energy between us. The unspoken words. The sexual tension. The lies. I can almost reach out and touch it. "You should know that if I have trouble sleeping tonight then it's because of you." His tone isn't so playful anymore.

I clear my throat. "Speaking of which, it's getting late."

"We should do this again some time."

"What? Send each other elevator porn?"

He laughs. "I want to get to know you better."

No, you don't. "Goodnight, Mason."

"Until next time, Sophia."

Chapter Forty Eight

Mason

"Aren't you going to compliment my dress?" Emily asks as I sit as far away from her as physically possible.

"We don't have to pretend until we're in there," I reply.

She laughs. "Wow, all work and no play makes Mason a dull boy. I wore your favorite color just for you." Even after all this time, she still believes that it's red.

"Did you find my grandpa's watch?"

She looks out of the window. "No. I looked everywhere."

"Then I guess I'll have to report it as stolen because I definitely didn't take it."

"I think you're being a little dramatic."

"No, I'm not. It was there before I left and now it's gone."

"I'll have another look."

"I'll come and look for it myself."

"Why don't you come back with me after the auction?" She moves her hand across the leather seat between us.

I stop it before it reaches my leg. "No."

"Not even for old times' sake?"

"No."

"But a woman has needs." She leans in and places her other hand on top of mine.

"Then make sure you tell the decorator. No means no."

She pulls both of her hands away and we ride the rest of the way in silence.

I jump out of the car as soon as we pull up outside the hotel. My frown is quickly replaced by a strained smile when I see other guests arriving. I walk around the back of the car and stop next to Emily, who is now smoothing out her dress. She smiles and holds her hand out to me and I have no choice but to accept it. I grimace when her thumb strokes the back on my hand. A year ago, I would have appreciated the small gesture but seeing as though she hasn't given me any kind of affection in a long time, I know she's only doing it to get a reaction out of me. I refuse to give her one. Instead, I smile, pose for photographs and imagine that her hand is somebody else's.

"Wow, brother, you're looking sharp," Buzz says with a grin.

"Why do you sound so surprised?"

"You usually wear the same old boring suits."

I look down at my midnight blue suit, which has always been my favorite color despite what Emily believes. "Yeah well I felt like mixing it up."

"That's the spirit. Change can be good."

"Will you be bidding on anyone tonight?" I ask. "Have you seen the line up?"

He raises his eyebrows. "Yeah, I've seen it. I'm guessing you haven't?"

"No, not yet. Any surprises?"

"Um, you could say that."

I scan the room and I'm pretty sure I forget how to breathe when I see a familiar pair of bambi eyes. Buzz follows my line of sight. "Did you not know she was coming?"

I ignore him and head in her direction. It's like a magnetic force is pulling me towards her. She looks other worldly, dressed in a floor length blue dress covered in hundreds of tiny diamonds. Even the slightest movement makes her look as though she's bursting with light. She smiles but it takes me at least half a minute to form coherent words. "I wasn't expecting to see you tonight."

She shifts from one foot to the other. "Well here I am. Surprise!"

"You look beautiful."

"You don't look too shabby yourself. You clean up well."

"You're color coordinating," Lori says. I hadn't even noticed that she was standing next to Sophia. "I must have missed the memo."

"Hello, Lori." She nods in response. "That color really suits you," I tell Sophia.

"It's my favorite color."

I grin. "Mine too."

"Champagne?" A waitress asks as she walks by. I don't usually drink but I could use a little something to calm my nerves. "Are you sure you can risk being around liquids when you're in such a lovely dress?" I ask Sophia. "First the wine, then the coffee."

She laughs. "A wise man once told me to take the risk or lose the chance."

I hold my glass up. "Cheers to that." We all take a drink. "I'm glad you could both make it. Will you be placing any bids this evening?" *Please say no, please say no, please say no.*

Sophia clears her throat. "Actually, people will be bidding on me."

My heart sinks. "Why?" Is the only thing I manage to get out.

"I want to help."

"You don't have to do that."

"I want to. You work with some wonderful charities."

What the hell am I supposed to say to that? *Forget about the charities and come home with me instead?* "You're right, we do. I just thought we had a full line up this year."

She winks. "Then it's a good thing I know people in high places."

"Who?" I'll fire them all. As if the news of Sophia putting herself up for auction isn't bad enough, I spot Emily making her way over to us. I silently will her to turn around or get intercepted by somebody but of course it doesn't happen. She walks straight up to us with a smug grin on her face. I try not to flinch when she threads her fingers through mine. "Aren't you going to introduce us, sweetie?" Emily asks.

There's a moment of silence as I stare at Sophia and she stares at our intertwined fingers. "Emily, this is Sophia," I say through clenched teeth. "Sophia, this is Emily."

"His wife," she adds. Sophia looks like she wants to be anywhere but here. The same as how I feel. "Have me met before?" she asks. "You look *so* familiar."

"No, we haven't," Sophia replies bluntly.

Emily leans her head to one side. "Are you sure?"

"Yes, I'm sure."

"So how do you know my husband?"

"Excuse us for a moment." I give Sophia an apologetic look before leading Emily away, all the time keeping a fake grin on my face. "What's with the Spanish inquisition?" I ask her.

"She's pretty," is all she says. "Don't you agree?"

"Please don't make this any more awkward than it already is."

"I didn't think she would be your type but apparently I was wrong. It's interesting."

I sigh. "What is?"

"It's interesting that you also seem to be *her* type."

"Emily, please."

"Please what?"

Please don't screw this up for me. "Let's just stay out of each other's way as much as possible and get tonight over with, okay?"

She makes eye contact with the band on stage and nods to the singer. "I wish you had mentioned something sooner."

The singer taps his microphone. "Ladies and Gentlemen, welcome to the fourth annual charity date night auction hosted by Hunter's Hotel. To kick start our evening, please could I ask Mr and Mrs Hunter to make their way over to the dance floor?"

Hundreds of heads turn to look at us but I only care about one. "What did you do?" I whisper as she takes my hand and leads me over to the dance floor.

"I just thought it might be nice, for old times' sake."

"Tonight is all about finding love," The singer announces as our wedding song begins to play. "I'd like to thank Mr and Mrs Hunter for helping us in our quest to find love and for being a shining example of how to keep that love alive. This one's for you." Emily begins to sway and I feel like I'm trapped in a bad dream. My eyes find Sophia's. She quickly looks away and downs the rest of her champagne.

"For old times' sake?" I ask, eyebrows raised.

"Yes. We used to be happy, remember?"

I remember. But I also remember how she violated my trust and without trust, we have nothing left, not even friendship. The next time I glance over at Sophia, she's gone. I desperately want to go and look for her but Emily gives my arm a gentle squeeze, reminding me of all of the people watching us.

"Whatever happens at the end of all of this," she says, "I hope we can stay civil. I just want the both of us to get what we deserve."

We don't talk for the rest of the song. The song which now fills me with sadness, regret and longing for a happier time. A happier me. It feels like we've come full circle and when the song comes to an end, everybody claps and cheers, oblivious to the fact that it's also the end of our marriage.

Chapter Forty Nine
Sophia

I don't know why I'm so angry. Maybe it's because I didn't expect to see Emily tonight. She could have mentioned that she was going to be here when she suggested that I come. Or maybe it's because she acted as though she was going to expose me right there and then. The sooner I can leave here, the better.

The door opens and Lori appears. "I hope you weren't planning on ditching me again, you know how worried I was last time."

"Of course I wasn't. It's too hot in there, that's all."

She leans in close to me. "Nobody knows about the divorce, remember? He has to pretend they're still together. It was just an act."

"What are you talking about?"

"Oh, come on. I saw the look on your face when they started dancing."

I shrug. "It's bad enough that I'm being forced to trap him without having to watch them dance to some ridiculously sappy love song."

"No wonder she doesn't want to tell anybody about the break up. They seem like the perfect little couple from the outside. What do you think Emily was doing putting you on the spot back there?"

"She probably thought she was being funny. Either that or she was actually trying to expose me."

"But I don't see how that would benefit her in any way."

"It'll be a power thing. Trying to show me who's boss."

"I wonder why Mason hasn't insisted that they tell people the truth."

"He said he was giving Emily time."

I know that. I just don't get *why* he's helping her. They've been separated for three months now. That seems like more than enough time."

I shrug. "It works in my favor if the public believe they're still together because I have more freedom. Once the paparazzi find out they're separated, all eyes will be on him. They'll be waiting for something to report. It was bad enough the other day."

The door opens again and Emily appears. "I'm not paying you to stand outside."

"Well I can't trap him while he's dancing with you, can I?"

"Touché." She grins. "You looked surprised to see me."

"I was. I didn't think you'd be here."

"Why not? The press are here and I'm Mason's wife. It would look strange if I wasn't here." She looks at Lori. "I'm guessing you're the sidekick?"

"I'm the best friend. I'd say nice to meet you but I'd be lying."

She rolls her eyes. "Calm down, we're all on the same team here."

"Are we?" I ask her.

"Of course we are."

"Then what were you trying to do back there? I didn't appreciate you putting me on the spot like that."

"Oh, come on. I was just having some fun with it."

I frown. "Having fun with the fact that you've hired me to catch your husband cheating? Are you enjoying this? Because I know I'm not."

"Of course not, but I'm not going to sit at home and cry for six weeks. You and Mason looked so serious. I was just trying to lighten the mood."

"We can't make him suspicious."

"Even if he did become suspicious, he has a penis and we all know how men are ruled by those ugly looking things. As long as he's attracted to you, he will conveniently push any suspicions he may have to the back of his mind. I can already tell that he likes you."

"Well he hasn't said or done anything to suggest that he does." Lori raises an eyebrow but it's gone in less than a second.

"What about your little date to the movies?"

"It wasn't a date."

"I was there too," Lori asks.

"So then he wants a threesome?"

"No. Buzz was there as well."

"Oh, it just keeps getting better and better. Buzz isn't a great influence."

"Well he's a great friend," Lori replies defensively.

"Then why wasn't he the one escorting Mason to the hospital?" She turns to me. "You didn't have to sit with him all night."

"It was all part of the plan to trap him," I lie.

"Well it sounds like you've got it all under control."

I wish.

The door opens again and this time it's a group of women. "Emily!" One of them shouts. "You look spectacular!" I use it as my opportunity to slip back into the main room.

"*Have you* got it all under control?" Lori asks.

I'm about to answer honestly when Buzz appears at her side. "There you are. Where did you two disappear to?"

"Jesus, we needed to pee, if that's okay with you?"

"Yes but I'd like an invite next time."

She shakes her head. "You're a creep."

"Hey, they need you on the stage," he tells me.

"Now?"

"Yep." I look over and see a small group forming. "They parade you around on stage so that people can choose who they want to bid on before it all starts."

"Oh great, that doesn't sound awkward in the slightest."

"It'll all be over soon," Lori says while giving me a knowing look.

I nod, take a deep breath and then make my way over to the stage.

Chapter Fifty
Mason

By the time I can excuse myself from an extremely riveting conversation about copy paper, Sophia is already on the stage with the rest of the volunteers. She looks nervous, playing with the number which has been attached to her wrist. I edge closer and stop next to a group of men who look and sound like they're already drunk.

"Look at the lips on number six," one of them says. My adrenaline starts to pump when I realize that he's talking about Sophia. He glances down at his watch. "In about three hours, they'll be wrapped around my dick."

The other men laugh. "Not if I outbid you," one of them replies.

"Bid on somebody else, she's mine."

She's mine? My blood starts to boil. There's no chance in hell that I'm going to let him or any of his friends take her on a date. I unclench my fists, pull my work cell out of my trouser pocket then pretend to take a call as I head outside. I walk as quickly as I can until I reach Eric at the main entrance.

He nods as I approach. "Can I help you with something, sir?"

"Yes, I need you to do something for me."

"Of course. Anything."

I nod and smile at guests as I walk straight back over to the group of morons. The stage is now empty, ready for the auction to commence. "Gentlemen, I don't believe we've met." I hold my right hand out to undesirable number one. "Mason Hunter."

"Ah, the main man." I shake his hand with a little more force than usual and fight the urge to crush his fingers. "Brad Lomas. It's good to finally meet you."

I wish I could say the same. I don't even bother to shake his friends' hands. "Are you enjoying yourselves?"

"Indeed. You have some incredible women here tonight. Tell me, how many of them have you fucked? You lucky son of a bitch." He grins and claps me on the back and it's a miracle that he's still standing when Buzz appears by my side a few seconds later. "Sorry to interrupt. Can I have a quick word, boss?"

I don't move or look away from Brad but Buzz pulls on my arm. "It's urgent." I let him lead me away without saying a word. "Keep walking," Buzz tells me. I do as he says until we're a safe distance away. "What the fuck was all that about?" he whispers.

"All what?"

"You were about two seconds away from knocking the dude out. What happened?"

"Brad Lomas," I simply reply. "Dig deep. Get as much dirt on him as you can then send it to his employer and his wife, if he has one." Buzz nods. "Don't let him out of your sight tonight and make sure he stays away from Sophia."

Chapter Fifty One
Sophia

"Next up we have number six," the auctioneer announces. "Please put your hands together for the very lovely Sophia."

After what feels like hours waiting backstage, I walk out to loud cheers and wolf whistles. I spot Mason and Lori standing next to each other. Mason smiles at me but I can tell that something is bothering him. He's shifting from one foot to the other and keeps looking over at the exit. Lori waits until he's not looking before giving me a little nod to let me know that our plan is still going ahead.

"Ladies and gentlemen, let's start the bidding at one hundred dollars." A guy standing on the other side of Lori immediately raises his paddle. "Thank you, sir. How about two hundred?" Another man standing in a small group of men holds his paddle up. "Two hundred dollars. Anyone for three?" Lori's bidder is about to make his move when the other guy beats him to it.

"Five hundred bucks!" he shouts. The crowd cheer and Lori uses it as her opportunity to whisper something to her secret bidder.

"Wow, five hundred dollars! Do you think we can get six?"

Lori's bidder holds up his paddle and shouts, "One thousand dollars!"

I raise my eyebrow but give Lori a huge smile. Even though we agreed to only bid up to five hundred, I can always count on her to have my back. "Thank you, sir," the auctioneer says. "Any advance on one thousand?"

The man standing in the group takes a step forward and shouts, "Five thousand dollars!" The crowd cheer as Lori frowns and mouths 'sorry' to me. Why the hell would anybody pay that much money to take me on a date? Even *I* don't think I'm worth that much. I try to catch Mason's eye but he's too busy burning a hole into the back of the guy's skull.

"Thank you very much! Any advance on *five thousand* dollars?"

"Ten thousand," a third bidder shouts from the other side of the room, close to the exit. He's dressed differently to the rest of the other guests. He's wearing a tailored jacket with gold buttons running down both sides and his hair is flattened to his head as though he's been wearing a hat. His face looks familiar but I can't think where I've seen him before.

"Wow, ten thousand dollars! The highest bid of the night so far! Thank you, sir. Do we have any other bids in the room?"

The group of men laugh and snicker as the guy who appears to be the ringleader holds his paddle up once more. "Fifteen thousand!" My jaw hits the ground but Lori gives me a look to say 'I told you so'. "Now can we just be done with it and skip to the date part?" he asks. I've never seen Mason look so angry as he turns and heads towards the exit. I have to stop myself from watching his every step.

The auctioneer laughs. "It sounds like somebody is very eager to take Sophia on a date. Let's put him out of his misery. Fifteen thousand dollars going once...fifteen thousand dollars going twice..."

"Thirty thousand," the bidder by the door shouts, just as Mason walks by.

The crowd goes wild and the other bidder shakes his head to signal that he's out. "Well, well, well! It looks like we have a high bidder! Thirty thousand going once...thirty thousand going twice...ladies and gentlemen, we have ourselves a date!" It's only then that the reality of the situation kicks in. I fully expected to be going home with Lori, like we had planned. It's a good thing I have experience going on dates with complete strangers. "Please give it up one more time for Sophia." He gestures for me to leave the stage and I walk off in complete shock at the huge amounts of money being spent here tonight. I guess I should have listened to Lori when she tried telling me that five hundred bucks is like spare change to a millionaire.

I instantly relax when I see Mason waiting for me backstage. His arms are crossed but he's no longer annoyed. In fact, he has a huge grin on his face. "Well you've certainly set the bar high for the rest of the auctions."

I look down at my feet. "I can't believe it."

"I can."

"I hope the high bidder isn't going to be disappointed."

"He won't be."

"But I'm not worth thirty thousand dollars."

"You're worth every last dime."

My cheeks start to warm. "Thank you. So when do I get to meet him?"

"Right now."

I nod and we stand in silence for a moment. "Where is he?" I ask while looking around.

"You're looking at him."

I stop breathing as his eyes burn into mine. "You…you're…you bid on me?"

"Well technically my friend bid on you but yes, it was on my behalf."

"The guy with the gold buttons?"

"Yes. My doorman, Eric."

So that explains his outfit and why Mason kept looking towards the exit. "I thought I recognized him from somewhere."

"I hope *you're* not disappointed."

I'm not. I'm just worried in case Emily finds out. "It's just…I don't…*why?*"

"Because our last outing turned into a trip to the hospital."

I shake my head. "Why, Mason?"

I can tell that he's having some kind of internal battle with himself. "Because…I owe you an ice cream, remember?" His smile isn't convincing.

"That's a very expensive ice cream." I find the courage to take a step closer to him. "No censoring, remember?"

He keeps his eyes locked with mine as he whispers, "Because I was lost. Before you, I was lost."

I let the truth of his words sink in, followed by the truth of how I feel about him. I sigh. "I'm still lost. And I can't see a way out." *Not for at least another five weeks.*

"Then let me find you."

His words hit me hard. "Mason, there are things you don't know…"

"I know enough," he interrupts. "I know how you make me feel. I know that I want to spend more time with you."

"And that's truly enough for you?"

"Yes, it is. I didn't see you coming, Sophia. I didn't see you coming, but I'm so glad that you did."

"But you're going through a break up. It's a tough time for you…"

"What's *tough* is watching other men try to take you on a date. And I've been going through a break up for the past year. I made my peace with it a long time ago. Is that what you're worried about? Do you think you would be some kind of rebound? Because you wouldn't be. Emily has nothing to do with this."

"Emily has *everything* to do with his," I reply. *More than you could ever imagine.*

He shakes his head. "Do you want me to go on stage right now and announce that we've broken up? Announce that I'm filing for divorce? Because I will."

"Jesus, no."

"Then what?"

"I don't want you to *do* anything."

"Do you feel it? Do you feel the connection between us?"

Say no, say no, say no! I sigh. "Yes, I feel it." What a selfish heart I have. I deserve any pain that comes my way at the end of all of this.

"Then what are you scared of?" We stare at each other for what feels like minutes and that's when it really hits me.

I'm scared of losing someone who isn't even mine.

The next auction ends and I take a few steps away from Mason when I see them walking off the stage. He thanks them for taking part and after half a minute or so of small talk, we're alone again. The silence is deafening. He closes the gap between us. "Let me find you, Sophia."

"What if you don't like what you find?"

He smiles sweetly. "Take the risk or lose the chance."

The door at the end of the hallway opens and the next person to be auctioned heads our way. I smile politely and wait for them to pass. "We should probably get back before Lori sends out a search party."

"Ah yeah, Buzz told me how worried she was the other night. My sister thought I was dead because I didn't answer my cell."

"Oh yeah, that reminds me." I pull his cell out of my purse. "You can have it back now that you've agreed to pay the thirty thousand ransom."

He laughs. "I was hoping you'd forgotten about it and left it at home."

"Why?"

"Because how am I supposed to send you elevator porn now?"

"You'll have to send them to someone else." We begin to walk down the hallway, back to the main room.

"I don't think they would know what the hell was happening. And there would definitely be some crossed wires if I asked somebody to text me a picture of a shaft. Speaking of which," he raises an eyebrow. "What did you think of my naked selfies?"

"I didn't look."

"Ah, so you passed your test after all?"

"Yep." A lie. I didn't pass anything. In fact, I failed miserably. After telling Lori not to snoop at his photos, I went straight to my bedroom and looked in every single folder in his gallery. There were no selfies, only a few pictures of him and his sister and a couple of random ones. I

183

was a very disappointed girl that night.

"Don't worry, you didn't miss out on anything. I was only joking about them." He winks. "They're all on my work phone."

We pause when we reach the door. "So when will we be going on our date?" I ask.

"Well, you haven't actually agreed to it yet."

I shrug. "It's for charity. What kind of person would I be if I said no?"

"For charity," he says, grinning. "Got it. Well seeing as though I'm going to be here all night, I think I'll bank it for now, if that's okay with you?"

"That's fine." He holds the door open for me. "Well…I hope you enjoy the rest of your evening."

"You too." His eyes burn into mine. "I meant everything that I said."

I nod. "Goodnight, Mason."

"Until next time, Sophia."

About an hour later, I'm back in the safety of my own bedroom, having some much needed alone time. I need to somehow try and process everything that Mason said to me. I don't even care if Emily has a problem with me leaving the event early. There was nothing in the contract which stated exactly how much time I have to spend with him.

For some reason, I didn't even tell Lori the full story of what had happened backstage. I only told her that he was the highest bidder because he wanted to make up for our failed movie night. Lori can be brutally honest and I'm not ready to admit my feelings out loud yet.

I look over at my bedside table and his little handwritten card catches my eye. I reach over and grab it then read his words over and over until they don't even sound like real words in my head anymore. I turn it over and my heart starts to race when I see a number. A phone number. How have I not noticed it before now? I spend the next fifteen minutes debating whether I should rip the card up or send him a message. I know what I *should* do but once again, my selfish heart ends up winning.

Chapter Fifty Two

Mason

"So are you going to tell me who Brad Lomas is?" Buzz asks when we're on the way to his house.

I loosen my tie and begin to unbutton the top of my shirt. "Shouldn't you be telling me?"

"All business, aren't you? He's thirty two, originally from Chicago, married with no kids. He used to work in computer programming but now he makes his money inventing apps."

"Did you find any dirt?"

He smirks. "I always do. Tell me what he did to piss you off first."

"I heard him telling his friends about what he planned on doing to Sophia once he won a date with her."

"No wonder you looked so angry. You should have told me, I would have found a way to get rid of him."

"It's fine. You kept a close eye on him like I asked. Now tell me what you found."

"Well I called a few of my guys and we did some digging and basically he's signed up to a website where you get matched up to have affairs."

"That kind of thing actually exists?"

"It's the internet, *everything* exists."

"So it's a dating site for cheaters?"

"Pretty much. When you sign up, you have to create a user profile where you list your stats, your likes and dislikes in the bedroom and oh yeah, what days and times you're free to cheat on your wife. It's pretty fucked up. There's even an option to search for people based on their dick or bra size."

"And you're sure he's definitely married?"

"Yep. He's been married to Jocelyn for eight years. She's a cop. Can you believe that? She's out risking her life while he's fucking other people and probably making use of her spare handcuffs."

"Bastard."

He nods. "Do you still want me to send the information over to her?"

"Does he have an active account?"

"Yes. He logged on yesterday and he's been paying the monthly subscription fee for the last eighteen months."

"Then yes, send her the proof. It's up to her what she decides to do with it."

He pulls his cell out of his jacket pocket. "Buzz and Mason, exposing cheaters since two thousand seventeen."

The sight of his cell makes me look at my own and all I can think about is how it's been inside of Sophia's bedroom. And maybe even her jeans. How is it even possible that I feel jealous of a cell phone? I shake my head at how ridiculous I'm being. I tap the screen and notice that I have a text message from an unknown number. I open it, expecting it to be spam but laugh out loud when I see a picture of an elevator shaft.

In case you're having withdrawal symptoms. S x

"What's so funny?" Buzz asks.

"Elevator porn."

"Ewwww, you're watching porn? Dude, I'm sitting *right* next to you. Can you at least wait five minutes?" I laugh even harder as he shuffles away from me, pressing himself up against the window.

Chapter Fifty Three
Sophia

"What are you reading?" Lori asks when we're sitting down eating breakfast.

"Oh, nothing."

She leans over and laughs. "It doesn't look like nothing."

"No, it *looks* like you should keep your nose out."

"And it also looks like you're stalking Mason."

I sigh. "I'm not stalking him. A story just popped up in my news feed. The media are going crazy because Mason and Emily left the auction in separate cars then they followed him to Buzz's house so they know they spent the night apart."

"Jeez, just because they're married, it doesn't mean they have to be joined at the hip."

"Exactly. TMZ are sticking to their secret baby storyline because why else would they leave in separate cars? It's *obviously* because he's living a double life."

"Oh yeah, I forgot you're his baby mama. How dare you not ask me to be your imaginary children's godmother?" I carry on scrolling until I reach a photo of them dancing. "I don't think it's possible for Mason to be standing any further away from her. He's not doing a very good job of throwing them off the scent, is he?" She smirks. "I wonder why that is."

"He probably doesn't care if they find out. It's Emily who wants to hide it, not Mason."

"I still can't believe he paid thirty thousand dollars just to stop you from going on a date with somebody else."

"Are you working today?" I ask.

"Nice little change of subject there. Yes, I have a half trap this afternoon. I was going to spend my night reading but maybe we should go out instead. You know, try and get some normality back into your life."

I wave her off. "I'm fine, honestly. You should read.

We can go out another time."

"You sure?"

"Of course."

She sighs. "Okay, if you're forcing me to read then I guess I'll have to."

Chapter Fifty Four
Mason

"Have you seen this crap?" I ask Buzz when he stomps into the kitchen the next morning.

"Jesus, give me chance. I've just woken up. Not everybody gets up at the crack of dawn like you, remember?" He walks over to the fridge and takes out some leftover Chinese. I dread to think how long it's been there. "Want some?"

"No thanks, I think I'll pass." I hold out my cell. "The paparazzi photographed me and Emily leaving the auction in separate cars last night then followed me here."

"The paps can suck my dick."

"And now TMZ are saying that it's proof I'm living a double life with my baby mama and three secret children."

"TMZ can suck my dick as well," he says through a mouth full of food.

I laugh. "Chirpy this morning, aren't you?"

He groans. "Apologies in advance if I'm a jerk these next few weeks."

"You're always a jerk and you never usually apologize for it."

"Well I'm probably going to be even worse than usual."

"Why?"

"Don't laugh."

"Go on…"

"I'm on a sex ban."

"Wait," I look out of the window. "I think I just saw a pig flying."

"Dude, it's not a laughing matter. I'm already struggling."

"How long has it been?"

"Three days."

I feign shock. "*Three* days? *Three* whole days? Have you checked that your dick hasn't fallen off? Will you even remember how to use it?"

"Don't worry. I've been training it every day. I've been watching so much porn that I almost spit on my hotdog the other day before eating it."

"You're disgusting."

"Seriously, I wouldn't wish this on anyone."

"I'm guessing Lori came up with the idea?" He nods. "How long is it for?"

"She didn't specify. She just said that we needed some time to connect mentally instead of physically."

"Smart girl."

"Smart? She could be getting the D twice a day but instead she wants to play Scrabble and watch *Pretty Little Liars*. You say smart, I say stupid."

"And *that* attitude right there is exactly why you're on a sex ban in the first place."

"And *your* attitude is exactly why you never get laid, even when you're not on a ban."

I shrug. "At least I don't have to get tested for STD's once a month."

"It's better to be safe than sorry."

"And it's better to use a condom than have herpes."

"Hey! I'm clean!"

I laugh. "Right now you are."

"Well I'll definitely be staying clean now that I'm on this stupid sex ban."

"So are you two exclusive?"

"No. She's made it quite clear that she's going to be seeing other people and that I should too. We're just hanging out and getting to know each other."

"So basically you've been friend zoned?"

"No, douchebag. It's all about the slow burn."

I raise my eyebrow. "The slow burn?"

"Yeah. Slow and steady wins the race."

"So you're not banned from sex, you're just banned from sex with Lori?"

"Technically, yes. But seeing as though Lori's the only person I want to have sex with then I may as well be banned from it altogether."

"Well I hope it works out for you. It's about time you found yourself a nice girl."

He nods. "Do you know anybody called Gideon?"

"Nope. Why?"

"I asked Lori if she wanted to do something tonight but she said she has a date with Gideon. Can you believe she would blow me off for somebody called Gideon? I mean, what kind of name is that? I bet he's a pretentious prick."

I laugh. "I like it. It's unusual."

"Oh, thanks for your loyalty."

"It's alright to feel jealous."

"Jealous? Jealous of what exactly? His stupid ass loafers or tiny dick?"

I raise my eyebrows. "How do you know he's got a tiny dick? The dude might be packing."

He throws his arms up in the air. "That's the total opposite of what I want to hear right now."

"If you feel bad about her going out with other guys then you should talk to her about it."

"Or I could just sabotage every date that she goes on."

"Because that would be the *adult* thing to do," I reply sarcastically.

"Exactly. I'm glad we're on the same page. Hey, can I borrow one of your baseball hats?"

"I thought you said your hair was too good to be hidden underneath a hat?"

"It is." He grins. "But I've always wanted to go undercover."

Chapter Fifty Five

Sophia

"Sophia, how are you?" Kristen asks when she calls me later that day. "Good, good," she says before I even get the chance to answer. "Emily wants to see both of us today."

I groan. "Why?"

"I'm not really sure. I think she wants to talk through what's been happening."

"*Nothing* has been happening."

"So just tell her that."

"Why can't you tell her over the phone?"

"You know what she's like. She's very insistent. I think it's best if we just appease her."

"Well what if I'm busy today?"

"Then she would probably want to see you tomorrow. Or the day after. Or the day after that."

I sigh. "What time?"

"Two o'clock. My office."

"I could have updated Kristen over the phone," I tell Emily a couple of hours later. "You know, like it says in the contract."

"Is there somewhere else you need to be right now, Sophia?" She raises one eyebrow. "Seducing my husband, perhaps?"

"Not right now."

"This is my marriage we're talking about. *My life.* Forgive me for wanting to talk to you in person."

I nod. "Well here I am. What would you like to know?"

"Start with last night."

"What about it? I hardly spoke to Mason. You heard the one conversation that we had."

"So that's the only time you spoke to him?"

"Yes."

"Are you sure about that?"

I fold my arms across my chest. "Yes."

"So then why did one of my friends see you two talking backstage?"

Shit. "Backstage? Oh, you must mean straight after the auction. I totally forgot about that. He was just thanking me for taking part."

"And?"

"And nothing."

"So why were you missing for almost ten minutes? Why didn't you come straight back into the main room?"

"I did."

"No, *you didn't.*"

I glance out of the window as I come up with yet another lie. "Oh, actually, I almost forgot."

"Sure you did," Emily interrupts.

"I asked him about the charities he supports so he told me about a couple of them."

She smirks. "Ah yes, he's very *giving.*"

My fingernails dig into my palms as I try to stop myself from scowling. "Anything else?"

"Yes. Perhaps you could help me understand how Mason's doorman has thirty thousand dollars to spare?"

"Eric."

"Who?"

"The doorman. His name is Eric."

She waves her hand dismissively. "It looks like Mason is overpaying his employee's if his doorman has thirty thousand dollars to spend."

"His *name* is Eric and he was bidding on behalf of somebody else." The truth.

"Who?"

"I don't know. Mason didn't mention any names. He just said that Eric had asked if he could take a little break to help out a friend."

"A friend. Interesting. I think I'll have a little chat

with Eric. I'm curious to find out who placed the highest bid of the night." I make a mental note to somehow warn Mason. "So that's another thing that you two talked about. Is your memory a little foggy, Sophia? Because you started by saying that he simply thanked you for taking part but then you remembered that you spoke about his charities and also about Eric. Could you be forgetting about other things too?"

"No, I couldn't."

"How much did you have to drink? I know you were drinking champagne."

"I had one glass. I wasn't drunk if that's what you're trying to suggest."

"I'm not trying to suggest anything. I'm just making sure that you're a reliable source."

"All my girls are reliable," Kristen adds. "And they know not to drink on the job."

She ignores Kristen and turns to me. "Why did you leave early if you didn't go on your date?"

I sigh. "I had a headache. I still do."

"You should have told me. I would have given you some Tylenol."

Never in a million years would I risk taking anything that she offered me. "It's fine. It wasn't the best place to trap him anyway, as you'll probably agree. There were far too many people there and like I've already told you, I hardly spoke to him."

"It may not have been the perfect place but you definitely couldn't trap him while you were sitting at home in your pajamas."

"Mason has never done anything to suggest that he would cheat on you." Regardless of what may be blossoming between the two of us, I honestly believe that he would never act on his feelings or even voice them if he was still in a relationship with Emily. "Maybe you should just accept it?"

"I'll accept it when the six weeks are up. When are you seeing him next?"

"I don't know. There's no planning involved. It's not

like we sit there and arrange a time and place."

"Well maybe you should."

"That's what I'm trying to tell you. He's not showing any interest in doing that. There are only so many times I can conveniently run into him or show up at his events."

"Well somebody must have planned the movie date."

"Yes, Buzz. Mason and I just got dragged along."

"So then work that angle. Get your friend to set up some more dates with Buzz."

I shrug. "I can ask but this has got nothing to do with her. She doesn't work for you, remember? She doesn't have to do anything she doesn't want to."

"I want more from you going forward."

"More? I'm not sure that I can give you more."

"You can give me a recording."

My stomach performs a somersault. "A recording of what?"

"Your conversations. I want to hear how he is with you."

I look at Kristen then back to Emily. "That's not in the contract."

"You told me that you would get the evidence. You said you would provide me with texts and photographs."

"And I meant it. Of course I would provide you with those if I had them but I don't. Mason isn't giving me anything to work with."

"So then record him. Prove it to me. Let me hear how loyal and trustworthy he is with my own ears."

"I'll see what I can do," I manage to get out through clenched teeth.

"Wear a wire the next time you see him. It'll be easier that way."

"No," I say with too much force. "I've already told you that it's too risky."

"None of your previous clients have discovered the wire so why would Mason?"

"It makes me uncomfortable. He would notice that I

was acting differently. I'm not going to wear a wire. I asked you to take it out of the contract for a reason."

"Fine. Do it your way, just get me something."

"Look Emily, I've been doing this job for two years now. I've trapped hundreds of men. I honestly don't believe that Mason is a cheater. I think it's a dead end."

"With all due respect, you may have been doing the job for two years but you've only known my husband for one week. He's managed to keep his dick in his pants for seven days, woopdedoo, give the guy a medal. I told you at the start that Mason wouldn't risk doing something straight away. There are five weeks left. I'm paying you a lot of money. *Get me something.*"

I stand up, unable to sit and listen to her crap any longer. "*Why?* Why do you want it so bad?"

Kristen clears her throat. "Maybe we should wrap this up, ladies. I have another appointment soon."

"Stop questioning my motivations and do your job," Emily says before turning her attention to Kristen. "I've been thinking about what we discussed the other day. I'd like to hire another one of your girls. Let's see if he can be tempted by a brunette instead."

"Does that mean you don't need me anymore?" I ask.

"No, it doesn't."

"But why do you need two of us?"

"Stop getting ahead of yourself. The other girl will just be for one night. She can try a different approach."

"Which is?"

She shrugs. "Get him drunk then offer it up on a plate."

"But I thought you said that Mason wouldn't risk a one night stand?"

"People change. Maybe he might be in the mood for one. Maybe he just doesn't like blondes. Or maybe he just isn't attracted to *you.*"

"So then what's the point in me carrying on?"

"Because I might be wrong. And because you've signed a contract."

"Don't you think it's too risky to involve another person?"

"Only as risky as it was to involve you in the first place. They'll sign a non disclosure agreement just like you did. They don't need to know about you."

"When will they do it?"

"Whenever I want them to."

I'm about to argue against it when Kristen catches my eye and gives a little shake of her head. "I'm sorry ladies but my next client is going to be arriving any minute now."

Emily stands up. "It's fine. We're done here anyway. I'll be in touch soon about your other girls."

Kristen nods and we both watch as she leaves the room. As soon as the door closes behind her, we look at each other in disbelief. I hold a finger up then crouch down and check under the table and chairs. I don't even know what to look for but nothing seems out of the ordinary. "I was checking to see if she's bugged the room."

"Hmmm, I wouldn't put it past her."

"Please don't send another girl to trap Mason."

"I'll have to. It'll look suspicious if I don't help her."

"Can you get them to sabotage it?"

"And risk Emily finding out? I don't trust the other girls like I trust you, Sophia."

I sigh. "At least send Carmen. She's not Mason's type." She's loud and loves the sound of her own voice. Mason would never be interested in her.

"She was interested in Leah the other day."

I groan. As well as being drop dead gorgeous, Leah has a degree in Astrophysics and is one of the funniest people I know. The thought of Mason flirting with Leah, or anyone else for that matter, makes me feel physically sick. "Just tell her that Leah is fully booked."

"I'll see what I can do."

"Please let me know when it's going to happen. I need to try and stop it."

"Do you?"

"Of course I do."

"Maybe we should just let it happen then all this will be over. We can wipe our hands of Emily for good."

"Let me know when it's going to happen," I repeat.

She rests her chin on top of her hands. "You really like him, don't you?"

"He's a good person."

"And so are you. Just be careful, Sophia. I know you're trying to protect him but I don't want you to get hurt at the end of all of this."

It may already be too late.

Chapter Fifty Six

Mason

"Stand up, you idiot," I tell Buzz when I find him crouched down behind a parked car. "I've been walking up and down the street for the past five minutes trying to find you."

"Good. That's the whole point of being undercover. I'm glad I decided to wear the camouflage after all."

I laugh. "You're wearing army pants. Do you even know how camouflage works?"

"Of course I do. Why do you think I'm hiding behind a *green* car?"

"Stand up before somebody calls the cops. You look like a total creeper."

"Did you bring the supplies?" he asks, ignoring me. I hold out the coffee. "Thanks, brother. What about the snacks?"

"I told you I wasn't going to bring food."

"Why not? I'm on a stake out. I could be here all night."

"Then it's your own fault if you go hungry. You should just go and talk to her."

"Gideon could be inside."

"*You* could be inside if you weren't so stubborn."

He smirks. "As much as I would love to, I'm banned, remember?"

"You're a moron."

"Hey! Are you here to support me or insult me?"

"A bit of both."

"Quick, get down." He grabs my arm and pulls me to the ground. "Somebody's there."

"Great, now the neighbors are going to report *two* creepy men to the cops."

He lets go of my arm. "Oh, it's only Sophia."

My ears prick up at the mention of her name. "Sophia's home?"

"No, I just lied about it for no reason." He raises his

eyebrow. "Yes, she's home. Bet you wish you'd brought snacks now, don't you?"

"Have you seen anyone else?" I ask.

"No, only Lori and Sophia so far."

Good. "What's in your pocket?" I ask, eyeing the bulge.

"Binoculars." He pulls them out and offers them to me.

"No thanks."

He shrugs and uses his T-shirt to polish the lenses. "Lori walked by the window about five minutes ago reading a book. She's probably passing the time until Shmideon shows up."

I laugh. "Schmideon? Is that the best you can come up with?"

"Yeah. I was trying to think of an adjective beginning with g but the only one I could think of was gigantic and after our conversation earlier, I definitely don't want to imagine any part of him being gigantic."

"Okay then, what about gentle?"

"No."

"Generous?"

"This isn't helping."

"Glorious."

"Dude, stop it."

"Gargantuan."

"Okay, you can leave now."

"I'm sorry, I'm sorry. I'll stop."

He shoves the binoculars back in his pocket then slowly gets to his feet. "Jesus, Mason, stand up. You look like a total creeper." I laugh and do as he says. He gestures to my T-shirt and sweat pants. "You need to cover up better next time. At least wear some of your fancy sunglasses."

"Next time? There won't be a next time."

"There could be."

"No, there couldn't. I'd call the cops myself."

His eyes widen. "Oh, shit."

"What?" I ask.

"Sophia's taking her clothes off."

My eyes shoot to her window and everything turns to slow motion as she pulls her shirt up and over her head. I know I should look away but my greedy eyes are glued to her. My whole body comes alive at the sight of her wearing nothing but a bra underneath.

"Nice rack," Buzz says, reminding me that I'm not alone.

"Look away," I tell him, refusing to take my own advice.

"At least let me wait until she takes off her jeans."

"Look away or I'll cut your eyeballs out."

He laughs. "Jesus, you get so protective over her."

I finally manage to tear my eyes away, mostly to check that Buzz has stopped watching. "We need to leave. This isn't right."

He nods then glances back at the window. "Are you sure? She's totally naked now."

My eyes dart back to the window. "You're a dick," I tell him when nobody's there.

"You got your hopes up, didn't you? Pervert."

"Says the guy who brought binoculars?"

"Failing to prepare is preparing to fail," he tells me with a smug look on his face.

"I'm sure the cops would love that little saying."

We both jump when my cell starts to ring. "Shhhh! I can't believe you didn't silence your phone before you came. What a rookie."

"Sorry. I'm not familiar with the rules of stalking." I quickly pull it out of my pocket and check the caller ID. I stand up a little straighter. "It's Sophia."

Buzz grins. "I didn't even know you had her number, you sly fox. What else have you been keeping from me?"

I tell him to be quiet before answering. "Hello?"

"Um, hey, it's me."

It's me. I like the familiarity of those two little words. I could get used to them. "How are you?" I ask.

"I'm okay. I was just wondering if you still have

paparazzi following you."

"No, I don't think so. They've probably moved on to their next victim. Why?"

"I think there might be some outside my house."

I immediately duck down, taking Buzz with me. "You think there are paparazzi outside your house?" I ask, to keep him in the loop.

"Yes. One of my neighbors just called to say there are some guys hanging about on the street. I looked outside and saw two men standing next to a parked car. They had their backs to me but I think one of them had a camera in his hand."

Buzz's binoculars. "Okay well don't worry. It won't be paparazzi. They don't know where you live. They don't even know who you are."

"Well maybe they've found out," she says, sounding worried.

"I doubt it."

"Do you think I should call the cops?"

"No! No, don't call the cops." I shake my head at Buzz. "Can you see them now?"

"Hang on, I'll look." I hear her footsteps and then, "No, they're gone. The parked car is still there."

"See, it's probably nothing. I can send Charlie round to check, if it would make you feel better. He knows most of the paparazzi."

"You'd do that?"

"Of course I would."

"Thank you."

"Are you home alone?" I ask.

"No, Lori's here too."

"Good. Are you going out anywhere or expecting guests?"

"No, we're having a quiet night in."

"Okay. Well I don't think you need to worry but maybe you should close your blinds, just in case." *And so that we can leave without being seen.*

"Yeah, I will. Thanks, Mason."

"It's fine. I'm sorry for worrying you."

"It's not your fault."

Yes, it is. "Well, I should go."

"Oh, yeah, okay. Sorry if I interrupted your evening."

"No, you didn't. I'm just hanging out with Buzz. Call me if you need anything."

"I will. Thank you."

"Any time."

The line goes dead before I can tell her goodbye. Buzz laughs then tries to imitate me. "Call me if you need anything. What are you hoping she *needs*?"

"Shut up," I tell him. "She's spooked. She saw us and wanted to call the cops. Your stupid plan almost got us caught." I slowly stand up and peek through the window of the parked car. Sophia's blinds are now closed. "Come on, we need to leave before somebody actually does report us."

"Did she mention Lori?" Buzz asks as he falls into step beside me.

"No, but I could hear her screwing Gideon in the background." I roll my eyes when he looks like he's just been punched in the gut. "I'm joking. They're home alone and not expecting company."

"That's what she told you."

"And I believe her." We walk in silence until we reach my car two blocks down.

"It's not going to magically open," Buzz says after we stand there for a few seconds. Even though I can hear him making noises, my brain doesn't process any of the words. The only thing I can think about is Sophia in her bra. Her red, lacy bra.

"Dude, I know you're used to Charlie opening the door for you but I'm sure as shit not going to do it." I shake my head, breaking free of the trance I was in. I unlock the doors and climb inside. "You were thinking of her rack, weren't you?" Buzz asks as I pull away from the curb. I turn the radio up to drown out the sound of his laughter.

Chapter Fifty Seven
Sophia

I don't hear from Mason for the next six days.

I spend the first couple of days convincing myself that it's because of our last phone call. He must have sent Charlie, realized that I was right about the paparazzi then distanced himself to make them back off.

I spend the rest of the week worrying that he's either met somebody else or he's found out what I'm doing and never wants to see me again. I can't decide which one would be worse. I even had a dream that he got back together with Emily. It felt so real that when I woke up, my pillow was damp.

He calls on the sixth day. "Hello?" I answer nervously.

"Hey, it's me."

"Hey, how are you?" I ask.

"Not bad. You?"

"Same."

"Sorry for the radio silence. I've been busy with work and family stuff."

"Oh, no, it's fine. I've been busy too. This week has flown by." *Lies.*

"You mean you haven't been sitting at home all week waiting for me to call? You haven't been falling asleep clutching your cell to your chest?"

I sigh. "Okay, I admit it. I've been a mess and you're a bastard for not calling me. At least text me next time, it only takes a minute."

He laughs. "Don't worry, there won't be a next time. Would it be weird if I told you that I've missed your voice?"

"Probably." *But I'd like it.*

"Hmmm, that's what I thought. Well just for the record, I haven't missed your voice. Not one bit. In fact, it's been awesome not having to listen to it. And do you know what's been even better? Not having to look at your face. I definitely haven't missed your horrible smile."

I laugh. "I haven't missed you either."

"Six days is a long time, baby mama." His voice is soft but serious. "Let's not do it again."

My stomach sinks at the thought of six days turning into forever once he finds out about me. "Okay," is all I can say.

"Have you got plans for this evening?"

I look down at the tub of Ben and Jerry's. "That depends."

"On what?"

"On whether eating ice cream and watching Channing Tatum dance to *Pony* counts as having plans."

"I don't have a clue what you're talking about. Come out with me instead."

"Where are you going?"

"Buzz is dragging me to the karaoke bar on California Street."

I groan. "Ugh, karaoke. I only sing in the shower."

"Well we can stay in and do that, if you'd prefer? That's fine by me."

"Sorry, I'm a solo performer."

"But a duo is so much more fun."

I laugh. "My shower stall is way too small for that kind of *fun*."

"My shower is very large. Just saying. It has awesome acoustics too; good for hitting all those high notes. I think you'd like it."

"It sounds very impressive. I still hate karaoke though."

"Buzz is asking Lori to go."

I sigh. Lori is the karaoke queen. "I guess I'll go if she goes."

"Well maybe I'll see you and your horrible smile later then."

"Maybe you will."

"I hope not. I'm not looking forward to seeing you *at all*."

I laugh. "I'm not looking forward to seeing you either."

"Good. I'm glad we're on the same page."

I hang up and face plant onto my bed.

I'm in trouble.

Chapter Fifty Eight
Mason

I tried to stay away from her.

It lasted less than a week.

It felt like a lifetime.

Never again.

On the first day, I kept myself so busy that I hardly thought about her. On the second day, the cracks started to show and I found myself thinking about her whenever I was by myself. On the third day, I spent the entire morning thinking about her. I have no idea what I was saying "yes" and "no" to in a Skype meeting, so it's a good thing I had Buzz with me. On the fourth day, I laid awake all night thinking about her. On the fifth day, my behaviour was nothing short of an addict's. I felt like I was having withdrawal symptoms and every single part of me craved her. It still does.

I don't even know why I put myself through it. Actually, that's a lie. I did it because I was scared of the feelings I was developing for her. Feelings that I haven't felt in a long time. Feelings that I'm not even sure are reciprocal. I was scared that it was too much too soon so I took a step back. I always knew that I wanted her but I didn't realize how much I *needed* her. It's funny how distance can sometimes bring us closer together.

"Beer?" I ask Buzz as we make our way over to the bar. I flinch when somebody tries and fails to hit a high note in their rendition of *I Believe In A Thing Called Love* by The Darkness.

"No. I need something stronger."

"That makes two of us if this is what I have to endure all night."

"Don't worry, the more you drink, the better the singers become. You'll be loving life in a couple of hours."

Another high note pierces through me. "I hope you're right." If Sophia wasn't coming, I'd have already left by now. We take a seat at the bar and I order two whiskeys. "Come on then, tell me why you need something stronger."

He sighs. "I don't know if I'm ready to talk about it yet."

"Okay, well you know that I'm here for you whenever you're ready." He puts his head in his hands and mumbles something. "I can't hear you."

He sits up straight. "I said my life is over."

"Come on bro, I'm sure it's not that bad."

"It is."

"What's happened?"

"If I tell you, you've got to promise not to tell anyone else."

"Have you broken any laws?"

"I don't think so."

"Then I won't tell anyone."

"Dude. I sexted my mom."

"*What?*"

"You heard. I sexted my mom. My own mother. The person who brought me into this world. How the fuck am I supposed to look her in the eye ever again?"

I have to stop myself from laughing but it's really difficult when he looks so distraught. "Can you give me some context or am I supposed to fill in the blanks myself?"

"I was drunk and horny."

"You've just made it sound ten times worse."

"I was supposed to text Lori. My mom is straight underneath her in my contacts."

"How bad was it?"

"Dude, it was bad. So fucking bad."

I can't hold the laughter in any longer. "I'm sorry."

He nods. "Me too."

"I bet it's not as bad as you think. Your mom's probably

209

forgotten about it already."

"She told me to go to church."

"Wow, so it *is* as bad as you think."

He groans. "Why did I have to go into so much detail?"

"What did you say?"

"What *didn't* I say? I know Lori loves to read so I was trying to be super descriptive. It was about six messages long."

"Did your mom at least critique you? Are there any areas you could improve on for next time?" I laugh and grab onto the side of the bar when he tries to push me off of my chair.

"No, Mason, my mom did not critique my sext."

"Does Lori know you're into incest?"

He huffs. "I knew I shouldn't have told you."

"I'm sorry, I can't help it. You would be doing the exact same thing if it happened to me."

"You're right. I can't even deny it."

"Did you tell Lori what happened?"

"No, I was too embarrassed."

"It's a shame she didn't get the message after you put so much effort into it."

"Oh no, she still got it. I copied and pasted it to her afterwards." I laugh then take a sip of whiskey. I hear a wolf whistle and turn around to see Sophia and Lori walking towards us.

"Hey, you," Sophia says.

I sigh. "Hey. I was hoping you wouldn't come."

"And *I* was hoping you would have left by now."

"Sorry to disappoint you."

"It's fine. I'm used to it."

"Your dress is horrible. You definitely made the wrong choice."

She laughs. "Thank you."

Lori frowns while Buzz shakes his head and says, "You two are weird."

Chapter Fifty Nine
Sophia

Mason laughs at me as I cringe the whole way through *Livin'* *On A Prayer.* "Don't worry. Buzz insists that they get better as the night goes on. Apparently they peak around midnight."

"They get better or he gets drunker?"

"I guess we're going to find out."

I groan. "Does that mean we're still going to be here at midnight?"

"Not if there's somewhere else you'd rather be," he replies, one eyebrow raised.

"Anywhere but here. That guy just butchered one of my all time favorite songs."

"We could go to the hotel, if you'd like?"

I laugh. "Stop trying to show me your shower."

"Who said anything about my shower?" His eyes twinkle with amusement. "You have a dirty mind, Sophia. Speaking of which, I googled Channing Tatum dancing to that horse song. I didn't know you were interested in that kind of thing."

"What kind of thing? Dancing?"

He laughs. "Oh, come on. He was hardly *dancing.* He was gyrating on women's faces."

"What the hell are you two talking about?" Lori asks as she sits down next to me.

"*Magic Mike.*"

"Who?" Mason asks.

"The dance is from the film *Magic Mike,*" I tell him.

His rolls his eyes. "You mean there's a whole film about him dry humping horny women?"

"It has an actual plot but yeah, there's lots of *dancing.*"

"If I knew that's what you classed as dancing then we'd be doing that tonight instead of karaoke."

"Oh and I suppose you have moves like Channing?"

He raises his eyebrow. "Oh, I have the moves." I take a

drink and try to think of something mundane to stop my mind from wandering to places that it shouldn't.

"The night is still young," Lori says. "I'm sure there will be enough time for you two to go dancing after we leave here."

"That's an excellent idea," Mason replies as I give her the side eye. "Don't you think, Sophia?"

I down the rest of my cosmopolitan. "I *think* I need another drink."

He laughs. "Me too. I'll get them. Same again?"

"Yes, please," Lori interrupts. "And one for me too, thanks Mason."

"Two cosmo's coming right up."

My greedy traitor eyes follow him as he walks over to the bar. "You should take a picture, it'll last longer," she says.

"And *you* should stop with the stupid comments. Don't encourage him."

She laughs. "I can't help it. I totally ship you two. I know you've struggled with all of this but Jesus Christ, you could cut the sexual tension with a chainsaw. I think actual sparks would fly if you two got together."

"Well it's never going to happen. I *can't* let it happen. Why did you tell him to get me another drink? You know I don't like to drink at work."

"Um, hello? You're not at work."

"Technically I am."

"I don't care about technicalities. You've already made it crystal clear that you're not going to trap him or help Emily in any way so no, you're not at work. We're just four friends hanging out on a Friday night. Stop feeling so guilty all of the time and have some fun." It's true. I wonder how much of what is weighing me down is actually mine to carry. "Answer me this, would you still want to spend time with him if you hadn't signed a contract?"

I sigh. "Yes."

"Exactly. You're not here because you have to be,

you're here because you want to be. Cut yourself some slack, Soph. Let your hair down for once."

I look over my shoulder and see Mason on his way back to us, a cocktail in each hand. He smiles sweetly when our eyes meet and I get a warm fuzzy feeling in the pit of my stomach. Multiple women turn to watch him as he walks by but his eyes stay firmly locked onto mine.

He places a drink in front of Lori and then carefully hands me the other, his fingers brushing against mine. "Thank you."

"What did I miss?"

I shrug. "Nothing."

"Hey, it looks like Buzz has finally chosen a song," Lori tells us. "It took him long enough."

"It's a very important decision," Mason jokes. "Life altering."

"Is he any good?" she asks.

"I'll let you be the judge of that."

"So that's a no."

"You might want to cover your ears," Mason whispers to me as the music starts to play. His hot breath sends a shiver down my spine. I take another drink while trying to regain my composure.

Buzz walks up to the mic and taps it three times. "Testing, testing. Can everybody hear me in the back?" A few people clap and cheer. "How y'all doing tonight?"

Lori rolls her eyes. "Jeez, he's acting like he's the headliner of his own show."

"I would like to dedicate this next song to my sweetheart, Lori." He points at her and she groans when several people turn around to look. "I can't think of a better song to sum up my feelings for you."

"Oh here we go," she says as he starts to sing *Hot In Herre*.

Chapter Sixty
Mason

The next hour consists of Buzz and Lori taking it in turns to dedicate songs to each other. Lori's first song was *We Don't Have To Take Our Clothes Off*, which Buzz then replied with R.Kelly's *Bump N' Grind*. Nobody else even attempts to have a turn at singing and based on the audience reaction, I'm pretty sure the owner is about ready to sign them up as an official act.

"It's like we're listening to the soundtrack of their relationship," Sophia says as Lori is half way through *You've Got A Friend In Me* – from the film *Toy Story*. The lyrics, which are totally contradictory to the lyrics in Buzz's song choices, earn a few laughs and cheers from the audience. Buzz broods through the entire thing, much to my enjoyment. He copes a lot better with her version of Katy Perry's *I Kissed A Girl*. I don't ask for the back story but it doesn't take a genius to work it out.

Several songs and drinks later and I'm feeling like my old self again. I'm care free, confident and happy – the happiest I've been in a long time. Buzz is now onto his final song of the evening and according to him, he saved the best for last. He thrusts and gyrates his way through Marvin Gaye's *Let's Get It On* and even gets a few dollar bills thrown at him.

"You know, this would be a great song to *dance* to," I tell Sophia.

"Would it now?" she asks, eyebrow raised.

I nod. "It definitely would. Buzz and Lori have chosen to communicate via song lyrics. You and I could express ourselves through the medium of dance."

She laughs. "Okay, Channing."

"Okay as in you agree to it?"

She leans her head to one side. "I thought you were a good boy."

"I am, most of the time. But I also have a bad boy

streak."

"Oh, really?"

"Mmmhmm. I can be *very* bad when I want to be."

"And when do you want to be?"

"Whenever I'm with you." Her eyes darken and the rise and fall of her chest quickens. The air around us feels charged, like it's full of emotion and unspoken truths. She looks like she's about to say something but stops when she notices someone behind me.

"Hello, Mason," a familiar voice says.

I manage to tear my eyes away from her and turn around to see who the voice belongs to. "Wow. Chantal. Long time no see."

She nods. "It's been eleven years."

"That's crazy. It's gone so fast."

"You haven't changed one bit."

"Don't say that." I laugh. "I was a scrawny sixteen year old when you last saw me."

"But still just as handsome." She looks at Sophia. "Is this your wife?"

"Oh, no, this is my…this is Sophia." I don't know why I have such a hard time calling her my friend. Maybe it's because she feels like much more than just a friend.

"Well I just recognized you and wanted to come say hi. Congrats on all of your success, by the way. You always were the smartest one in our group."

"Thanks, Chantal. It was good to see you again." She gives a little wave then walks away. I turn back to Sophia. "Sorry about that."

"No, it's fine. Is she an old friend?"

"Kind of. She was my first ever girlfriend."

"Oh, cute."

"I lost my virginity to her."

"Ah, the time you can't remember because it was over so quick."

I laugh. "Thanks for reminding me."

"Poor Chantal."

"Poor Chantal? Poor me. She broke up with me the day after."

Her hand flies up to her mouth, presumably to hide her laughter. "That bad, was it?"

"Yes, it was. I'm not even going to try and deny it. It's okay, you can laugh. I've come on a lot since then."

She laughs some more. "Is that a pun?"

I sigh. "There you go with your dirty mind again. And no, it wasn't a pun. Tell me about your ex. How long ago did you break up?"

"Two years ago."

"Have you dated since?"

"Nope."

"Why not? I bet men have been falling over themselves to take you out on a date."

"Um, not really. It's complicated. My job takes up a lot of my time and to be honest, I haven't been interested in dating."

"And is that still how you feel?"

She pauses and I hold my breath waiting for her answer. "No, I don't think it is." *Good.* "What about you? Have you been on any dates since separating from Emily?"

"No. I haven't been interested in dating." I look her dead in the eye, willing her to ask me the next question.

"And is that still how you feel?"

"No, Sophia. Not anymore."

"Do you still love Emily?" she asks, blurting it out as though she has no control over her tongue.

"No, I don't. I care about her and I probably always will but there's no love left."

"Tell me more about her."

She's not you. I clear my throat. "What do you want to know?"

"How did you meet? You seem so…different."

"You're right, we are different. We were opposites in every way, which I liked to begin with. It was different and exciting. She used to challenge me and question everything but I believe that opposites can only attract for so long. She was a waitress in a restaurant. She used to be independent and ambitious but the money changed her, like it does to a lot of people. We're not interested in any of the same things and most importantly, our morals and values don't line up."

I nod. "Do you think your marriage ended because of Emily's affair?"

"No." She looks surprised by my answer. "I believe that if you truly love someone, nothing will get in the way of it. Nothing can stop it. Not time, distance, money or deceit. You will love who you love."

"And you really believe that?"

"I do. I think that when you find the one, separation isn't possible."

"So when did you know that it was over?"

"Deep down, I knew not long after the wedding. I was embarrassed and didn't want to believe it. We were supposed to be happy, not needing therapy a few months after getting married. She couldn't understand why I wasn't happy. She thinks that happiness can be bought. I tried, I really did. I only wanted to get married once."

"Would you ever get remarried?"

"Yes, I would. Even though it didn't work out with Emily, I still believe in marriage. I think it would depend on the other person too. They might not want to marry me with all the baggage I have."

"We all have baggage."

"But some more than others. I can't even have an allergic reaction in peace these days." She laughs. "I do worry that my lifestyle may scare people off. And I also worry that I might be seen as a failure because I couldn't save my marriage."

"You're not a failure, Mason. Not one bit."

"Would it be weird if I told you that you make me happy?"

She laughs. "Probably. But not as weird as you telling me that you miss my voice."

217

"Well in that case, you don't make me happy. You make me miserable. I haven't been this miserable in a long time. Nobody can make me feel as miserable as you do."

"I've been trying to fight it but the truth is that you make me miserable too."

"Please don't fight it."

"I wish we had met at a different time, under different circumstances."

"But if we had, we wouldn't be sitting here right now telling each other how miserable we are." She laughs. "Your turn now. How long were you with your ex?"

"Three years."

"What's his name?"

"Scott Parker. He wasn't your decorator by any chance, was he? Sorry, I shouldn't joke about it."

I laugh. "Now wouldn't that be something? But no, his name isn't Scott. Did you think that he was the one?"

"At the time, yes. But looking back, it's clear that we weren't right for each other. We got into a routine and I think we were together out of habit in the end. Even though I loved him, it was never exciting. It was an ordinary, convenient kind of love. Not that there's anything wrong with that but I don't want ordinary love. Not anymore. I want to drown in passion."

"You could have taken the words right out of my mouth. Emily thinks that I have given up on love but it's the total opposite. I made the decision to leave *because* I'll never give up on love. I don't want to settle. Some people have okay jobs, okay relationships and okay lives and that's fine, but I don't want an okay life. I don't want an okay love. I want a great love. We're only here once. I would rather risk everything I have for the smallest chance that something amazing could happen. The next time I say I love you to somebody, I want it to feel different, like it's the first time I'm ever saying it."

She nods. "Well technically you've just said it to me."

I laugh. "All in good time, Sophia. We have so much

more to learn about each other. What's your last name, by the way?"

She sits up a little straighter. "It's Hamilton."

"Hamilton." A slow grin spreads across my face. "So if we ever get married, your initials would stay the same."

She laughs. "All in good time, Mason. I mean, jeez, you're still married to somebody else. I might have to start calling you Ross Gellar."

I laugh. "So that would make you Rachel."

"She *does* have awesome dress sense but I'm probably most like Monica."

"Ewwww, no, you can't be my sister."

"What are you guys talking about?" Buzz asks as he sits down next to me.

"Where have you been?" I ask him, changing the subject.

He smirks. "We needed some *air.*"

"You okay?" Lori asks Sophia. She nods in response.

"It's your turn to sing," Buzz says.

"Nah, I'm sticking to dancing tonight. Isn't that right, Sophia?"

She raises an eyebrow. "Apparently so. I hope you enjoy dancing on your own."

I chuckle. "Oh, I do but I'd much rather dance with you."

"You can't dance for shit," Buzz interrupts.

Both Sophia and Lori burst out laughing. "What?" he says. "It's true. He has no rhythm."

I shake my head. "Stop talking, Buzz."

"But everybody knows it's true. You're too stiff."

I think I see actual tears of laughter running down Sophia's face. "Please stop before I pee on myself," she says.

"He doesn't know what he's talking about," I tell Sophia, trying to keep a straight face but failing, miserably. "Honestly. I'm a very skilled dancer. Let me prove it to you."

"Yeah," Buzz says. "Why don't you prove it to her right

now. We can all watch and laugh."

"Oh, this is too much," Lori says when she can catch a breath.

"How many drinks have those two had?" Buzz asks me as he pulls his cell out of his pocket. "They're acting crazy. I need to document it. Say hello to everybody on Snapchat, ladies."

"Don't you dare," Lori says.

He laughs. "I'm only joking. I'm sure I have a video on here of Mason dancing. Let me find it so I can show you how lame he is."

My eyes snap to his as Sophia and Lori break out into another fit of laughter. "Don't you have anything better to do?" I ask. "Perhaps you could text your *mom.*"

The grin instantly falls from his face and finds its way onto mine. He stands up. "I'll get some more drinks instead."

Chapter Sixty One
Sophia

I don't know how many cocktails I've had but I *do* know that it's way too many. My head is spinning and I'm at the stage where everybody is my new BFF. I'm giving out free hugs and I'm pretty sure I swapped numbers with a girl in the restroom all because she let me use her hairbrush.

"Mason?"

"Yes, Sophia?"

I giggle. "I like it when you say my name like that."

"Like what?"

"All sexy and brooding. Wait, is that even a word? Brooding? It sounds funny. Have I just made it up? Brooding. Brooooo-ding. Oh my god, I've just invented a word. I need to write it down before I forget. I'm sure I have a pen somewhere." I open my purse and take out my phone and lipstick. "Nope. No pen."

"Sophia..."

"Can I borrow your pen?"

He laughs. "I don't have one but…"

"Pfft, call yourself a businessman? Lor, do you have a pen?"

"No, sweetie. Why do you need a pen?"

"I've just invented a new word."

"Wow! What is it?"

I narrow my eyes. "Shit. I've forgotten. That's Mason's fault for not having a pen."

"It was brooding," he tells me.

"No, that wasn't it. It was…it was…oh, I remember! It was brooding." Mason laughs. "Brooding. Broo and then ding, like the bell. Brooooo-ding. Brooo-ding ding ding." Lori joins in with me.

"It's a real word," Mason says.

"I know it because I just invented it. I bet you haven't invented any words have you, Mr Big Shot?"

"Sophia, it's a…"

I turn to face him. "Mason, I'm being serious now. You're going to have to stop saying my name like that because it's doing all kinds of funny things to me."

Chapter Sixty Two
Mason

Sophia.

Sophia.

Sophia.

Sophia.

Sophia.

Sophia.

I want to carry on saying it all night. Her face is so close to mine. So close that I can feel the warmth of her breath caressing my lips. It would be too easy to lean in and kiss her right now. God, I want to kiss her so bad. I swallow hard.

"You say that like it's a bad thing."

"It *is* a bad thing," she replies.

"Why?"

"Because I like you."

I laugh. "I like you too, Sophia."

"No. I don't like you. Well I *do* like you but I don't *just* like you. I *like you* like you."

I pretend to be deep in thought. "So hang on a minute, do you like me or not? That was a little confusing."

"Yes. I like you too much."

"I don't think that's possible."

"You're wrong. It is possible."

"But why would that be a bad thing?"

She throws her arms up. "Because I don't want to trap you, Mason. You don't get it."

"Trap me? What are you talking about?"

"Soph," Lori says, straight faced. "I think it's time for us to go home."

"I don't want to do anything that could potentially help her in any way," she tells me, ignoring Lori.

"What? Help who?"

"Sophia," Lori says with more force this time. "Stop it. You're drunk and not making any sense. Let's go home."

"I'm having fun like you told me to."

"I know but it's getting late and we've all had a lot to drink."

"I don't want to go home."

Lori turns to me. "Please help."

"I think it's time for bed," I tell Sophia.

She wiggles her eyebrows up and down. "Of course you do."

I try to keep a straight face. "Let me rephrase that. I think it's time to leave. I'm going to call Charlie and ask him to come get us and take us home, is that okay?"

She nods right before throwing up all over my shoes.

"On a scale of one to ten, how much do you want to kiss me right now?" Buzz asks Lori.

"Hmmm…about a minus ten," she replies.

"At least you had to think about it."

"Yeah, I had to think about how much you repulse me."

"I don't think you understood the question."

"I understood just fine, thank you."

I turn back to Sophia who has her eyes closed and a paper bag on top of her lap. "Hey," I say softly. "We're just pulling up outside your house now."

She opens her eyes. "I'm sorry, Mason. For everything. I didn't mean to get myself into this mess."

"You don't need to apologize. You're not the first person to get drunk and throw up on me." I give Buzz a pointed look.

"Will you forgive me?"

I chuckle. "Of course I forgive you."

"Let's get you to bed then, party animal," Lori says, looking a little on edge. "Thanks for the ride, Mason."

"Any time." I jump out of the car and hold a hand out

to Sophia. I gasp when she threads her fingers through mine in such a small yet intimate gesture. It feels completely natural, like we've done it hundreds of times before. I'm not sure how I'm going to cope when it's time to let go. I don't have long to think about it because her legs give way as soon as she takes a step out of the car. She seems to have gotten considerably worse in the last half hour and puking hasn't sobered her up in the slightest. She squeals when I bend down and scoop her up into my arms. "I think this is the safest bet," I tell her.

She closes her eyes and sighs. "Oh, Mason. Why do you have to be so goddamn perfect?"

I laugh. "I'm not perfect."

"You're pretty damn close."

"So are you."

"No, I'm definitely not."

"Well you're perfect to me, Sophia."

She groans. "There you go again saying my name like that. Do you know how turned on I am right now?"

I'm hard in less than five seconds. It doesn't help that my hands are gripping her bare thighs. I take a deep, steadying breath. "Probably not as turned on as I am." Her glazed doe eyes turn dark, mirroring my own.

"Where was my offer to be carried?" Lori asks Buzz as we reach the front door. "Why couldn't you be a gentleman like Mason and help me out of the car?"

"Because I'm not Mason and I'm not a gentleman." He holds both of his hands up and spins around. "This is me. What you see is what you get. I'm impulsive and intense. I'm spontaneous and sarcastic. I'm loud and loyal to a fault. And I like to live my life the same way as I like to fuck - hard and fast. I know I'm not your usual type but you're single for a reason, sweetheart. You can't ignore your feelings forever. Jump aboard the Buzz train and I promise to give you the ride of your life."

She rolls her eyes. "You missed modest off of the list. Here, hold this so I can look for my keys." She shoves her purse towards him. "I can't hold it and look at the same time. It doesn't help that it's so freaking dark."

"It also doesn't help that you're Mary fucking Poppins. I can't believe how much stuff you carry around with you. Have you packed the kitchen sink in there too?"

"No, but I have mace somewhere."

"Yeah well you'd have to find it first."

She scowls. "Hold still and I will."

"What the hell is this?" He pulls out something shaped like a large bullet.

"Lipstick."

"Why is it so big? And is that a switch?"

"It's my BOB, idiot."

"What's a BOB?"

"Battery operated boyfriend. Hold still."

"A fucking vibrator? Why the hell do you have one of those when you've got me?"

"Because I can turn a vibrator off."

"But it's much more fun turning me *on*."

"I can turn that thing on too, whenever and wherever I want. And it doesn't talk."

"Hey, I can be as quiet as a mouse. I must admit, I do usually enjoy a bit of dirty talk but if you want me to be quiet then that's fine by me."

Just when I think Sophia's fallen asleep, she opens her eyes. "Am I dreaming or are they actually talking about vibrators?"

I chuckle. "You're not dreaming."

"Can I ask you something? It's important," she says in an almost whisper.

"Of course."

"How did Buzz get his nickname?"

I laugh. "That's important? He would kill me if I told you."

"I won't tell anyone, not even Lori. Pinky swear."

"Hmmmm, what do I get in return?"

"Elevator and shower porn on tap."

"Well in that case…" I hold my pinky finger out and check that he's not listening. He's too busy making fun of Lori for having a bottle of mouthwash in her purse. "I once heard about this guy who lost his virginity," I tell her quietly. "He had been watching *Toy Story* earlier that day and apparently when he came, he shouted 'To infinity and beyond!'"

"No way!"

I shrug. "Rumor has it that there's video proof."

"Oh my god! That's so much better than I could have ever imagined." She laughs until she's gasping for breath and I have to grip her even harder to stop us from falling over.

"Hey! Let us in on the joke," Buzz says.

"Oh, I'm pretty sure you already know it," she tells him, trying to keep a straight face but failing miserably. I turn my back to him and place a finger to my lips. "Okay, I have another question. How did you get so beautiful?"

"I don't know anything about that," I reply.

"Oh, here we go," Buzz says. "Please don't inflate his ego any more than it already is."

She ignores him. "Surely you own a mirror. Seriously, who do I need to thank?"

"Well, a lot of people say that I look like my mother."

"Does she have Twitter? I'll tweet her."

I laugh. "No, Sophia, my mother does not have a Twitter account. She probably doesn't even know what it is."

"Why can't *you* be kind like Sophia?" Buzz asks Lori, eyebrow raised. She jangles her keys in his face. "Found them. You can go home now."

"Point proven. Aren't you going to invite me in for a coffee?"

"It's almost one, why the hell would you drink coffee at this time of night?" He wiggles his eyebrows up and down. "Goodbye, Buzz."

"Wait, can I use your bathroom? I really need to go."

She sighs as she unlocks the door and pushes it open. "I guess so. It's at the bottom of the hallway. Make sure you put the toilet seat down afterwards."

I carry Sophia inside. "Hey, is your dog home? I didn't see him last time."

She laughs. "We don't have a dog."

"Oh, I thought you said you had a black lab."

"We *had* a dog," Lori says. "But we had to give it away because of my allergies."

"Yeah, she's allergic to animals," Sophia adds. "All of them."

"Oh. Well that sucks. Which one is your bedroom?" I ask Sophia.

"Second on the left."

My heart beats faster and faster with every step that I take and I'm convinced that she must be able to feel it trying to hammer its way out of my chest. We reach the second door on the left and I use my foot to gently push it open. And just like that, I'm standing in Sophia's bedroom. My eyes dart straight to her bed. Her *double* bed. Lord give me strength. "If I'm being honest, this isn't how I imagined it would be seeing your bedroom for the first time."

"How did you imagine it?"

I laugh. "Well you were sober, for one. And my shoes didn't have puke on them." She groans again. "And we were both wearing less clothing."

"Why were we wearing less clothing?"

"I don't know. Maybe it was a hot day."

"So why wasn't the AC on?"

I shrug. "It was broken."

"Why didn't we just go to your place instead?"

"Because I was here to fix it."

"What did we do afterwards?"

"We took a shower because we were all hot and sweaty."

"I've already told you that my shower is only big enough for one person."

I walk her over to the bed and lay her down as gently as I can. "Well I proved you wrong." I hover over her and it takes all of my strength not to lean down and kiss her.

"Did you now?"

"I did."

"And how was it?"

I think back to when she rated me out of ten the first time we ever met. A slow smile spreads across my face. "A solid six point five."

She laughs. "You don't have much of an imagination if it was only a six point five. Tell your imaginary self to try harder next time."

"Maybe it was you who didn't put the effort in. Just saying."

She gasps. "I *always* put the effort in."

"Good to know."

"You'll find out soon enough." My dick twitches and her eyes shoot straight to it. Our bodies are so close now. *Too close.* "I don't think I can hold out for much longer."

"You're drunk," I say, in challenge.

She slowly brings her eyes back up to mine. "I'm only saying what I think when I'm sober."

Walk away. Walk away. *Walk the fuck away.* "In that case, we'll carry on this conversation another time."

She throws her head back and a small frustrated moan escapes her lips. It becomes my undoing and without thinking, I lower myself onto her, letting her feel the full weight of my body. I'm not sure if the pounding against my chest is coming from my heart or hers but I instantly know that *this* is how it's supposed to feel. *This* is what I've been missing out on all of these years. Two bodies becoming one. Two hearts beating as one. Our lips are inches apart and I groan when she bucks her hips. I close my eyes and try to regain any trace of willpower left inside me. I try to memorize the feel of her body against mine before I push up on my forearms and climb off the bed. "Until next time, Sophia." She turns over and buries her face in her pillows. I take a deep breath and adjust my pants as I glance around the room, trying to gather any extra snippets of information about her. My eyes are drawn to a little card on her bedside table. A little card which happens to have handwriting on it. *My* handwriting. I smile like an idiot at the fact that she's kept it and that it's right next to where she sleeps. I look at her one last time before I force myself to walk out of the room.

She calls my name just as I'm about to close the door behind me. I turn back around. "I never want to hurt you."

"Shhhh, get some sleep," I tell her.

"You're my game changer. She changed the rules but you changed the whole game."

"Sweet dreams, Sophia." I close the door gently then press my forehead up against it. "You're my game changer too."

Chapter Sixty Three

Sophia

I wake up with a pounding headache, sore throat and birds nest hair. I look down at my pajamas and have no idea how or when I got into them. Thank god I have Lori to take care of me. "I'm never drinking again," I mumble to myself before reaching for the delicious looking glass of water on my bedside table. Too lazy to even sit up, I grab it with one hand and carefully bring it down to my mouth. I tip the glass up just as a memory of last night flashes through my mind like lightning. I'm lying on the bed and Mason is on top of me. I feel how hard he is and lift my hips up to meet him, desperately craving more contact. Did we…

"Shit!" I shout as I get covered in water. I sit up too fast and curse again when the room starts to spin. I close my eyes and consider crawling back under my covers for the rest of the day but now I'm wet as well as thirsty. And more importantly, I need to ask Lori what happened last night. I mentally curse myself for getting so drunk. I slowly stand up, feeling like an old lady, and steady myself before heading to the kitchen.

I jump when I see Buzz sitting at the kitchen table. "What are you doing here?" I quickly cross my arms across my chest.

He laughs. "Good morning to you too. You're almost as welcoming as Lori."

"Where is she?"

"Getting dressed," he answers with a smirk. "Even though I told her there was really no need." I walk over to the fridge and grab a bottle of water. "I didn't realize we were having a wet T-shirt competition," he says. "Mason is going to be so bummed that he missed out."

I take a long drink, my cheeks heating at the mention of his name. "I spilled my glass of water."

"Oh yes, you conveniently spilled it all over your pajama top when you knew I was alone in the kitchen."

"I didn't know you were here. I *still* don't know why you're here."

He laughs. "Look, Sophia, maybe in a different lifetime you and I would be together and have beautiful babies but I kind of have a thing for your best friend and *my* best friend kind of has a thing for you. So maybe you could back off a little, yeah?"

"Shut up, Buzz." I try to act normal but my heart is going crazy at his comment.

"Did Mason go home last night?" I ask casually, trying to fit the puzzle pieces together.

He smirks. "I don't know, you tell me."

"Tell you what?" Lori asks as she walks into the kitchen and pulls me into a hug. "Good morning," she says for Buzz to hear before whispering, "Don't worry, Mason went home. Everything is fine. I'll fill you in later."

"Well isn't this a delight for my eyes," Buzz says.

"Pervert," Lori replies. "We're going for lunch, do you want to come with us? Buzz is paying, aren't you?"

"Apparently so."

"Lunch? What time is it?" I ask.

"Almost twelve thirty."

I didn't realize I slept for so long. "Thanks but no thanks. I need to get a shower. My hair smells like vodka…and puke. Wait, did I throw up?"

Buzz laughs. "You don't remember?"

"No but that would explain why my throat is burning."

"Do you want to tell her or should I?" he asks Lori.

She shrugs. "You puked. It's not a big deal. Been there, done that, bought the T-shirt."

"You puked *on Mason*," Buzz says.

My eyes widen. "What?"

"Only on his shoes," Lori adds. "It's fine. He wiped it off."

"Oh my god! I'm mortified." I sit down and rest my head on the table. "Please don't let me drink ever again."

"Nah, I like drunk Sophia," Buzz says. "I think Mason

does too."

"Why does it sound like I was the only drunk one?"

"Probably because you kept drinking my cocktails as well as your own. Mason tried to cut you off but you wouldn't listen to him. Do you want me to bring some greasy food back with me? It should help with the hangover."

I groan. "Yes, please."

"Okay. Well I'll see you in an hour or two. Call me if you need anything. Your cell is in your purse, next to the coffee machine."

I wave at her without bothering to lift my head off of the table. Buzz laughs. "Enjoy your hangover."

My wave is quickly replaced by my middle finger.

I wake up to the sound of Justin Bieber serenading me in Spanish. I have no idea where I am or what day it is. It takes me a good few seconds to realize that I must have fallen back to sleep at the kitchen table and that the music is coming from my cell. I stand up and walk over to the coffee machine. I pull my cell out of my purse and feel like I'm going to throw up again when I see Mason's name flashing across the screen. "Hello?" I answer, trying to sound as normal and awake as possible.

"Hey, party animal. How's your head?"

I groan. "It feels like an elephant is standing on it."

He laughs. "I'm not surprised. Have you taken anything for it?"

"No. I think we ran out of Tylenol."

"Do you want me to bring some over?"

"No, no, it's fine. I'll get some later."

"I hope you don't mind me calling you. I was waiting to make sure I didn't wake you up but then Buzz mentioned that he saw you."

"I don't mind."

"He also mentioned something about a wet T-shirt competition."

"Just ignore him."

"Yeah, I usually do." He laughs. "It's not as easy in the week though, what with us working together."

"He told me about last night. Do I owe you a new pair of shoes?"

"No, of course you don't."

"I'm sorry. I'm so embarrassed."

"Don't be. I had a great night. You were just having fun. You were very…complimentary."

"Oh god. In what way?"

He chuckles. "You may have called me perfect a couple of times." *Why, Sophia? Why?* "You even said that I was beautiful and wanted to thank my mom on Twitter."

"You're lying."

"I'm not, I swear."

"You didn't tell me her username, did you?"

He laughs. "No, she doesn't have one."

"Thank god for that. I better check that I didn't post anything stupid to anybody else."

"I think you were probably too drunk to use your phone."

I groan. "I never usually drink that much."

"That's what they all say."

"Honestly. I hardly ever drink. I just got carried away for some reason." Probably because I've been so tightly wound these past couple of weeks and needed to let off some steam.

"You're allowed to have fun, Sophia."

The way he says my name brings back another memory. "How many times did I tell you that I was horny last night?"

He laughs. "Only once."

"I'm sorry if I was too…forthcoming. Things got a little heated before you left, unless I dreamt it all."

"Are you saying that you dream about me, Sophia?"

Yes. "If you weren't actually on top of me last night then yes, I dream about you."

"Luckily, that wasn't a dream." There's a long pause and I'm sure I can feel the sexual tension through the phone line. Why do I have to be so attracted to him? "But I can pretend it was, if you'd prefer?" he asks softly. "I can try and forget that it happened."

Another pause before I reply honestly. Selfishly. "No."

I swear that I hear a sigh of relief. "Would it be weird if I told you that I missed you already?"

My stomach flips. "Probably."

"Well it doesn't matter anyway because I don't miss you. Not even one percent. It was such an inconvenience having to carry you to your bed last night. I hope I don't have to do it again anytime soon. I also hope that I don't have to lie on top of you ever again."

I laugh. "I hope you don't either."

"Good. I'm glad we're on the same page."

If only that was the truth then all of this would be so much easier.

I hear Lori cursing as she locks the front door behind her. "What's happened?" I ask when she sits down and places the burger and some Tylenol in front of me. "Thanks. I'm starving." I start to unwrap it straight away. "You even got me some Tylenol. You're the best."

"I didn't get the Tylenol. It was in the mail box."

Mason. I smile.

She groans as she looks at her cell. "I can't decide if I want to strangle him or rip his clothes off."

"Who?" I ask.

"Who do you think? Only one person can make my blood boil like this." I laugh. "Don't laugh. Look at what he's done now." She holds her phone up to show me his

Facebook profile. I shake my head, not having a clue what I'm supposed to be looking at. "He's just updated his relationship status," she says through gritted teeth.

Buzz Miller is in a relationship with Lori Campbell.

I take a bite of the burger. "I didn't know his last name was Miller."

"Oh, *that's* the thing you decide to pick up on?"

I laugh. "You know what he's like. He's probably just doing it to push your buttons."

"We've been out for lunch *one* time and he's already made us Facebook official."

"Well did anything happen last night? I was shocked to see him here earlier."

"We talked a lot and cuddled. That's it."

"Aww, you cuddled?"

"Yes." She sighs. "I'm a complete masochist. I'm supposed to stop seeing him in a few weeks."

I don't tell her how guilty that makes me feel. "How do you feel about that?"

"Not good. But let's face it, he was never going to be a long-term option anyway, not that I want anything serious right now."

"His Facebook status says otherwise."

She rolls her eyes. "Anyway, enough about me. If I've got any extra gray hairs today, it's because of you, not Buzz."

"I'm sorry. Did I do anything stupid?"

"What, like telling Mason that you don't want to trap him?"

My eyes nearly pop out of my head. "Nooooo!"

"Exactly."

"What…why…"

"You were talking about how much you like each other. No, wait, let me get this right…you don't just like him, you *like him* like him." I groan. "And then you said it was wrong and when he questioned you, you got pissy and told him

236

that you didn't want to trap him. He didn't seem weird about it. He must have just thought you were talking crap because you were drunk."

"It's way too risky drinking around him." She nods in agreement. "Oh well, it could have been worse. At least nothing bad happened."

"It didn't while I was with you but you were alone in your bedroom at one point. He seemed like he was in a very good mood when he left."

"No, nothing happened in my room." *Even though I wanted it to.*

"You sure?"

"Yes. I was drunk but not *that* drunk. I would have remembered."

She laughs. "It was nice to see you having fun. You two are a good match."

"Lor," I warn.

"What?" she asks, innocently.

"You know what. Nothing's changed."

"Okay, okay, you keep telling yourself that. So what's the plan?"

I take the last bite of my burger, already feeling a lot more human. "The plan is to forget all about boys and have a pajama day." She claps and takes off her jacket while humming to *Hot In Herre*. I laugh. "Now *that* I remember."

Chapter Sixty Four

Mason

Why is it that every time a phone rings, even if it's not my own, my heart rate goes through the roof and I automatically assume that it's Sophia? I need to calm the fuck down. I feel like the world's worst friend for feeling disappointed when I see Buzz's name flash up. "Hello?" I answer.

"Hey. Are you free to talk?"

"Of course I am. Is everything okay?"

"I'm not sure. I need to tell you something."

I laugh. "Please don't tell me you sexted your mom again."

"No. I found something last night."

"Maybe you could be a little more specific."

"I found something in Lori's bedroom."

"I'm not sure I want to know."

"No, it's nothing like that. Jesus, I wish it was. I tried to act normal and didn't bring it up but now I can't stop thinking about it."

"Are you waiting for the ominous background music to kick in before telling me?"

"I found a file."

"Okay. What kind of file?"

"It was like a case file for some random dude. It had his personal details like his weight and height and stuff about his marriage."

"Who is he?"

"His name is Nicholas Keating."

"I've never heard of him. Run a background check."

"I already have. He lives a couple of blocks from the office. He's in his forties and has three kids to three different women. He has a couple of DUI's from years ago but apart from that, nothing shady."

"Then you need to talk to Lori about it."

"I can't."

"Why not?"

"Because then she'll know I was snooping around in her shit and never want to see me again."

I sigh and drop down onto the sofa. "Where did you find it?"

"In a drawer."

"Shit, Buzz. Why were you looking through her drawers?"

"I was looking for condoms."

"Bullshit. You're on a sex ban."

"I wanted to see if she had them to use with somebody else."

"What were you really looking for?"

"I don't even know. I really like her and it just seems too good to be true. It doesn't matter what I was looking for, it matters that I found something."

"Maybe it's her ex. Or a relative. I have no idea."

"Maybe she's stalking him."

I laugh. "I doubt it."

"It's weird because she doesn't always answer my calls. And she's hot and cold with me. One day she's fine then the next she has this wall up. Jesus Christ, I sound like a fifteen year old girl."

"If you have trust issues then you need to address them. Just try and talk to her about it."

"Like you did with Emily?"

"That was different. We were married and she was fucking the decorator. She probably still is."

"You're right. I'm sorry."

"You should be honest with her."

"And you don't think she will run a mile?"

"Maybe, but what's the alternative? You can't let it stew, it will drive you crazy."

"You're right. Thanks for the advice, brother."

"Any time."

"What happened with you and Sophia last night?"

"Nothing."

"Oh, come on. You were in her bedroom and she was

practically begging for it."

"Watch your mouth."

He laughs. "I forgot how protective you get over her. What's the deal with you two?"

"I get the impression that she's not comfortable with the whole Emily situation."

"Just serve the divorce papers and be done with it. Sophia seems like a really good girl."

"I already know that. Hey, I forgot to ask you, what did Lori say when you told her about your nickname?"

"What do you mean? I haven't told her."

I laugh. "Oh, I just assumed she knew because she chose to sing the *Toy Story* song last night."

"No, that was just a coincidence."

"I may have told Sophia."

"Bro! Are you fucking with me?"

"No, but she probably doesn't remember because of how drunk she was. She couldn't remember much when we spoke earlier."

"I can't believe you told her. I'm going to expose your secret as payback."

"Which is?"

"That you've got a tiny dick."

I laugh. "So when you refer to it as a secret, it's actually a lie."

"You wish I was lying."

"Go ahead and tell her. There's only one way I can prove you wrong."

He grins. "That's the spirit."

"Dude, I just had a thought…what if Lori's a hitman?"

"Then my heart may get broken in more ways than one."

Chapter Sixty Five
Sophia

I'm grocery shopping the next day when Mason calls. "It's time to cash in our date," he says in greeting.

"When?"

"Right now."

"Where?"

"The hotel"

"You're inviting me to your hotel room?"

"No, I'm inviting you to my penthouse suite."

"Is this a date or a booty call?"

He chuckles. "It can be whatever you want it to be."

"I'm at Walmart right now. I haven't washed my hair in four days and I'm not wearing a bra."

"You say that like it's a problem. I'm totally okay with you not wearing a bra."

I laugh. "Sure you are."

"If it makes you feel any better, I'm not wearing any pants."

My imagination comes alive. "Oh yeah, much better."

"You can wash your hair when you get here, if you really want to. You can test out my extremely large shower."

"Solo act, remember?"

"Of course. Tsk tsk, you and your dirty mind."

"Give me a couple of hours and I'm all yours."

"Say that again."

"What? Give me a couple of hours?"

"The last part, Sophia."

"And I'm all yours." *Oh.*

"Don't keep me waiting too long, will you? I've just sent the nurse away."

"The nurse? What nurse?"

"From the eye hospital."

"What are you talking about?"

"I had my laser eye surgery this morning. I need you to come and look after me."

"Oh, so you're just using me?"

He laughs. "You can use me in return. In any way you'd like."

"Why did you send the nurse away?"

"Because I don't need her. You're coming over."

"But you didn't know that at the time."

"I knew I could rely on you. I'd much rather get a sponge bath off you."

"A sponge bath? Mason, you've had an operation on your *eyes*."

"Exactly, so I can't *see* what body part I'm washing."

I laugh. "Jeez, you'll be asking me to wear a nurse's uniform next."

"Well now that you mention it, yes, that would be perfect."

"For you, maybe. Do you need me to buy anything while I'm here?"

"No, unless you want to choose us something for breakfast."

"Breakfast? It's almost time for dinner."

"*Tomorrow's* breakfast."

"That's very presumptuous of you."

"What?" he asks innocently. "The nurse isn't coming back until tomorrow afternoon so I thought you could stay with me until then. I can hardly see anything. I'm just sitting here in the dark, all alone."

I sigh. "I'll be there in an hour."

Around forty five minutes later, after abandoning my shopping cart and running home for the world's quickest shower, I'm standing outside Mason's room. I untie the belt on my trench coat and knock on the door. A few seconds later, I hear a voice followed by footsteps. And then I hear a second voice. I panic and begin to fumble around with my belt. I curse when I pull it too hard and have to start threading the end of it back through the loops.

The door opens and Mason's jaw hits the ground as soon as he sees me. "Fuck, Sophia. I was only joking about the nurse's uniform."

I raise my eyebrow. "I thought you couldn't see anything." I knew I shouldn't have let Lori talk me into wearing her nurse's costume. It was supposed to keep the mood light, especially after our last encounter, but judging by the fire in his eyes, it's had the opposite effect.

"And I thought you said one hour."

"I rushed over here," I tell him as I finally manage to tie the belt.

"Who is it?" I hear a woman ask. "Come and sit down, you should be resting." A beautiful woman with a short blonde bob appears next to him. "Oh, hello."

"Hi." *Who are you and why are you here?*

"Are you the nurse?"

Mason smirks. "No. This is my…this is Sophia."

Her eyes widen in recognition. "Ah, Sophia. I've heard a lot about you."

She has? Mason clears his throat. "Well it was good to see you, mom."

Mom? MOM? How the hell did this turn into a meeting with his mother? And how does she look so young? "I'll come back later," I tell them as I take a step backwards.

"No!" Mason shouts. "My mom stopped by to check on me but I keep telling her that I'm fine. She was just leaving, weren't you, mom?"

"Yes. We should grab lunch some time, Sophia." I smile politely, not knowing what to say. *Oh, I don't think you would want to. I've been hired by your son's wife to try and steal all of his money.* She kisses Mason on the cheek. "Bye, sweetie."

He waits until the elevator doors completely close before turning around to face me. His eyes twinkle as he holds out his hand. "Let me get your coat."

Chapter Sixty Six
Mason

Dreams really do come true. "I always imagined you as a nurse."

She ignores my outstretched hand and walks straight past me. "I abandoned my cart for you."

I laugh as I follow her inside. "What?"

"I abandoned my groceries. I went straight home because I thought you actually needed my help."

"Does that mean you didn't buy us any breakfast?"

"I won't be here for breakfast."

My eyes fall to the bag she brought with her. "You sure about that?"

"Yes."

"So what's in the overnight bag?"

"It's not an overnight bag. It's just a bag."

"Okay. What's in your suspiciously large not-an-overnight bag?"

"Just stuff I thought I might need. A book, a blanket, some snacks."

I laugh. "You do realize that this is a hotel, don't you?"

"Yes, Mason. It's pretty hard to miss the huge sign on the side of the building."

"Then why did you think you'd need any of those things? We have a library, two restaurants and the softest blankets money could buy."

"Well I didn't know how bad your eyes were going to be so I came prepared. I didn't know you had a library."

"I can show you if you'd like."

"Thanks but I already have my book."

"You know, we also have extremely comfortable king-sized beds if you decide to change your mind about breakfast."

"I won't change my mind. You don't need me."

"I do need you," I tell her, all joking aside. She holds my gaze for a long moment then shakes her head, as though trying to shake our connection.

"Did you even have surgery or was it just a ploy to get me here?"

"Yes, I had it done this morning. I stayed there for a couple of hours after, until the burning and stinging died down."

"Are they sore now?"

"Not sore, just a little uncomfortable and sensitive to the light."

"I wondered why the blinds were closed. Have you got any drops you need to be taking?"

"Yes, they're over on the kitchen counter. I need to take them three times a day. I've also got some other stuff to keep my eyes lubricated which I can take as often as I like."

"Drops three times a day, eye lube as much as you want, got it."

"Now you look *and* sound like a nurse. I'm looking forward to finding out what your bedside manner is like."

I love it when I make her blush. "I bet you say that to all the nurses."

"Trust me, I don't. Are you going to stay in your coat all day?"

"No."

"Good."

"I'm going to get changed. I packed some other clothes."

"Dammit. Okay, if you must."

"Well?" she asks after a few seconds of us staring at each other.

"Well what?"

"Which room do you want me to get changed in?"

"This one." My laughter follows her down the hallway.

245

"This place is gorgeous," she says as she walks back into the room wearing a baggy T-shirt and some yoga pants. She looks so casual, like she's right at home. It makes me grin from ear to ear. "Who needs a house when you can live somewhere like this, rent free?"

"Exactly. But while I'm using it, nobody else can. I'm a greedy, selfish man."

"That's true. I guess there are hundreds of other rooms you could be using instead."

"But none that have this view."

She laughs and nods to the blinds. "Shame we can't see it."

"We can open them when it's not as bright. The sun should be setting soon. It's even prettier at night time."

"I'll look forward to it." She flops down beside me then pulls her feet up until she's sitting on them.

"Interesting position."

"Yeah, I seem to get myself into all sorts of weird positions." She groans when I raise my eyebrow. "Not like that. Get your head out of the gutter."

"But I like it in there. I can't believe you didn't let me see you in your nurse's outfit one last time."

"So your mom seems nice," she says, changing the subject. "She's very beautiful."

"Yes, she is." I smirk. "Hey, you forgot to thank her."

"Well maybe you can do it on my behalf seeing as though you talk to her about me." She raises her eyebrow in question.

Thanks, Mom. Still embarrassing me at twenty seven years old. "Oh, take no notice. I may have mentioned you a couple of times in passing. You know what moms are like." Her shoulders slump. It's so subtle that most people wouldn't even notice, but to me, it's glaringly obvious. She attempts to hide it with a smile. "Hey, are you okay?"

"Yeah, no, I'm fine. It's just…oh, never mind. I don't want to bore you with family stuff."

"Are you joking? You wouldn't be boring me. I can't

246

get enough of you."

"Sweet talk me all you want but I'm not putting the nurse's uniform back on."

"I'm being serious, Sophia. You can talk to me about anything. Please tell me."

She looks at the floor. "I was just going to say that I don't actually talk to my mom anymore, or my dad for that matter."

"Is that your choice or theirs?"

"Theirs. We call each other a few times throughout the year but we're not close like we used to be."

"What happened?"

"Nothing happened. They don't approve of my career choice."

"So they just cut you out of their lives?" I ask, completely taken aback.

"Yeah, pretty much. They told me that I'm welcome back if I decide to get a real job."

I shake my head. "Jesus. That sucks. I'm sorry to hear that."

"Don't be. It hurt at first but not anymore. I have Lori now. She's like family to me."

"You have me, too." She smiles but her eyes become glazed. "I mean it. I'm here for you."

"Thank you."

"I think they are completely out of order."

"They're entitled to their opinion."

"There's a difference between having an opinion and being batshit crazy. I mean, just look at you. You're magnificent. Who wouldn't want you in their life?"

She blushes, which wasn't even my intention. "I think they only did it for shock value to begin with, hoping that I'd quit and get a different job."

"But you didn't quit and now they've lost the best thing to ever happen to them."

"It's a little more complicated."

"No it's not. It's *your* life. You're a grown woman doing

what you want to do. You're a writer, chasing your dreams."

She sighs. "No, I'm not. I started doing my job because it was what I wanted and needed to do two years ago. I'm good at it and it pays the bills but it's taking over my life. I don't want to do it anymore."

"I didn't know you felt that way."

"It's not easy for me to talk about. Maybe one day we can talk more about it."

"I'll be here."

"I hope so. Just know that when I quit, it will be my choice. It will be for me, not my family."

"Will you try to build bridges with them?"

"Probably not. I've learned the hard way that family doesn't always have to be blood. I would never turn them away but I won't be running back to them. I want to be around people who accept and support me no matter what."

"I agree. I feel a similar way about my father." I very rarely talk about him but I trust Sophia and want to open up to her like she has to me. "He abandoned us when I was five. I didn't see him again for twenty years. He turned up at my office a couple of years ago. He just strolled right in and asked me to go to lunch with him. I agreed and listened to what he had to say. Turns out he only wanted my money. He had a gambling addiction and when I said no, he made threats against my mom and sister. That didn't go down too well with me."

"Wow. I'm sorry."

"We're better off without him. Walking out on us was the best gift he could have given to us. I grew up having a super close bond with my grandpa which probably wouldn't have happened if my father had stuck around. My papa was the greatest man I have ever met. He would have liked you."

"I'm sure I would have liked him too." She moves her hand closer to mine until our pinky fingers are touching. "When did he pass?"

"Two years ago this fall. I miss him so much."

She nods. "It must be really difficult for you."

"They gave him nine months to live but he fought for an extra two years. We worked through his bucket list together. We climbed the bay bridge one time."

"You *climbed* it?"

"Yeah, we climbed right to the top."

She shudders. "Rather you than me."

"It was amazing. He did more in those two years than most people do in their entire lifetime. I'll be forever grateful that we got that extra time with him." I nudge her gently. "I'm sorry if this is a little too heavy for a first date."

She smiles. "You have nothing to apologize for."

"I've been thinking about him a lot recently and feeling guilty."

"Guilty? You have nothing to feel guilty about."

"He left me his watch and now I can't find it."

"His watch?" She sits up a little straighter. "Have you definitely lost it?"

"Well I last saw it over at the house a few months ago. I definitely didn't bring it over here but apparently Emily doesn't know anything about it. I wouldn't be surprised if she's thrown it in the trash."

My eyes widen as she places her hand on top of mine. "I'm so sorry, Mason. For all of it." I turn my hand over and slowly lace my fingers between hers, sending sparks of electricity throughout my entire body. "It's going to find its way back to you," she says.

"I hope so."

We sit in silence for what feels like hours. I close my eyes and try to soak in everything to do with this moment. Everything to do with her. "I could get used to this," I tell her.

"What? Not having to listen to me talk?

"No way, your voice is my favorite sound."

"I'm still not putting the nurse's uniform back on."

I laugh. "I could get used to holding your hand. I could probably get used to dating you as well."

"Oh, you could *probably* get used to it?"

"I could *definitely* get used to it."

"Well maybe you should slow down a little, Romeo. This is for charity, remember?"

"I remember. But a date is still a date."

"That's true."

"Tell me Sophia…do you kiss on the first date?"

She laughs. "No, I don't."

"When do you?"

"It depends on who I'm dating but I think the third date seems pretty reasonable."

"Got it." She's about to say something else but gets interrupted by the sound of three loud beeps and then - *"The sun is expected to set in approximately five minutes."*

Her eyes widen as she quickly lets go of my hand. "What the hell was that? I thought somebody else was in the room with us."

"I'm sorry. It was my AI."

"Your what?"

"Artificial intelligence. I forgot to switch her off."

She raises an eyebrow. "*Her?*"

"Yes. Suri."

"Oh, you mean Siri? Like on my iPhone?"

"No, I mean Suri. As in, Siri's younger sister."

"You swapped Siri for a younger model who just so happens to be her own sister? You bastard!"

"I couldn't say no. She's ridiculously intelligent."

"She's ridiculously creepy. *And* she interrupted our conversation."

"Some notifications are set to automatic. She can respond to thousands of commands."

"Yeah well there are plenty of things she can't do."

"Like what?"

"Lots of things. Physical things."

I grin. "Are you jealous of my AI, Sophia?"

She huffs. "Of course not. That's just ridiculous."

"Suri, play us a song." I laugh when Marvin Gaye's *Sexual Healing* starts to play. "I swear I didn't program her to do that. It's on shuffle."

"Pfft. What is she, your wingman? Or should that be your wingrobot? I don't like her."

"Suri, stop the music and pay Sophia a compliment."

"Sophia, you are the most beautiful human I have ever seen."

I laugh. "Oh, thanks a lot."

"Okay, maybe I like her a little bit more now." She whispers, "Can she actually see things?"

"No. She's just sucking up to you because you called her creepy. Suri, power down." I stand up and extend my hand. "Come on, I don't want us to miss the sunset." She uncurls herself then takes my hand. "Yep," I say. "I could definitely get used to this." I lead her over to the balcony and slide open the door. She gasps as the San Francisco skyline explodes in front of us. I gesture for her to step out first. "After you." She walks straight over to the edge of the balcony. "Now do you see why I'm so greedy?"

"Yes. I never want to leave."

"You don't have to." I mean it.

"It's so beautiful," she whispers.

"The most beautiful thing I have ever seen," I reply, my eyes fixed firmly on her.

"It doesn't look real. It looks like a painting or something out of a movie."

I laugh. "What, like somebody has CGI'd the sunset in?"

"Exactly."

"Okay then. So if we were in a movie right now, what would happen next?"

She frowns as she ponders the question. I love how she takes the time to properly think about it, as though it requires a serious answer. "I guess it depends on what genre it is."

"What genre would you want it to be?"

She grins. "We're standing in front of the most spectacular sunset I have ever seen. It has to be a romance movie."

"So no zombies?"

"Definitely no zombies."

"Okay, so it's a romance movie and we're standing in front of the most spectacular sunset that *either* of us has ever seen. What would happen next?"

"You tell me, Mason."

"I'd probably look straight into your eyes and tell you that the sunset pales in comparison to your beauty."

She nods in approval. "Very good. Cheesy, but good. Then what?"

I slowly reach out with my free hand. "And then I would tuck this loose strand of hair behind your ear." Her breath catches as my finger brushes against her skin.

She laughs nervously. "It looks like somebody has been watching far too many romance movies."

I grin. "All in the name of research."

"What would happen next, Mr Director?"

"I'd tell you that I can't stop thinking about you and the way your body felt under mine."

She grips my hand a little tighter. "Then what?"

"Then there would be a flashback to two nights ago. It would show me on top of you, our lips so close I can almost taste you. It would show you bucking your hips, desperate to feel every inch of me. It would show the desire in your eyes as you moan in frustration."

"Carry on," she says, her voice breathy, eyes glazed.

"Then it would cut back to the present. I would tell you that I can't wait until I'm on top of you again. I would tell you that next time, I won't be getting off. I would ask if you remember telling me how horny you were."

"I remember," she whispers.

"I would ask if it was the truth or if it was the alcohol talking."

"It was the truth."

"I would ask if you remember telling me that you can't hold out for much longer."

"I remember."

"Tell me what happens next, Sophia."

She closes her eyes. "I…I'm not…I think I should go."

"Is that what you want?"

"No."

"Then stay. Talk to me. What's on your mind?"

She sighs. "We need to wait."

"Until what?"

"Emily."

"We're getting divorced. You know the situation."

"You're right, I do. There's a line and once we cross it…"

"What?" I interrupt. "What will happen?"

"People could get hurt."

"Are you talking about Emily again because I've already told you…"

"No, I'm not talking about Emily."

"Then who? I would never hurt you."

Her eyes fill with tears. "I know you wouldn't."

"So who are you talking about?"

"It's complicated."

"Then let me uncomplicate it."

Chapter Sixty Seven

Sophia

He leans in and suddenly everything turns to slow motion. "Mason…" He stops in an instant. He looks at me with honest, genuine, desire-filled eyes. "I don't know if I can do this." I'm already in deep water. I already feel too much for him. If we take the next step, it would be so much harder when he eventually finds out about me and never wants to see me again. I let go of his hand. "I'm sorry, I can't do this." I turn around and walk away from him. Away from temptation.

"Sophia, wait!" I don't stop. I walk straight over to the front door. I need to get out of here before I give in to my desires and let my emotions get the better of me. "Sophia, please stay and talk to me."

"I'm sorry," I tell him again as I open the door and rush over to the elevator which brought me up here. I push the button and watch as it turns green. "Come on," I mumble and press it a few more times. "Come on, come on, come on!" I need to get out of here ASAP. I don't trust myself around him anymore. Why the hell is the elevator taking so goddamn long? I look around for the fire exit just as Mason appears, bag in hand. "You forgot this." I swallow hard. Why did he have to come after me? Every single part of me, from the top of my head to the tips of my toes, is consumed by him. My mind, my body and my soul craves Mason Hunter. "Please come back inside," he says. "I want to understand you. Please come and talk to me."

The elevator doors finally open behind me. My heart is pounding and my hands are shaking as I try to decide what to do. I walk backwards and sigh, disappointed in myself and my decision. Disappointed in the whole situation. "I don't know what to say. I'm sorry." I step inside and push the button to take me down to the lobby.

"What are you running from Sophia?" he asks as he walks towards me.

"Myself. This isn't about you."

He laughs. "Are you really using the 'it's not you, it's me' line right now? We haven't even finished our first date and you're already breaking up with me."

The doors start to close. "It's not like that. I *want* to…"

He holds his arm out. "Then what's stopping you?" The doors beep as they open again.

"Emily." Shit, what am I doing? I can feel the truth bubbling up inside of me. I could tell him everything right here and now but by telling him the truth, I would also have to tell him goodbye and I'm definitely not ready for that.

"If it were up to me, we would have gotten divorced three months ago. I haven't served the papers yet out of courtesy, no other reason. I'll serve them right now if you want me to."

"It's not about that."

"You're right, it's not. This is about *us*. Just you and me. I know you feel what I feel. Forget about everybody else and tell me what you want." He drops my bag when the doors start to close again and steps inside. "If you don't want this, if you truly don't want me, then I'll walk away. Just tell me what you want." The doors close and we start to descend. His gaze is so intense that in this moment, nothing else matters. Nothing else *exists*. This is the moment I've been dreading but always knew would come. "Tell me what you *want*, Sophia."

"I want you," I whisper.

"Say it again."

"I want *you*."

He hits the emergency stop button and we shudder to a halt. He closes the gap between us and walks us backwards until I'm pressed up against the wall. He takes my face in both of his hands and looks apprehensive as he leans in, carefully watching my reaction, as though he's waiting for me to stop him again. But I don't. Not this time. Whether it's right or wrong, I can't deny how much I want him. As soon as our lips meet, he lets go of any reservations. He kisses me like he owns me, and in this moment, he does.

The next few minutes pass in a blur.

He kisses my neck.

I moan in delight.

His hands travel up my T-shirt.

My nipples harden.

His eyes go wide.

I groan when his lips leave mine.

He smirks as he takes my nipple into his mouth.

I wonder if he can feel how fast my heart is beating.

He sucks harder.

I fist his hair.

He gently bites down.

My legs turn to jelly.

His hands grab my ass as he lifts me up.

My legs wrap around his waist.

His hard cock presses into my stomach.

I'm desperate for him.

"I have a new favorite sound," he tells me as his eyes burn into mine. "Your heartbeat." He bends his knees and carefully places me down on the floor. He looks at me for a long moment before kissing me. Hard. Fast. Gentle. Slow. Every possible way that a person can be kissed.

He pulls away and works his way down my body, trailing kisses in his wake. I feel like I'm going to explode with anticipation as he reaches my stomach. Luckily, he doesn't keep me waiting too long and moves further south. He keeps his eyes locked on mine as his mouth finds its intended target. He strokes and kisses me through my yoga pants and *oh my god*, if it feels this good through clothes then how will it feel on my bare skin? I throw my head back and moan when he closes his mouth around me and begins to suck. He laughs which sends little vibrations through me, resulting in
even more pleasure. I raise my hips and ride his mouth until I feel the pressure starting to build. "Take my fucking pants off, Mason."

"Yes, Ma'am." He takes off my shoes then slips a hand into my waistline. He strokes me before pulling both layers down in one go. His eyes light up as he growls. "I need to taste you."

"Then what are you waiting for?" He smirks before burying his head between my thighs. I shout out in pure ecstasy when his skilled fingers and tongue work in unison. It doesn't take long before I'm bucking my hips and calling out his name as the world explodes around me. He milks every last shudder out of me and then slows the pace. "What are you doing?" I ask after about half a minute when it becomes obvious that he has no intention of stopping. It feels one hundred times more sensitive than it did a few minutes ago and I squirm around, which causes his stubble to rub up against me. He chuckles as his fingers carry on in a slow and steady rhythm. He gently pushes down on my lower stomach as his fingers speed up.

"What does it look like I'm doing? I'm making you come." That's all it takes to spark my second orgasm. I call out his name as I ride the waves which ebb and flow. He watches me in awe then sits up and licks his lips with a devilish grin on his face. It's almost enough to make me have orgasm number three. I know without a doubt that I will never, ever, be the same person after tonight. I will forever crave his touch. "You taste just as delicious as I'd imagined."

I lean up on my elbows. "Is it my turn to taste you now?"

"I think that's the greatest question anybody has ever asked me." I sit up and crawl over to him. He takes hold of my face and kisses me slowly. "I could definitely get used to *this*. In fact, I think I'm already used to it."

I laugh. "Stand up."

He does as I ask. "I like your bossy side. I'm not used to taking orders." I pause for a moment and look up at the magnificent man standing in front of me. My heart shatters at the fact that I will never be able to do this again. Why did I have to develop feelings for the one person who is off limits? I reach up and undo the button on his jeans just as a man's voice fills the elevator. "Mr Hunter, are you in there, sir?"

I panic and grab my underwear. "That's not another AI, is it?" I whisper as I quickly yank them back on.

He laughs and shakes his head in answer. "Yes, I'm in here."

"It's Darnell from maintenance."

"Hello Darnell."

"Are you okay, sir? We've had a problem with the hotel servers and we've just been alerted that the emergency stop button was engaged ten minutes ago. Is there an emergency?" My cheeks heat in embarrassment as I put my pants and shoes back on.

"No. I'm fine. I was just…taking care of something." His eyes dance with amusement.

"In that case, I'm sorry for interrupting. For some reason, we can't access the live stream for the camera in there." My eyes widen as I look around. "It's running about half an hour behind and it's not letting us skip to present time. IT are working on it now."

"I'm fine. Tell IT not to worry."

"I will. Enjoy your evening, sir."

"You too."

"You didn't tell me there were cameras in here," I say.

He holds his hands up. "I'm sorry. It didn't even cross my mind. I got a little carried away."

We both did. I flatten my hair. "What happens in twenty minutes when the footage is all caught up?"

"I won't let it." He presses the stop button again. The mechanics begin to whir and we start to move a few seconds later.

"But what if somebody sees us?" I groan as I'm filled with regret. How could I have been so stupid? I listened to my heart instead of my head and now I've
put us both in jeopardy. "What if they leak it?"

"Sophia, nobody will see it. I promise." He wraps his

arms around me and pulls me closer to him. "Do you want to wait in the bar while I take care of it or go back up to the penthouse?"

I stiffen. "Um, I think I'll just go home."

He frowns. "Oh. Oh, okay. Are you sure?"

"Yeah, I'm getting tired."

"You can spend the night here, if you want? We could even stay in separate rooms."

"Lori doesn't like to be alone in the house at night."

He peers down at me. "Are you okay?"

I nod, trying to keep a poker face. "Of course I am."

He kisses me softly. "Thank you for tonight. It was the best first date I have ever had. In fact, it was one of the best *nights* I've ever had."

"So much for not kissing on the first date, huh? Now you have real life elevator porn," I joke, trying to keep the mood light. Anything to stop my real emotions from showing.

"When can I see you again?"

"I don't know."

"I want to take you out to dinner. We can slow things down if you would prefer."

"I'll call you."

He nods and kisses me on the forehead right before the elevator doors start to open. "I'll be thinking about you."

"I'll be thinking about you too," I reply in an almost whisper.

"Will you let Charlie drive you home?" he asks as we step out of the elevator.

"No, it's fine. I'll walk." I smile. "I could use some fresh air." He laughs softly. "Goodbye, Mason."

"Until next time, Sophia."

I manage to make it out of the hotel before the tears start to fall. My heart aches at the realization that very soon, there won't be a next time.

Chapter Sixty Eight

Mason

Half an hour later, I head back up to the penthouse after making sure that all of the footage got wiped. Nobody even questioned the order – one of the perks of being the boss. I'd be lying if I said that I wasn't tempted to keep a copy for my own personal use. But if I get my own way, I won't need to watch a recording of us because I'll have the real thing. I get hard thinking about the way she called out my name as she came all over my fingers and mouth. It was beyond anything I could have ever imagined and even though we were interrupted, I got my own pleasure from pleasuring her.

I feel like after tonight, our connection runs even deeper and I'm determined to get her to open up to me. I'll do whatever I can to help her through her struggles.

I step out of the elevator and get a shock when I see Buzz leaning against the front door, Sophia's bag at his feet. "There you are," he says.

"Here I am," I reply as I walk over to him.

"Where were you?"

I pull the keycard out of my pocket and unlock the door. "I went to see IT. They have a problem with the servers."

He yawns. "I stopped listening as soon as you said IT."

"How long have you been here?" I ask as he follows me inside.

"About fifteen minutes. Eric told me that you were in the building so I just thought I'd wait."

"You should have called first."

"I never call first."

I take the bag off of him. "Well maybe you should. What if I was busy?"

"*Were* you busy?"

"No but I could have been."

He narrows his eyes and looks around the room. "Why are all of the blinds closed?"

"Because I've had my eye surgery."

"I thought your surgery was next week."

"No, it was this morning."

"Are you sure?"

"Yes, Buzz. I'm pretty sure somebody sliced open my corneas this morning."

"You're acting strange."

I laugh. "I'm acting strange? *You're* acting strange. Did you come here for a reason or are you just going to question me?"

"What's in the bag?"

"So you're just going to question me."

"Whose bag is it?"

"Mine."

"Why did you leave it outside?"

"I forgot that I put it down. I was just coming back up to get it."

"What's inside?"

"Stuff."

"What kind of stuff?"

"Jesus. Just stuff. Snacks and a change of clothes. I was going to stay over at Indie's. She broke up with Ted Spielberg."

"Who?"

"The movie director."

"Is he related to Stephen Spielberg?"

"No, it's just a joke."

He perches on the edge of the sofa. "So let me get this straight. This is *your* bag and you were going to stay over at your sister's house?"

"Yep."

"Then why the fuck has it got a nurse's uniform inside? You better start talking."

I laugh. Why does he have to stick his nose into everything? "You looked in the bag?"

"No, it was just a lucky guess. Of course I looked. It was just left outside your door. What if there was a bomb inside? I was trying to help. You should be thanking me."

"Thanks for trying to help but if there was a bomb inside, you probably would have set it off by handling it. You should have called me before looking."

"You're only saying that because of the kinky shit inside. Are you going to tell me the truth or do I need to report you for incest?"

"You're blowing it out of proportion. It's just a dumb costume."

"What about the book?"

"What about it?"

"I read some of it to pass the time. It's pure filth."

I raise my eyebrow. Sophia reads erotica? I didn't think it was possible to want her any more than I already do. "It is?"

"Yes. Explain."

"I can't believe that you actually read something other than a playboy magazine."

"I also have to read your boring ass emails every day at work. Now stop trying to avoid the question and tell me what's going on."

I sigh. "Fine. It's not my bag."

"Okay. This is the part where you tell me whose it is."

"It's a friend's. She came to visit earlier and left it by accident."

A huge shit eating grin takes over his face. "And she brought a nurse's uniform with her?"

"No, she didn't bring it…she was wearing it."

His eyes nearly pop out of his head. "Even better! Did you get laid?"

"No."

"Don't lie."

"I'm not."

"Which friend was it? I thought I was your only friend. Wait a minute…was it Sophia?"

"No."

"I had phone sex with Lori about an hour ago and she

mentioned that she was home alone."

"So?"

"So she was home alone because Sophia was at your apartment wearing a nurse's uniform!"

"She could have been anywhere."

"She could have been but she wasn't. How was the sex?"

"I've already told you, we didn't have sex."

"Whatever. A woman shows up dressed as a hot nurse and you don't have sex? You really think I'm going to believe that?"

"Believe what you want but it's the truth."

"So then how did the costume end up in the bag?"

"She got changed into some other clothes."

"So she got naked in your apartment."

I'd never actually thought about it that way. Great, now I'm horny again. "Remind me why you're here."

"To hang out. I need to get my mind off of Lori's secret file. Even the phone sex didn't work." His eyes turn sad. "And because it's the anniversary tomorrow."

The anniversary of his brother's death. I nod. "I was going to ask if you wanted to go somewhere or do something."

"I'm having breakfast with my family and lunch with Lori but I'm pretty sure I'll want to get crazy drunk at night."

"You know I'm here for you, brother. Whatever you need, just ask."

"Thanks, man. Do you really mean that?"

"Of course I do."

"Okay then, in that case, I need you to tell me what the sex was like with Sophia. Was it as good as you'd imagined?"

I roll my eyes and walk out of the room. "You told me to ask!" he shouts after me.

Chapter Sixty Nine
Sophia

"Lor?" I shout as I lock the front door behind me.

"I'm in here," she shouts from her bedroom. I walk in to find her crouched down on the floor taking photos of some lipstick.

"What are you doing?"

"Buzz asked me to send him some nudes. Who am I to say no?"

I'm about to try and make a joke when out of nowhere, I burst into tears. I've been trying my hardest to stay strong over the past few weeks but after tonight, it's all become too much. Her eyes fill with worry. "Oh, sweetie." She leads me over to her bed. "Shhhh, it's okay. Sit down and tell me what happened."

"I'm a terrible person," I tell her.

"Of course you're not."

"We kissed." She gasps then slaps a hand over her mouth. "See, even you think I'm a terrible person."

"No I don't. I'm just shocked."

"Well there's more. One thing led to another."

"And?"

"And he went down on me."

Her eyes widen. "And there's me thinking that you've told him the truth."

I bury my head in my hands. "That's what I should have done. I should have come clean. He's going to find out soon enough anyway so why not tonight?"

"He might not."

"If Emily doesn't tell him then I will. I couldn't live with a secret like that. It's already killing me after a few weeks."

"I'm sure he will understand when you explain the whole situation to him. You have genuine feelings for each other."

"I doubt it. He's huge on honesty and trust. I've lied to

him and kept secrets."

"But you haven't trapped him."

I raise my eyebrow. "Haven't I?"

"Of course you haven't. You might have been hired by Emily but you haven't helped her at all. You haven't provided her with one piece of information, despite her pressurizing you. You could have taken photos of him a week or two ago and been done with it. You could have called Emily after tonight but you haven't. Sure, you've gotten close to him but you certainly haven't trapped him."

"He's going to hate me. I shouldn't have let it turn physical."

"Sometimes you can't help it. And even when he does find out, somehow I don't think that he's going to regret making it to third base with you." She grins. "How was it?"

I groan. "Mind-blowing. I never wanted it to end."

"I knew it," she replies excitedly. "When you're ready to talk about it, I need details." I roll my eyes at her. "I'm only joking…kind of."

"Now what am I supposed to do?"

"That's for you to decide but I think it would be a shame to walk away. You're great together."

"It doesn't matter if we're great together. We all know how this is going to end. Mason isn't my happily ever after."

"Who says it needs to end?"

"Everything comes to an end. He won't want anything to do with me when he finds out."

"That's for him to decide. You only have a couple of weeks left then you can sit him down and explain everything."

"I don't think I'm strong enough to be around him anymore. It's not fair on either of us. I'm going to do more harm than good."

"What are you saying?"

"I'm saying that I need to put an end to this, once and for all. It's going to kill me saying goodbye but I can't carry on like this. If there's a chance that Mason will hate me a little less by ending things sooner rather than later then I need to at least try."

"Are you going to tell him?"

"Yes, but I need to talk to Emily first."

Chapter Seventy
Mason

I fall to sleep thinking about her.

I wake up thinking about her.

I think about her when I'm in the shower.

I think about her when I'm eating my breakfast.

I think about her when I'm getting dressed.

I don't just think about her when I step into the elevator. My mind is *bombarded* with images of her. How the hell am I supposed to ride an elevator like a normal person ever again after last night? We joke about elevator porn but now I can't even look at one without getting hard. I pull out my cell and call her. It rings and rings and just when I think it's about to go to voicemail, she answers. "Hello?"

"Guess where I am?" I ask.

"Um, it's Monday morning so I'm guessing you're at work."

"No. I'm in the elevator. Well, I'm just about to get out of it actually." She laughs softly. "I wish you were here."

"What, so Darnell could spy on us?"

"I'm thinking of getting the camera taken out."

"That's very presumptuous of you, Mason."

"No, it's wishful thinking," I reply as I head to the lobby. "How are you feeling today?"

"I'm fine." She doesn't sound very convincing.

"Are you sure?"

"Yeah, I'm just tired," she says, which reassures me a little. "I didn't get much sleep last night."

I smile. "Neither did I. What are your plans for today?"

"I'm working."

I wave at Eric then nod in thanks when he opens the door for me. "What about lunch?"

"I'm having lunch with Lori today."

I get a sinking feeling in my stomach. Didn't Buzz tell me that he was having lunch with Lori today? "Are you going anywhere nice?"

"I'm not sure. I think Lori has booked a table at some Italian place."

"Well I hope you have a nice time." I pat Charlie on the back as he opens the car door for me. "I'd ask you to dinner but I've already made plans with Buzz."

"It's fine. I'm busy tonight anyway. I'm having a *Gilmore Girls* marathon."

"I have no idea what you just said. Give me more girls?"

She giggles. "No, Mason. That sounds naughty. *Gilmore girls* is a TV show. You should watch it."

"Maybe we could watch it together some time."

"Maybe."

I can tell that something's on her mind but I don't want to push too much. I hope she's not having any regrets about yesterday. Maybe she's worried about the CCTV. "I took care of the camera footage, by the way. I wiped it all. You have nothing to worry about."

"Good. I don't want to make things any more difficult." I can't help but analyze her choice of words. *'Any more* difficult'. I wasn't aware that things *were* difficult. Sure, we're not in an ideal situation but when we're together, it comes so easy. It would be so easy for me to love her. Maybe she can't get past the fact that I'm still married and that Emily is still in my life whether I like it or not. Disappointment floods through me.

"I meant what I said yesterday, Sophia. We can take things slow. I just want to spend more time with you and get to know you better. I would love to take you out to dinner and I still owe you that movie, remember?"

"Oh yeah, I forgot about that."

"I didn't." I hesitate before speaking my mind. "Please don't shut me out. I think we could be on to a good thing here."

She pauses. "I'm trying my best to process everything."

"That's all I can ask of you."

"In the end, I've got to do what's best for me."

"I understand. If you need some time or space, just let me know."

She sighs. "Thank you. I should go. Goodbye, Mason."

"Until next time, Sophia."

I just pray that there is one.

"We're going drinking," Buzz announces when he shows up at my door that evening with a bottle of liquor in each hand. "And I'm not taking no for an answer."

I laugh. "Can I be the designated driver?"

"No. That excuse doesn't work when you've got your own goddamn chauffer. Plus, I don't want you judging my bad choices."

"So you want me to make them with you instead?"

"Hell yeah!" He takes two glasses out of the cupboard and starts to pour.

"Why don't we just stay in and order a take out?"

"Because we're not an old married couple."

"But why do we need to go out? You're already drunk."

"I'm not drunk enough. I want to feel completely numb."

"Why don't we go down to the hotel bar?"

"Because I don't want to embarrass you or get fired."

"You know you can talk to me, don't you? You don't have to drink your problems away."

"I don't want to talk about it. I don't even want to think about it." He takes a sip and hands me the other glass. "Hence the alcohol."

Whether I agree with it or not, if getting crazy drunk is going to help Buzz get through tonight then I'm all in. "Okay. Where are we going?"

"That's more like it."

"Maybe we should invite Sophia and Lori."

He laughs. "Oh. I haven't told you yet, have I? I spoke to Lori about the file."

"When?"

"Today at lunch."

Lunch. My heart sinks. Why did Sophia lie to me? "Was it just you and her?"

"Yes, until she walked out."

"What happened?" I ask Buzz, trying to force my own problems to the back of my mind.

"She never wants to see me again."

"Did she actually say that?"

"Yeah, right before she told me to delete her number."

I take a drink. "Well I wasn't expecting that. Did you at least find out why she had the file?"

"No, she wouldn't tell me anything."

"She's probably just upset."

He groans in frustration. "This is why I don't do relationships. My head is fucked. I don't even know why I tried. I'm not a relationship kind of guy. I'm always going to be the one night stand or maybe one day I'll get promoted to fuck buddy."

"Don't say that."

"It's true. I told her that I was finally ready to commit and she ended it. I should have known it was too good to be true."

"I'm sorry, brother. Maybe she just needs some time."

"She made it very clear that she can't be in a relationship with me. What does that even mean? She *can't*. Can't or won't?"

"If it's meant to be…"

"Don't start with all of your fate and destiny bullshit," he interrupts. "If it was *meant to be* then Lori would be my girlfriend right now but instead I'm single as fuck. I'm practically a born again virgin. Anyway, I don't want to talk about it anymore. Tell me what's been happening with you. When I listen to your problems, it always makes me feel better about my own."

"Oh, thanks."

He laughs. "You know what I mean."

"There's not much to report…oh, just that I think I'm falling in love with Sophia."

"What the fuck, man?"

"Exactly. I can't stop thinking about her. Everything I see or do reminds me of her. I can't even listen to the radio without somehow finding a way to relate all of the song lyrics to her. It's driving me crazy."

"Woah, you're obsessed. Have you told her how you feel?"

"No and I'm not going to. Not yet. For whatever reason, she seems to have this huge wall up. I don't want to scare her off."

"Dude, you need to knock that motherfucking wall down. You deserve to be happy."

"I know. I'm going to try."

"Don't just try. *Do it.*"

I hold my glass up. "To knocking down walls."

He grins and chinks his glass with mine. "Does that mean I'm allowed to call you Yankee now?"

Chapter Seventy One
Sophia

"*Gilmore Girls*!" Lori shouts when she arrives home from her latest trap. She flops down beside me. "I can't believe you're watching it without me."

"I'm sorry. I've saved *Pretty Little Liars* to watch with you."

"In that case, I forgive you." She takes off her jacket.

"What does chapter fifty five mean?" I ask, eyeing her T-shirt.

"*A Court of Mist and Fury*. If you know, you know."

I laugh. "I *don't* know. How's your day been?"

"Crap. What about yours?"

"Crap."

"Do you want to talk about it?"

"Not really. Do you?"

She laughs. "Not really."

"If you change your mind, you know where I am."

"Same."

We spend the next half hour watching *Gilmore Girls* in silence until my phone rings. My stomach flips at the thought of it being Mason. I'm half relieved, half disappointed when I see Kristen's name. "It's Kristen," I tell Lori. "She's probably checking up on me because I still haven't met Emily's demands."

"When are you planning on visiting her?"

"Tomorrow." I sigh. "Hello Kristen. Tell Emily that I don't have any updates for her."

"This isn't about Emily. I need to ask you a really big favor."

"Okay?"

"I'm sorry to do this but I double booked Jenna and all of the other girls are on traps or unavailable."

I groan. "You want me to go on a trap?"

"Will you?"

"Do I have a choice?"

"Of course you do. I'll just have to reschedule it. The girlfriend is pretty desperate though. Her fiancé called their wedding off."

"When and where?"

"Thank you, thank you, thank you! You need to be at Anderson's in an hour."

"An hour? Thanks for the notice."

"I'm sorry. His name is Scotty. I'll text you a photo."

"Is it a full trap?"

"No, just a half. I'm sure you'll be home after an hour or two. He sounds like a real dick."

"Oh, great."

"Aww, come on. Just treat it as a bit of practice. I don't want my best girl getting rusty now, do I?"

"I've already agreed to it, you don't have to sweet talk me."

She laughs. "You're a star. Check in with me afterwards."

"Do you want me to go instead?" Lori asks as soon as I hang up.

"Nah, you've only just got back from one. Plus, I could use the distraction."

"Do you even remember what to do?"

I laugh. "Of course I do."

So much for a quiet night in.

An hour later, I walk into Anderson's wearing one of my favorite red dresses. The thought of flirting with someone other than Mason feels wrong, like I'm cheating on him, which I know is completely messed up. Maybe tonight is what I need to remind me that there's a life outside of the Mason Hunter bubble.

I approach the bar and realize that I haven't even looked at Kristen's text because I've been in such a rush. I pull my cell out of my purse and open up the text just as somebody calls my name. I turn around and come face to face with Scott Parker. Scott Parker who cheated on me and broke my heart. Scott Parker whose photograph is now on my phone screen.

Fuck. I've been hired to trap my ex.

"I thought it was you," he says as he looks me up and down. "You look incredible."

I don't know what to say. The last time I saw him, he was inside another woman. "It's been a long time," I reply, wondering if the girlfriend who hired me is the same one he cheated on me with. Karma's a bitch.

"Too long," he replies.

Not long enough more like. I used to think that Scott Parker was the most handsome man I had ever laid eyes on but now he just looks like a little boy compared to Mason. "Are you alone?" he asks.

"Yes." I gesture to my cell as I place it back inside my purse. "I was supposed to be meeting a friend but she's just cancelled."

He smirks which pisses me off more than it probably should. "Good thing I'm here then, isn't it? What a coincidence."

If you mean a planned coincidence which has been paid for by your fiancée, then yes. "What about you?" I ask. "Who are you here with?"

"Just a couple of my work buddies. Do you want to join us?"

Time to get to work. "Maybe later. I'd rather us have some time alone. We have a lot of catching up to do."

His eyes fall to my chest. "We do. You're a woman now."

I laugh. "And I wasn't before?"

"You know what I mean. You were just a girl back then. Now…your curves…wow. I was an idiot for what I did to you."

"Yes, you were."

"If only I could turn back time."

Then you still would have cheated on me. "It's all in the past."

"You know, my dad still has your poster framed above his fireplace."

"What poster?"

"The one of my face on a leopard's body."

"It's a cheetah's body. You know, because you *cheated* on me."

"Ohhhh, I get it now. I always wondered what that was all about." I have to stop myself from rolling my eyes. "Well my dad framed it to remind me of what I lost and to make me think twice before disrespecting another woman."

Too bad it's hanging up at his dad's house and not his own. "I always liked your dad."

"He always liked you too. I think he probably liked you more than he liked me."

"And did you learn your lesson?"

"Of course I did. I was really hurt by it all. It took me a long time to get over."

He was hurt? "So are you dating anybody?"

He hesitates and I fully expect him to lie to me but instead he sighs. "Yes. We're going through a rough patch but I really want to make it work." I'm caught off guard by his honesty. "She wants to get married but I'm not ready. She's a few years older than me. I keep reminding her that I'm only twenty four."

"And? What exactly are you waiting for? What's going to be different in five or even ten years time?"

"I'm not exactly sure."

"Do you love her?"

"Yes, I do."

"Can you live without her?"

"I wouldn't want to."

"Then what's the problem?"

"I'm scared."

"Of what?"

"Of losing her like I lost you."

275

You only lost me because you couldn't keep your dick in your pants. "You can't let the past ruin your future. It's different this time. You've grown up since then. Plus, your dad still has my poster on his wall to stop you from doing anything stupid."

"True."

"But please don't marry her if you think you might hurt her."

"I wouldn't…I won't." He smiles. "Thank you for being so wonderful, Sophia. I'm glad we ran into each other today." He pulls me into a hug and finally after two years, I get the closure that I hadn't even realized I needed.

"You should go and talk to her," I say as I pull away. "Just be honest with her about everything."

"You're right." He laughs. "Hey, where do I claim my reward?"

"Huh?"

"On the poster you put that you'd give a million dollars to the person who could find my respect for women…" I stop listening to him when I glance over his shoulder and see a familiar pair of eyes watching me.

Chapter Seventy Two

Mason

I stop breathing when he wraps his arms around her. It looks familiar, like they've done it hundreds of times before. My adrenaline kicks in and I want to shout at him to get off of her. That's the second time she has lied to me today. She lied about going to lunch with Lori and she lied about staying home tonight.

Buzz claps me on the shoulder. "Dude, who the fuck is that?"

"I'm about to find out."

"Want me to come with?"

"Nah, I've got this. Go and get us a drink."

He laughs. "You sure? Don't do anything stupid."

I ignore him and head in their direction. Sophia's eyes go wide when she spots me. "I know I said we could take things slow but this isn't what I had in mind."

She laughs nervously. "Are you stalking me?" One thing I've noticed is that she's always making jokes when she's uncomfortable.

"Who's your friend?" I ask, keeping my eyes on hers.

"I'm Scott," he says, holding his hand out. "Parker," he adds just as I'm about to shake his hand. I stop and instead fold my arms across my chest.

You have got to be kidding me. What the hell is she doing with her ex? Maybe that's why her walls have been up. Maybe she's still seeing him. I raise my eyebrow at her. "So when you said you were having a *Gilmore Girls* marathon, what you actually meant was Netflix and chill?"

"No," she replies, looking hurt and offended.

"Well I just came over to say hello. Enjoy the rest of your evening." I turn around and walk straight out of the bar. I can't be in there with them.

A few seconds later the door opens and I sense her before I see her. "Mason?"

"You got dressed up for him."

277

"No. I don't dress for men. I only dress for myself."

"You look way too beautiful to be in this crappy bar. You don't belong here." I become hypnotised by the heavy rise and fall of her chest.

"Then where do I belong?"

"We both know the answer to that. You belong with me."

She shakes her head. "You've been drinking."

"I've had three measly glasses of Jack Daniels. Besides, what was it that you said to me last week? I'm only saying what I think when I'm sober."

"Maybe we should talk in the morning."

"Are you getting back together with him?"

"What? No!"

"So then what are you doing here with him?"

"He's getting married. I think he…"

"Realized that he was making the biggest mistake of his life by not marrying you?"

"No. I think he needed closure."

"Well you shouldn't have given it to him. He doesn't deserve even one minute of your time."

"I think maybe *I* needed closure too."

"You mean you didn't get it when you walked in on him fucking another woman?"

She raises her eyebrow. "No, obviously I didn't. Just like you didn't get it when you found out that your wife was fucking somebody else. It doesn't always work like that and you know it."

"Fuck, I'm sorry. I shouldn't have said that. I don't want to see you with anybody else. I just want to make you happy."

"You already do," she whispers. "But I don't think I can return the favor."

"That's bullshit. I haven't been this happy in years, Sophia. Please don't shut me out. Why did you lie about staying home tonight?"

"I didn't lie. I got a call about an hour ago. It was a last

278

minute thing."

"And what about lunch time?"

"What about it?" she asks nervously.

"Why did you lie about going for lunch with Lori?"

She sighs. "I'm sorry. I didn't want to say no and hurt your feelings. I needed some space to sort my head out and think about what I really wanted."

"And what is it that you want, Sophia?"

"I think you already know."

"I know what *I* want. Tell me what *you* want."

She shrugs. "Does it really matter?"

"Of course it matters."

"Why? We can't always have what we want."

I close the gap between us. "You can have me, if that's what you want."

"Mason…"

"In fact, you *already* have me."

She looks over my shoulder. "There are people watching us."

"I don't care anymore."

"You won't be saying that when we're front page news tomorrow."

"Yes, I will be. I'm done with the lies. I just want to be honest from here on out."

Her shoulders slump. "We can't do this here."

I point to Charlie who is parked up across the street. "Let's talk in the car. Or Charlie could drive us somewhere if you'd prefer."

"I really don't have that much to say, Mason."

"Then we won't do much talking."

She raises her eyebrow just as her douchebag ex appears behind her. "Is everything okay here?"

"Everything is fine," I reply bluntly, keeping my eyes on Sophia.

"Soph, are you okay?"

Soph? I roll my eyes. The thought of her being in love with this guy makes me sick to my stomach. "Yes, we're fine.

You should go back inside."

"I know you," he says to me. "You're the hotel guy."

"I know you too. You're the cheater guy."

His eyes widen while Sophia looks half shocked, half amused. "I…we…that was a long time ago."

"Yeah well it still happened."

"Aren't you married?" he asks, looking from me to Sophia. "Where's your wife?"

"Aren't you engaged?" I shoot back. "Where's your fiancée?"

He ignores me. "Are you two friends or something?"

I hold my breath as I wait for her to answer. "Yes." I immediately want to know if she answered yes to us being friends or yes to us being something else. "Just go back inside, Scott. Or better yet, go home to your fiancée."

He pulls her into his arms while keeping his eyes locked with mine. "It was good to see you again, Soph." He strokes her back, intentionally goading me, which has the desired effect as my blood starts to boil.

Buzz appears next to me and narrows his eyes at them. "You okay, brother?"

"Perfect."

"Look after yourself," Scott says, looking at me one last time before walking away.

"Well he seemed like a massive dickhead," Buzz says. "Who is he?"

"My ex."

"Well that explains it."

"I hate that he calls you Soph," I tell her.

"Why?"

"It sounds too familiar. He never deserved you."

She shrugs. "Emily never deserved you."

"Please come for a drive with me."

"I don't think that's a good idea."

"Well how about I just give you a ride home instead?"

"What about Buzz?"

"I can come too, if that's what you're worried about,

Soph." I glare at him. "Jesus. I'm joking. I'll be fine, my buddy Jack is in there. I have more than one friend, unlike Mason." He winks at me. "I'll text you if we move on to a different bar."

I nod then lead Sophia over to the car. I gesture for Charlie to stay in the driver's seat as I open the door for her. She climbs inside, and a true gentleman would look away but I don't feel like being a gentleman tonight. Her body always looks amazing but her skin-tight red dress and matching stilettos are destroying me. "Take us to Sophia's house, please Charlie," I tell him as I climb in after her. I slide closer to her then watch as she nervously smoothes her dress down. "Why did you think it would be a bad idea to go for a drive with me?"

"I didn't say it was a bad idea. I said I don't think it's a *good* idea."

"Isn't that the same thing?"

She sighs. "I turn into somebody else when I'm around you."

"How do you mean?"

"I'm usually rational and sensible."

I laugh. "Are you trying to say that I'm a bad influence?"

"Yes. I don't trust myself when I'm around you."

"What about your feelings for me? Do you trust them?"

"Yes, that's why it's a lethal combination."

I lean over and press the button to activate the privacy screen. "No offense, Charlie." A few seconds later, the screen is up and we're completely blocked off from the rest of the world.

She swallows hard. "Is that really necessary?"

I chuckle. "Charlie and Buzz have been known to gossip." I take hold of her hand. "It's pretty obvious that you've got a lot on your mind at the moment. I just want you to know that I'm here for you. I'm not going to push you but I'm also not going to back off unless you tell me to. I really like you, Sophia. I can be patient but all I ask in return is that you don't shut me out. I know this will be worth the wait."

"I'm pretty sure that I'm going to fuck this up before it's even started."

"It's already started."

"I'm scared, Mason."

"Don't be. Don't let the fear win. Just take a deep breath and know that everything you want is on the other side of it." A single tear rolls down her cheek and it breaks my heart. Before I even have time to think about what I'm doing, I lean in and kiss it away.

"Everything I want is right in front of me," she whispers.

My heart feels like it's going to hammer its way out of my chest as I lean in and gently kiss the corners of her mouth. "You know, the Buddhists say that if you meet someone and your heart pounds, your hands shake and your knees go weak then they're not the one for you. They say that when you meet your true love, you'll feel calm and at peace." I take her hand and place it against my chest. "I call bullshit. How can we ever be sure that we've met the one for us unless our hearts show us?"

She kisses me but this time there's nothing gentle about it. It's hard and fast. It's desperate and clumsy. It's rushed, as though our time is running out.

I pull her on top of me and she yanks her dress up so she can straddle me properly. She gasps at my rock hard erection then manoeuvres herself until it's right where she needs it to be. She kisses me again and starts to rock her hips back and forth. I push the straps of her dress down then pull her closer to me, taking a nipple into my mouth. The harder I suck, the more she moans. The more she moans, the harder I become. She's full on riding me now and it's causing enough friction to make me moan along with her. I switch to her other nipple as she reaches down and starts to unbutton my jeans. I take her face in my hands. "Are you sure?"

"Yes, I'm sure." She drops to her knees in front of me

and frees me from my jeans and boxer shorts. I almost come right there and then when I see the look of pure hunger in her eyes. I watch her every movement as she takes me into her mouth and slowly begins to move up and down. I fist her hair and keep my eyes locked on hers as she teases me with her tongue.

"Sophia. I want to be inside you." She laughs and takes me out of her mouth.

"You already are." She swirls her tongue around the tip of my cock and I'm not sure how much longer I can last.

"You know…what I…mean," I somehow manage to reply. She kisses me right on the tip then looks at me with those hungry eyes again as she climbs back on top of me. "I don't have a condom," I tell her.

"I'm clean. I have an IUD."

I nod. "We don't need any more children just yet, baby mama." She moves her panties to the side and takes hold of me. The anticipation is almost enough to make me explode as she leans up then slowly lowers herself on to me.

I moan and grip her hips when she takes my full length. "You are so beautiful," I tell her. She leans forward and kisses me as she increases the pace. I move my body in time with hers and before long, I start to feel a familiar build up. I pull her even closer to me and kiss every inch of her exposed skin. She closes her eyes and throws her head back as she rides me even faster. "Come for me, Sophia." As if waiting for my order, she moans then calls out my name. Her body goes limp and I find my own release as she rides the waves of hers. I wrap my arms around her as she places her head against my shoulder. "I wish we could do this every day," I say as I trace patterns against her arms and back.

"Yeah but maybe not in the car."

"I'm not fussy." She laughs and slowly climbs off of me. I button up my jeans and watch as she pulls her dress down and rearranges the straps. When she's finished, I pull her towards me and wrap my arms around her. She holds on tight, as though she never wants to let go, and if it was up to me, she wouldn't have to. I hadn't even noticed that the car had stopped. I stroke her hair and kiss her on the forehead. "It's all going to be okay."

She looks up at me. "I hope so."

"Take the risk or lose the chance."

She smiles but I can tell that she's still trapped in her own thoughts. "I guess this is the hard part."

"What is?"

"Saying goodbye." She kisses me one last time before reaching for the door handle. "Goodbye, Mason."

"Until next time, game changer."

She smiles but the last thing I see is the sadness in her eyes.

Chapter Seventy Three
Sophia

I open the door and jump when Lori shouts, "I knew it!"

I place my hand against my chest. "Jeez, you scared me."

"I knew it was Mason's car! Why were you with him?"

"He showed up at Anderson's."

"Was Buzz there? Wait, don't answer that. I'm not bothered."

"Guess who I…"

"Actually, just tell me. Was Buzz there?"

"Yes."

She nods. "Sorry, go on."

"Guess who I was hired to trap?"

"Was it finally Channing?"

"No. It was Scott Parker."

"Your douchebag ex Scott Parker?" I nod. "Woah, I hope you trapped that motherfucker."

"I didn't. He said he wants to make his relationship work. Apparently he called the wedding off because he's scared of fucking it up like he did with me."

"And you believed him?"

"I can't believe I'm saying this but yes, I did."

"Would you have preferred to trap him and get your revenge?"

I shrug. "No, not really. It was nice to hear that he actually learned his lesson. At least there's some hope, even for people like him. I would hate for him to go around doing what he did to me."

"Did Mason see you with him?"

"Yes. He wasn't very happy about it."

She grins. "I bet he wasn't. Why were you sitting outside for ten minutes?"

"We were just talking." I'm not sure why I don't tell her the truth. Maybe it's because I'm too ashamed. She saw me break down after what happened in the elevator but then I took it one step further tonight.

"Was Buzz in the car too?"

"No, he stayed at the bar. Mason's going back to find him now."

"He's probably already gone home with someone. So what's the next step? Are you still going to see Emily tomorrow?"

I sigh. "Yes. I've already let it get too far. It's time to face the truth."

Chapter Seventy Four

Mason

I walk back into the bar to see Buzz surrounded by women. He cheers as I approach. "You're back!" The blonde sitting on his lap turns around and I'm shocked to see that it's his ex, Stacey.

"Can I talk to you for a second?" I ask.

"You can say whatever you want to say in front of us, Mason," Stacey replies.

I ignore her and raise my eyebrow at Buzz. He lifts Stacey off of him then stands up. "I'll be back in a minute, ladies. Try not to miss me too much." He throws his arm around me as I lead him away from the group. "Glad you're back, brother. How did it go with Sophia?"

"Great."

"Did you knock any walls down?"

I smile. "I think so. I *hope* so."

"You're really good together."

"You know who *isn't* good together? You and Stacey."

He laughs. "Don't worry. I'm just having some fun. She's a good distraction."

"What about Lori?"

"What about her? She doesn't want anything to do with me. At least Stacey wants to fuck me. Lori didn't even want to do that."

"Please don't do anything stupid. You'll regret it in the morning."

"No, I won't. I won't *remember* anything in the morning."

"Let's fly somewhere."

"What?"

"If you need a distraction then let's fly somewhere. We could go to Vegas."

Two of the women who were sitting at his table appear next to us. He laughs. "I was gone for less than a minute."

"We miss you already," one of them tells him.

The other one laughs when I roll my eyes. "You're Mason, right?" I nod. "Buzz was talking about you. I'm Carmen."

"Nice to meet you."

She looks down at my hand. "Are you single?"

My mind instantly jumps to Sophia. "No."

"Married?"

I hesitate. "Yes."

"Are you happy?"

"Yes." It has nothing to do with being married but I'm the happiest I've been in a long time.

"Then you're one of the lucky ones."

"I'm very lucky."

"I could never get married. I get bored too easily. I wouldn't like to fuck the same person day in, day out for the rest of my life. Don't you get bored, Mason? Don't you ever feel like mixing things up?"

"It's impossible to get bored when you're with the right person. I don't want to have sex with anybody else ever again." I would be the luckiest son of a bitch if I got to have sex with Sophia for the rest of my life.

She leans forward, revealing even more cleavage. "Not even for one night?"

"No."

"Dude, is the offer still on?" Buzz asks.

"What offer?" I ask.

"Vegas."

Carmen's eyes light up. "Are you going to Vegas?"

"Hell yes!" Buzz replies. "And you two are invited! I'll go and tell the others."

I sigh. "I need to talk to you again. Excuse us, ladies." I take hold of his arm and pull him away. "We're leaving."

"Yeah, we are! Vegas baby!"

"No, we're not going to Vegas. We're going home. If you want to drink until you pass out then fine, but you can do it back at the hotel. I'm not letting you sabotage a good thing."

He stops. "A good thing? What are you talking about? I don't even have *a thing* anymore, let alone a good one."

"You just need to give her some space. Since when do you give up so easily?"

"Why are you so bothered?"

I give him a little nudge and lead him over to the exit. "Because I know how much you like Lori and I also know how long it's taken you to find her."

"Exactly. It's taken me years to find her but only seconds to lose her. I'm a massive fuck up. It's over."

"Even if it *is* over, you still deserve someone better than Stacey. She didn't treat you right and I won't let that happen again. You're my best friend."

"Thanks for having my back, brother. I love you."

"I love you, too. Now let's go back to the hotel and order a pizza. You can stay the night if you want. I need to make sure that you don't choke on your own vomit."

"Aww, how sweet of you. Hey, are you going to wear the nurse's uniform while you look after me?"

Chapter Seventy Five
Sophia

The next morning, I wake up with puffy eyes and a heavy heart. I wish that I could hide under my covers all day but I know what needs to be done.

"Morning, sweetie," Lori says as I walk into the kitchen. "How are you feeling?"

"Like crap."

"Is your plan still going ahead?"

I nod. "Today's the day. I can't put it off any longer."

"Do you want me to come with you?"

"No, I'll be okay. Will you be here when I get back?"

"Of course I will be. I'm not working today." I sit down opposite her and nibble on a piece of toast. "What time are you meeting her?"

"I don't know. I'm going to call her in a minute."

She takes a drink of coffee then begins to choke. Her eyes widen as she begins to tap on her phone. "Oh my god!"

"What?"

She holds the cell out to me. It's a photo of Buzz surrounded by about five or six women. I sigh. "Is that from last night?"

"Yes. Look closer."

I take the cell off of her and properly look at each woman in turn. I groan when I spot his ex. "I didn't realize it was Stacey. What is he doing with her?"

"Keep looking."

I gasp when my eyes land on the last woman. "It's Carmen." I get a sinking feeling in my stomach. "Oh no."

"What?"

"Emily was talking about hiring more girls to trap Mason. She wanted to hire Leah but I told Kristen to send Carmen instead."

"Well judging by the photos, you don't need to worry. Mason isn't even on any of them. She probably hooked up with Buzz. Maybe they had a threesome with Stacey." She sneers. "He changed his relationship status back to single."

"Are you going to talk to him today?"

"No, it's over. Oh well, I only have myself to blame. It was nice while it lasted."

I sigh and pray to god that I won't be saying the same thing about Mason in a couple of hours.

I take a deep breath and call Emily. "Hello?" she answers.

"Hi, it's Sophia. Are you free to meet? We need to talk."

"Have you got some information for me?"

"Yes, I have."

"Is it worth my time?"

I sigh. "Yes."

"Then I'm free."

"Twelve o'clock at the office?"

"Hmmm, could you come to the house instead? I'm not feeling too great. Don't worry, it's nothing contagious."

"I don't think that's a good idea."

"Why not? I can call Kristen and ask her to come too. Or I guess we could just leave it until another day."

I don't want to drag it out any longer, especially after last night. "I'll come over."

"Excellent. Do you have a pen?"

"For what?"

"My address."

"I already know it."

She laughs. "Oh yes, I forgot you're an expert when it comes to my husband."

"It was in his file."

"See you at twelve. You're doing the right thing, Sophia."

"I know I am."

Take the risk or lose the chance.

Chapter Seventy Six

Mason

I stand over Buzz's slumped body. He's been sound asleep on the bathroom floor ever since he stopped throwing up at around three A.M. I lean in close to him and focus on his chest, checking to see if he's still breathing. I wait for a few seconds but don't see any movement. I go to check his pulse when he opens his eyes and shouts, "BOO!" I jump so high I almost hit the ceiling. He laughs until he's coughing and spluttering, which nearly makes him throw up again.

"Remind me not to bother checking that you're alive the next time you drink yourself into a stupor."

"You can't get rid of me that easily. Plus, when I die, I'm going to haunt you."

"Please don't. One lifetime is more than enough. I'm going to order breakfast, what do you want?"

"I'll have whatever you're having."

"Okay. Make sure you have a shower, you stink of puke."

"Did you throw up too?"

"No?"

"So then what's your excuse for smelling so bad?"

"Oh, that's not me. That's the smell of bullshit coming out of your mouth."

He laughs. "I deserved that." He calls my name just as I'm about to leave the room. "Thanks for looking after me last night."

"I've got your back, brother."

"Did I call Lori?"

"No but you tried to. I took your phone away from you."

"Good. I have a lot of grovelling to do today."

I'm on the penthouse line ordering breakfast when my cell rings. I rush to finish the order then pull it out of my pocket excitedly. My whole body sags when I see who is calling. "Hello Emily."

"Long time, no speak. Do you miss me yet?"

"What do you want?"

She laughs. "I miss you too, darling." I shouldn't have even answered her call. "I need to talk to you about a few things."

"To do with what?"

"To do with our marriage, Mason. Or rather, our failed marriage. I want to discuss the terms of the divorce before we make it official."

"We can do that through our lawyers."

"Oh, come on. I know you're not an unreasonable person. I don't want some big formal thing. Just stop by the house later. I won't keep you for long, I promise."

I sigh. "What time?"

"About twelve."

I look down at my phone. 10:37 A.M. "We're just waiting on breakfast but that should be okay."

"Who is *we*?"

"Buzz stayed over last night."

"Wild night, was it?"

An image of Sophia riding me flashes through my mind. "I had a lot of fun."

"I bet you did. How many women did he bring back with him?"

"None."

She snickers. "Oh, I don't believe that."

"I don't care."

"See you at twelve." She hangs up and I already regret agreeing to meet her.

Chapter Seventy Seven
Sophia

I hesitate as I climb out of the Uber and contemplate asking the driver to take me back home. Even now, I'm unsure whether I'm doing the right thing or if I'm about to make the biggest mistake of my life. I close the door behind me and watch as they drive away. There's no going back now.

I walk up to the huge double gates and press the intercom button. They open almost immediately as though Emily has been waiting for me. I look down at the file in my hand and tell myself that I can do this. I *must* do this.

She opens the front door and gestures for me to enter. She looks happy to see me and even a little bit smug. I stop at the bottom of the huge wooden staircase and look up at the ornate chandelier above my head. "Thanks for coming," she says. "Follow me." She leads me through a formal dining room and into a small sitting area. "Sit down, make yourself comfortable." I perch on the edge of the sofa and glance around. I don't think I'll ever feel comfortable around her, especially when I'm in the house that she once shared with Mason. She picks up a remote and pushes a few buttons. Soft music begins to play as she eyes the file in my hand. "So you finally have some information for me?"

"I do."

She holds her hand out. "Well?"

"Before I show you, I want to know why you hired me."

"What do you mean? I hired you for the same reason all the other women hire you. To see if Mason would cheat on me."

"Are you sure about that?"

"Yes."

"And there's no other reason?"

She leans her head to one side. "What other reason would there be?"

"Oh, I don't know…something about a prenup,

maybe?"

She raises an eyebrow. "Spit it out, Sophia."

"I know about the clause in your prenup. If one of you gets caught cheating, the other person gets one hundred percent of everything."

She sits up straighter. "Where did you hear that?"

"Does it matter?"

She glances down at the file. "I guess not anymore. Yes, it's true about the clause."

"So you used me to get the evidence you needed?"

"It depends on how you look at it. You once told me that you can't force a man to cheat. If Mason didn't take the bait then I wouldn't have been able to take his money, would I?"

"And you still believe that it's cheating even though you're getting a divorce?"

"So you know about the divorce too. What else has Mason told you?"

"He told me that you've been separated for almost four months and that there's no chance of you getting back together."

She shrugs. "The papers haven't been served yet. He's still my husband."

"He's not a cheater and we both know it."

"The evidence in your hand suggests otherwise. Speaking of which, are you going to keep me waiting all day?"

"We haven't finished talking. I'll show you when I'm ready."

"Moody today, aren't you?" She gestures for me to carry on.

"Mason is a good person. He's one of the most honest and trustworthy men that I have ever met. He doesn't deserve what you're doing to him."

She laughs. "What *we're* doing to him."

"No. I never chose this. I want out."

"Well give me the evidence and it will all be over."

"Did you ever love him?"

"Of course I loved him."

"Then how can you do this to him?"

She shrugs. "It's nothing personal."

"Are you joking? Of course it's personal. You're trying to ruin his life. He's worked so hard to get where he is today and you want to take it all away from him. If you truly loved him then you wouldn't go through with it. I'm here to ask you to nullify the contract."

She laughs. "Nullify the contract? Why the hell would I do that?"

"Because it's the right thing to do."

"What's in it for me?"

"A clear conscience and whatever you're actually entitled to. Whatever you *agreed* to when you signed the prenup."

"I signed the prenup when I was madly in love and when I thought we would be married forever." My stomach churns. "But things change. People change. I'm not a naïve little girl anymore. I'm only *entitled* to five percent of his whole empire. I'd come out with less than three mil. This house is worth more than that. Does that seem fair to you?"

"Actually, it seems more than fair."

"Are you joking? I put my whole life on hold for him."

"That's your own fault."

"Excuse me?"

"He never asked you to do that. He never asked you to quit your job. Just like he never forced you to play golf and go to lunch with your friends every day. Stop blaming him for everything."

"But he *is* to blame. He became emotionally unavailable. He didn't show me any affection for well over a year."

"Was that before or after your affair?"

"Oh wow, apparently you're an expert on my life now. It's nice to know that he's still hung up on the affair. How childish of him to keep going on about it."

"Of course he's still hung up on the affair. You betrayed him. You broke his trust. You made him question everything, not just about your relationship but about his intuition, his judgement and his self respect. So no, he's not childish to want to talk about his trust issues or insecurities which stemmed from you not being able to keep your panties on."

She starts to slow clap. "Bravo. Nice little speech there. Why are you so bothered? This is your job. This is what you do."

"No it's not. I catch *cheating* men. Mason isn't a cheater. You've been broken up for months."

"Jesus. I should have just hired Carmen from the start. She didn't question me like you always seem to do."

"And did she trap him?"

She smiles. "No. Apparently he told her that he's the happiest he's been in a long time. Hey, at least you've made him happy while screwing him over."

I take a deep breath. "I'm giving you one last chance to nullify the contract. If you won't do it for Mason then at least do it for karma."

"I don't believe in karma."

"Well you should. Let me rip these photos up."

"What photos?" My head spins around and I gasp when I see Mason standing in the doorway, drained of all color. "What are you doing here, Sophia?"

Emily laughs. "Well isn't this cozy?"

I didn't hear his footsteps because of the music. "Did you set this up?" I ask her. "Did you tell him to come here?"

"Yes. I thought it might be nice for us all to get together. I've always wanted a threesome, haven't I, Mason?"

He ignores her completely, looking only at me. "Sophia?"

"I was going to tell you today, I swear. I was going to explain everything."

"What's happening?" he asks.

"Aww, did you think that Sophia was actually interested

297

in you?"

"Mason, let's go somewhere else. I'll tell you everything."

"Oh no," Emily says. "I want to see the look on his face when he finds out the truth."

"The truth about what?"

"Sophia is my employee," Emily announces as she snatches the file out of my hand. I don't even have the strength to stop her. My whole body feels limp. I've dreaded this moment for weeks but the look in his eyes is way worse than anything I could have ever imagined. "I hired her to seduce you. To trap you."

I see the exact moment his heart breaks and even though I tried to prepare myself for this, I feel my own heart shatter into a thousand tiny pieces. He shakes his head. "No. I don't believe you."

Emily laughs as she walks over to him. "It's true. Look." She shoves the file in his face. "All the evidence is in here." She opens it and quickly glances down at the first page. "I have photographic evidence of you cheating on me. Tsk tsk, Mason. If only you could have waited until we got divorced. Maybe if you had been more of a man and had sex with your own wife, you wouldn't have been so desperate to shove your dick inside the first woman to pay you a bit of attention." He looks at the photograph and frowns. She turns the page without looking. "There are pages and pages of them. Keep an eye out for the divorce papers, darling."

He looks at the second page and then looks at me in question. I shake my head. "Not here." He takes the file off of her then walks out of the room.

"Hey! Come back!" she shouts. "I'm guessing you made copies?" she asks me.

I ignore her and chase after Mason. He doesn't stop walking, even after leaving the house. "Mason, wait." I have to jog to keep up with him. "Please let me explain."

He finally stops when we're completely clear of the

front gates. "Is it true what she said?"

"Mason…"

"Is it true?"

"Yes but…"

He covers his face with his hands and crouches down as though he can't bear to stand. I see his pain. I feel his pain. I *am* his pain. "You lied to me. All of this has been a lie. I thought we had something real."

"We did. We do. It was all real for me. I didn't help her. I didn't tell her anything."

"Why did you agree to do it in the first place?"

"I…it's my job…it *was* my job. I'm going to quit."

"You told me you were a writer."

"I majored in English and Creative Writing. I hated lying to you. It tore me up inside."

"So your real job is to seduce men?"

I sigh. "I catch cheaters. Women hire me to find out if their husband is cheating on them. I didn't know you were getting divorced. I would never have agreed to help her. As soon as you told me you were separated, I tried to stay away."

"You didn't try very hard."

"I did. That was the problem. I tried really hard but the more I got to know you, the more I liked you. I couldn't stay away."

"Why didn't you just tell me?"

"She made me sign a contract. A non-disclosure form. She threatened to sue me if I told anybody. I came close to telling you a few times."

"I wouldn't have said anything to Emily."

"I know that now. I was scared of losing you. I knew you wouldn't want anything to do with me once you found out."

"That's for me to decide."

"I know. I'm so sorry, Mason."

"What else was in the contract? Did she order you to fuck me last night?"

"No! No, of course not. I swear to you it was all genuine. I didn't want to help her in any way. That's why I was so worried about the camera in the elevator. I thought somebody might sell it then Emily could use it against you. She kept pushing for photos and asked me to wear a wire but I wouldn't help her."

He holds the file up. "Did you take these photos?"

"No. One of my friends owed me a favor. She used to work for the agency as a photographer but now she's a private detective."

"And Emily doesn't even know that these are of her?"

"No. I let her believe they were photographs of you. I was going to show her and make her call the whole thing off but then you turned up."

"You didn't have to do all of this."

"I wanted to. It wasn't fair that she was accusing you of cheating and trying to take your money when she was the one dating somebody else. I swear to you that I was going to come and see you after I was done here. I was going to tell you everything."

"Why should I believe you?" I reach into my purse and pull out the watch. His eyes widen in complete and utter shock as he takes it from me. "My grandpa's watch. Where did you get this?"

"I got it from a pawn shop a couple of weeks ago. She pawned your stuff, Mason. I found out and bought it back, before I even knew whose it was or what it meant to you. I couldn't afford any of the other things. I've been desperate to give it back to you since you told me it was your grandpa's."

He shakes his head. "I told you how guilty I felt about it the other night but you still didn't tell me."

"I didn't know how to. I'm so sorry. I wish I could turn back time."

"Me too."

My heart aches as Charlie pulls up beside him.

"Please believe me, Mason. I never wanted to hurt you.

I came here today to try and put an end to it all. She wanted to take everything away from you."

"She already has." His eyes burn into mine and I'm not sure where his pain ends and mine begins. "Goodbye, Sophia." He opens the car door and climbs inside. My eyes fill with tears at how final his goodbye sounded. I watch him drive away, taking part of my heart with him. I drop to my knees and let the pain wash over me.

Chapter Seventy Eight
Mason

"Dude, you can't just leave," Buzz tells me as I throw an empty suitcase onto the bed.

"Watch me."

"Where are you even going?"

"Sydney," I tell him as I start to fill it with clothes.

"*Australia?* What about work?"

"What about it?"

"We have clients over from London in a couple of days, remember?"

"I trust you to hold down the fort."

"You shouldn't," he mumbles.

"You've done it plenty of times before."

"What about your mom? And Indiana? Aren't you going to say goodbye to them first?"

"I'll call them when I land."

"And what about me?"

"I'll call you when I land too."

"That's not what I meant."

I stop packing and turn to him. "Buzz, you'll be fine."

"But you're my best friend."

"And nothing is going to change that."

"Not even seven thousand miles?"

"No."

"I'm worried about you, brother. I've never seen you like this."

"Don't be. I just need some space."

"Then go to The Hamptons. Why have you got to go to the other side of the world?"

"Because I like it there."

"How long are you going for?"

"I don't know."

"But you're coming back?"

"Probably."

"*Probably?* I don't like that answer. This isn't you."

"I don't even know who I am anymore. It feels like a part of me is missing."

"You don't know who you are? I'll tell you who you are. You're Mason Hunter and you're a fucking gladiator. You're the strongest person I know. You're the *best* person I know. You can get through this."

"I don't know if I can."

He shakes his head, looking genuinely worried. "What the fuck has she done to you?"

"She's changed me."

"Please just stay tonight."

I close the suitcase and zip it shut. "No."

He groans. "You're running away from your problems."

"I'm not *running* anywhere. I'm taking the jet."

"See, you just made a little joke. You're fine. Stay. We can get through this together."

"I'm not in a good place, Buzz."

"Don't let Emily win."

"Emily? I don't care about Emily. I expected something like this from her. She's fucked with my head but Sophia has fucked with my heart." I lift the suitcase off of the bed. "Keep an eye on Indie while I'm gone."

"If I say no, will you stay?"

"No, I'll just hire somebody to do it."

He sighs. "Of course I'll look out for her."

"Please don't make me bankrupt." I joke as I hold out my hand. He ignores it and pulls me into a bear hug.

"I love you, brother." A huge lump forms in my throat. "Do whatever the fuck you need to do and get your ass back here as quickly as possible."

I nod and turn away from him just as a lone tear trickles down my face. I walk away and don't look back.

Chapter Seventy Nine

Sophia

"Please eat," Lori says.

"I'm not hungry."

"It's been two days and you've hardly eaten."

"I'm not hungry," I tell her again before hiding under the covers.

"Sophia, you need to eat something," Lori says as she opens the blinds.

I cover my eyes. "I'm not hungry."

"It's been three days and you've hardly eaten."

"I had a pop-tart last night."

"Oh, wow. In that case, you won't need to eat for the rest of the year."

"I had some cheetos too."

"Soph, please. You need some real food. Why don't we go out for lunch?"

"I'm not hungry," I tell her again before hiding under my pillow.

"Here, eat this," Lori says as she shoves a bagel in my face.

"I'm not hungry."

"It's been four days and you've hardly eaten."

"Just leave it on the floor."

"Sophia…"

"Lor, please don't. Not again." She nods, kisses me on the forehead and leaves.

"Get up," Lori says.

"I don't want to."

She yanks the covers off of me. "It's been five days."

"And?"

"And I'm not letting you do this anymore."

"I can't."

"Yes, you can." Her eyes fill with tears. "I know you're hurting but seeing you like this is hurting me too. You're my best friend. I can't see you like this anymore. Let me help you. *Please* let me help you."

I nod and slowly climb out of bed.

Chapter Eighty

Mason

"The wanderer returns," Indie says as I pull her into a hug. "Don't you dare do that again. I was worried about you."

"I'm sorry."

"At least take me with you next time. Look at your tan."

"How's mom?" I ask.

"Furious. She's been talking about putting you up for adoption." I laugh. "She's fine, just worried. She's out of town at some Zumba conference or something. You know I don't like to ask too many questions in case she tries to rope me into it."

"And is everything okay with you?"

"Yes but I'm not here to talk about me. I'm not the one who ran away to Australia. Be honest with me. How are you?"

"I'm okay. I just needed some time to process everything and think about what I want."

"And what do you want?"

"I want to be happy."

"I want that too. You deserve to be happy. Buzz told me everything. He also had to physically stop me from going to see Emily."

I shrug. "Don't waste your energy on her. The divorce papers have been served. She's not getting a cent. She will be out of our lives very soon."

"Good. I can't believe she had the audacity to hire somebody to catch you cheating when she's the one who cheated on you when you were still together. Buzz told me how Sophia refused to tell her anything." I nod. "Have you spoken to her since you found out?"

"No."

"Are you going to?"

"Yes. I won't be able to move on with my life without talking to her first."

"Look, I don't want to get involved but..."

I chuckle. "But you're going to anyway?"

"I just want to say my two cents and be done with it. I hate that Sophia agreed to help Emily in the first place. I hate that she lied to you and kept things from you. And most of all, I hate that she hurt you. But she refused to help Emily. She rode in an ambulance with you and spent all night at the hospital. She bought Grandpa's watch back when she didn't even know how much it meant to you. She didn't need to do any of those things. She brought back the old Mason. She gave me back my big brother. When you met her, something inside you changed. It's like you came alive. Life doesn't always give us second chances so if you're lucky enough to get one, don't waste it."

I ruffle her hair then sling my arm around her. "I've missed you, Dr. Phil."

Chapter Eighty One
Sophia

"I've just spoken to Buzz."

I take a bite of my sandwich. "That's good. How did it go?"

"A lot better than last time. We're having lunch tomorrow."

"Ah, that's awesome. I'm so happy for you."

"Are you sure you're okay with me seeing him?" she asks.

"Of course I am. I want you to be happy."

"I know you do. I just don't want it to bring back any bad memories for you."

"I have good memories too." She nods but it's obvious that something is on her mind. "What's up?" I ask.

"Buzz told me something about Mason."

My heart aches at the mention of his name. "Go on."

"He's been in Australia."

I start to imagine hundreds of different scenarios. "Has he met somebody?"

She frowns. "No. At least, I don't think so. Buzz told me that he's flying home today. I just thought you might want to know."

I shrug. "Why? He doesn't want anything to do with me."

"You don't know that."

I push the rest of my sandwich away from me. "Yes, I do. It's been three weeks. Jesus, he travelled to the other side of the world to get away from me."

"Maybe you should try and talk to him now that you've both had some time to process everything."

"No."

"Soph…"

"Lor, stop it. This isn't one of your romance novels. I'm not going to rush to the airport so I can declare my undying love for him. This is real life. It was only last week that I finally managed to leave the house without breaking down. I can't take any more heartache. If he wants to talk to me then he knows where I am."

I gasp when my cell starts to ring. Lori's eyes widen. "Is it him?" My heart plummets when I see that it's Kristen. A perfect example of why I need to try and move on with my life.

I sigh. "Of course it's not him. Hello Kristen."

"Sophia, how are you?"

"I'm getting there," I tell her, surprised that she actually let me answer for once.

"I need your help."

"No."

"Please, Sophia."

"No. I've told you, no more traps."

"I know you have and I've been very patient with you. It's been three weeks and I haven't asked you for a thing. But you're still my employee for one more week. I'm in a very tight spot and I promise I won't ask you again. This is the last trap you will ever have to go on. If you agree to do it then your employment will cease tonight."

"I want it in writing."

"Deal. Swing by the office first and you can have it."

I sigh. "Where do you need me to be?"

"Scoma's. Seven thirty."

Scoma's. The place where Mason and I first met. I close my eyes and think back to a much simpler time. Before I agreed to take part in Emily's evil plan. Before I broke an honest man's heart and broke my own in the process. I would do anything to be given a second chance but unfortunately, we don't always get them. "Can we meet at a different place?"

"Come on, Sophia. You know we don't get to choose the location."

"Fine. What's his name?"

"Um, one second, let me check… it's Andy. I don't

have a photo but I'm sure he will stand out, he's got long blonde hair down to his shoulders and he's six foot five."

"Great, I'm trapping Thor."

She laughs. "Thank you, Sophia. It's going to be okay, you know. It might not feel like it now but in the end, it will all be okay."

I think back to when she said something very similar a few weeks ago and look how that turned out.

Something isn't right.

The restaurant is completely empty and I can't even see a member of staff. I frown and head in the direction of the bar to no avail. "Hello?" I shout. Kristen must have sent me to the wrong place. At least I can leave; it's already starting to bring back memories of Mason. I pull my cell out of my purse and call Kristen as I make my way outside. It starts to ring just as I push through the double doors. I glance around and stop dead in my tracks when I see Mason sitting on the bench, watching me. He smiles and it feels like home. "Hello, Sophia."

I try to talk but no words come out. I clear my throat and try again. "Mason, what are you doing here?"

"I'm here to see you."

My heart feels like it's about to leap out of my chest. "I thought I was here for a trap." I cancel Kristen's call.

"I asked your boss for a favor. Well, it was more of a guilt trip. She agreed to do it for you, not me."

"She's not my boss after tonight."

"You quit?"

"Yes."

"Why?"

"Because I don't want this life anymore. I meant what I said that night at the penthouse. My priorities have changed."

He pats the bench. "Will you sit with me?" I nod and walk over to him. The air becomes considerably thicker and I feel the familiar buzz of energy between us. "It's strange being back here, isn't it? It's like we've come full circle."

I nod. "I wish I could go back to that first night."

"Me too."

We sit in silence for what feels like minutes. "When did you get back?" I ask.

"A few hours ago."

"Did the time away help?"

"Yes, it did. I've had a lot of time to think and I actually want to apologize to you. I left before I even gave you the chance to properly explain. I was in shock and I didn't want to believe that you had anything to do with Emily so I ran away as far as I could go."

"You have nothing to apologize for. I'm the one who should be sorry. I swear to you that I would never have agreed to help her if I had known what she was up to. To me, it was just another job."

He nods and pulls a box out of his jacket pocket. I recognize it straight away. He takes out his grandpa's watch then removes the velvet insert, revealing a piece of paper underneath. "Can I share something with you?"

"Of course you can."

"This is a note from my grandpa. I've always kept it in here and it means more to me than the actual watch does. That's why I was so upset when I thought that I had lost it. He gave each of his grandchildren a piece of advice. He told my cousin to live for the moment and never give up on her dreams. He told my sister to always be herself and to stand up for what she believes in. He could have chosen any piece of advice to give to me but this is what he thought I needed to hear the most. *'There is no love without forgiveness, and there is no forgiveness without love.'* When Emily cheated on me, I was so close to walking away but this note is what made me stay. I tried to make the words fit the situation but I realize now that it was never about Emily. I forgave her because I deserved peace but I forgive you because you actually deserve forgiveness. You're a good person and I know you were only doing what you had to do. I believe you came into my life for a reason but I'm sitting here now through choice. I choose you, Sophia. I will always choose you. It has taken me twenty seven years to find you and I'm not willing to let you go. It might be a bumpy ride but I can guarantee it will all be worth it in the end."

My eyes fill with tears. "I thought I'd lost you."

"I *was* lost but you never lost me."

"Can we start over?"

"I can't think of a better place to start over than right here on this bench, where it all began." He takes my face in his hands and kisses me like he's trying to make up for lost time. "Sophia?"

"Yes?"

"Would it be weird if I told you that I've fallen in love with you?"

I beam with happiness. "No, Mason. No, it wouldn't."

The End.

Acknowledgements

To Ivan. Thank you for your continued love and support.

To my babies, Dexter and Isla. Thank you for giving me the motivation to work so hard. I hope I can make you proud and inspire you to chase your own dreams one day.

To Roxy, aka my book bestie. Thank you for always being there for me and for cheering me on. I can't wait until we finally get to meet up and fangirl over Rhysand!

To Allura, Courtney and Melissa. Thank you for being the best beta readers a girl could ever ask for. This book wouldn't be what it is without all of you. It would also be a lot less American! Melissa - thank you for all of the awesome teaser pictures!

To my wonderful blogger friends. You are all rock stars! Your support means the world to me. Thank you so, so much.

And last but not least, to my amazing readers. My favourite part of being an author is without a doubt getting to talk to all of you. This book means so much to me and I hope you love it as much as I do!

About the author

Karli Perrin is a twenty something, English Language and Linguistics graduate from Manchester, England. She has always been a big lover of books and was inspired to write her debut novel in 2013. She is a huge believer of fate and is a sucker for a happy ending. Her ultimate goal in life is to live in a house made entirely out of books with her fiancé and two children.

...Hogwarts is plan B.

Stalk Karli

Facebook – authorkarliperrin
Instagram - @karliperrinauthor
Twitter – @karli_perrin
karliperrinauthor@hotmail.com
Goodreads.com/karliperrin

Follow Buzz on Twitter - @buzzhasarrived
Check out Sophia's Pinterest board - search Karli Perrin

Printed in Great Britain
by Amazon